SCAVENGER OF SOULS

ALSO BY JOSHUA DAVID BELLIN

Survival Colony 9

SCAVENGER OF SOULS

JOSHUA DAVID BELLIN

MARGARET K. McELDERRY BOOKS
New York London Toronto Sydney New Delhi

MARGARET K. McELDERRY BOOKS
An imprint of Simon & Schuster Children's Publishing Division
1230 Avenue of the Americas, New York, New York 10020
This book is a work of fiction. Any references to historical events, real people, or real places are used fictitiously. Other names, characters, places, and events are products of the author's imagination, and any resemblance to actual events or places or persons, living or dead, is entirely coincidental.
Text copyright © 2016 by Joshua David Bellin
Jacket photo-illustration and design by Sonia Chaghatzbanian
Jacket photograph copyright © 2016 by Sean Mosher-Smith
All rights reserved, including the right of reproduction in whole or in part in any form.
MARGARET K. McELDERRY BOOKS is a trademark of Simon & Schuster, Inc.
For information about special discounts for bulk purchases, please contact Simon & Schuster Special Sales at 1-866-506-1949 or business@simonandschuster.com.
The Simon & Schuster Speakers Bureau can bring authors to your live event. For more information or to book an event, contact the Simon & Schuster Speakers Bureau at 1-866-248-3049 or visit our website at www.simonspeakers.com.
Interior design by Sonia Chaghatzbanian and Irene Metaxatos
The text for this book is set in ITC Stone Sans Std.
Manufactured in the United States of America
First edition
10 9 8 7 6 5 4 3 2 1
CIP data for this book is available from the Library of Congress.
ISBN 978-1-4814-6244-0 (hardcover)
ISBN 978-1-4814-6246-4 (eBook)

For David Mayer

ACKNOWLEDGMENTS

Everyone says writing your second book is harder than writing your first, and everyone is right. Without the people I'm about to name, I don't think I could have done it.

Four women top the list. My agent, Liza Fleissig of Liza Royce Agency, continues to astonish me with her energy, passion, and commitment to me and my books. My editor, Karen Wojtyla, is not only a great editor but a great teacher: she sees the potential in what I write, and she makes me work hard to realize it. Assistant editor Annie Nybo is able to sum up in very few words exactly what needs to be fixed in a manuscript. And my wife, Christine Saitz, has listened to me ramble for several years about Skaldi and a guy named Querry, yet she still supports what I do. If you're wondering why I gravitate toward strong women in my writing—well, wonder no longer.

This book wouldn't be anywhere near as beautiful as it is if not for the dedicated and creative people who helped prepare it for publication, including copy editor Brian D. Luster and cover designers Sonia Chaghatzbanian and Irene Metaxatos. Thanks for making my words just right and for bringing the visions in my head to life.

The writing life would be much more confusing if not for the wonderful friends I've made. These include the members of the Fall Fourteeners—Austin Aslan, Kristine Carlson Asselin, Kate Boorman, Jaye Robin Brown, S. L. Duncan, Amy Finnegan, Joy N. Hensley, Kendall Kulper, Kristen Lippert-Martin, Shallee Macarthur, Lisa Maxwell, Kat Ross, and Sarah J. Schmitt—and the incredibly supportive community of writers with whom I share Pittsburgh as my home: Sally Alexander, Laura Lee Anderson, Linda M. Au, Jonathan Auxier, Caroline Carlson, Joe Coluccio, Nick Courage, Carrie Ann DiRisio, Erin Frankel, Joy Givens, Larry Ivkovich, Stephanie Keyes, Leah Pileggi, Thomas Sweterlitsch, Diane Turnshek, and many more. I also want to give a shout-out to the members of the KidLit Authors Club (especially Dianne Salerni) and to the many agency siblings who have supported me along the way: Kaye Baillie, Jenny Bardsley, Kerry O'Malley Cerra, Darlene Beck Jacobson, and (again) Sarah J. Schmitt. Thanks to all for being part of my extended writers' family.

The local chapter of the Society of Children's Book Writers and Illustrators, headed by Marcy Canterna, Kate Dopirak, and Nora Thompson, has put me in touch with some great people and opportunities, as have the librarians and teachers (too many to name) in area schools. I also need to mention five local bookstores that have supported me, both by hosting events and by displaying my work on their shelves: Mystery Lovers Bookshop, Classic Lines Bookstore, the Penguin Bookshop, and the Barnes & Noble stores in the Waterfront and Settlers Ridge. Thanks for embracing a local writer!

Jen Rees was the first to read the manuscript and give it the thumbs-up. Two close writer-friends, Tom Isbell and Kat Ross, read the book at a later point and provided me with valuable feedback. My thanks to them not only for taking on this task but for their own novels, from which I've learned much.

I'm fortunate to have parents who filled my bookshelves and my mind when I was just getting started. Thanks, Mom and Dad. I'm also fortunate to have children who love my stories and understand my need to write them. Thanks, Lilly and Jonah.

This book is dedicated to my first high school English teacher, who was also the first teacher to suggest that I might make a career of writing. Sadly, he is no longer alive, and so I can't show him how much his words and example influenced me. But this book is for him. Every published writer has such a teacher. Every aspiring writer needs one.

And finally: my readers. I can't name you here (I'm sorry, but the acknowledgments would be too long!), but I can't thank you enough for your reviews, your questions, your emails, your drawings, your everything. You're why I keep writing. Drop me a line and let me know how you like this one.

PART ONE

NORTH

Aleka looked out over the land and frowned.

She stood at the crest of a low hill, squinting in the sunlight, the lines deepening around her mouth. I tried to read her expression, but as usual I failed.

This was Aleka, after all. Her close-cropped, graying blond hair framed a face she could turn into a mask at a moment's notice. I'd been studying that face for the better part of a week, and I still had no idea what was going on behind her deep gray eyes.

Aleka. My mother. And as much a mystery to me as my own past.

After a long minute she spoke the name of her second-in-command. "Soon."

Soon, a big guy with what might have been called a potbelly in a different time, came up beside her.

Aleka surveyed the unforgiving landscape, the lazy glint

of river the only sign of movement in the waste. "How long?"

"A week. Maybe two if we're extra careful." He searched her face, but he must have come up empty too. "Why?"

She didn't answer. The others had edged closer, listening. Any conversation that hinted at our dwindling supply of canned goods got their attention.

But after another long look over the barren land, she turned and strode back down the hill, refusing to meet any of our eyes. Everyone watched her go in silence, until she disappeared behind a clump of rock that stood at the base of the hill.

"Well, that was enlightening," Wali said.

There were sixteen of us, the last survivors of Survival Colony 9. Five grown-ups counting Aleka, Soon, our camp healer Tyris, our craftswoman Nekane, and the old woman whose name no one knew, a wraith with wild white hair and a threadbare shift the same drab gray-brown as our uniforms. For the past week we'd been carrying her on a homemade stretcher, while she gripped her late husband's collection container, a scuffed, bottle-green jar overflowing with scraps of his hair and fingernails. She was amazingly heavy for a woman who'd dwindled to skin and bones.

The rest of us were teens and younger. Wali, with his shaggy hair and bronzed muscles, the oldest at seventeen. Nessa, the only teenage girl left in our colony since the death of Wali's girlfriend, Korah. Then there was Adem, a tall skinny awkward guy who communicated mostly with gulps and blushes. And the little ones, seven of them total, from ragged five-year-old Keely to knowing Zataias at age ten, with straggly-haired Bea in the middle.

And that left only me. Querry Genn. Fifteen years old last week, and thanks to an accident seven months ago, with no memory of the first fourteen.

Only my mother held the secret to who I was. But she wasn't talking.

She hadn't said a word to me the whole week. That entire time, we'd been creeping across a desert landscape of stripped stone and yawning crevices, the scars our ancestors had cut into the face of the land. For six of those seven days we'd been carrying the old woman. Aleka had driven us at a pace unusual even for her, with only short rests at the brutal height of day and long marches deep into the night. What she was hurrying for was another thing she wouldn't talk to me about.

When we'd left our camp by the river, the old woman had babbled on about mountains somewhere to the north, licking her lips while she talked as if she could taste the fresh air. She'd described green grass as high as our knees, wind rippling across it so it seemed to shimmer like something she called satin. She'd told us about yellow flowers and purple ones, trickling water so clear you could see brightly colored fish darting among the submerged stones. Clouds, she said, blanketed the mountain peaks, cool and white and soft, unlike the oppressive brown clouds that smothered the sun but almost never rained in the world we knew. At first I refused to believe her, told myself that half of what she said had to be exaggerated or misremembered or just plain crazy. But like everyone else, I'd fallen in love with the picture she painted. None of the rest of us had seen mountains, not even Tyris, who'd been two or three years old when the wars started. After a lifetime in the desert, the prospect of mountains rearing up out of nowhere, white and purple and capped with gold from the sun, was irresistible.

By now, though, it seemed even the old woman had forgotten where we were headed. She'd lapsed into silence, except when she stroked her collection jar, mumbling to it. She slept most of the time, sometimes beating her hands against her chest and mouthing words no one could make out. But even when her eyes opened, her glassy expression showed no awareness of anyone or anything around her.

We set her stretcher down in the best shade we could find and stood there, waiting for Aleka to return. Nessa held the old woman's gnarled hand and sang softly, something the old woman had sung to her when Nessa was a kid. I tried to organize a game with the little ones, but they just flopped in the dirt, limbs flung everywhere in postures of dramatic protest. I'd learned the hard way that you couldn't get all seven of them to do anything at once, but occasionally, if you got one of them doing something that looked interesting enough, the others couldn't stand to be left out.

Today, though, it wasn't going to happen. A fossil hunt usually got them going, but this time even Keely wouldn't bite when I told him an old, rotting buffalo skull was a *T. rex*.

"I don't want to play that game, Querry," he managed weakly, before putting his head down and closing his eyes. "It's boring."

Without warning, Aleka stalked back to the group. To my complete surprise, she took my arm and pulled me away from the others. I stumbled to keep up with her long strides. When we reached the rock where she'd hidden herself before, she stopped, so suddenly she just about spun me around.

"Querry," she said. "We need to talk."

"We've needed to talk all week," I said under my breath.

She heard me. She always did. "That will have to wait. This is priority."

"Something else always is, isn't it?"

We faced off for a moment.

"I'm asking you to be patient," she said. "And to believe I'm working on this."

"Fine." I wished for once I could meet her on even ground, but she had a good six inches on me, not to mention at least thirty years. "Let me know when you've got it all worked out."

If I thought I'd get a reaction from that, I was wrong. Her face went into lockdown, and I was pretty sure the conversation was over. But then she asked, "What is it you want, Querry?"

"Answers," I said. "The truth." "Answers aren't always true," she said. "And the truth isn't always the answer you want."

"Whatever that means."

She glared at me, but kept her voice in check.

"It means what it means," she said. "For one, it means that Soon's estimate is wildly optimistic. I've checked our stores, and we have only a few days of food left. If we're even stingier than usual. Which is a risk, since there's nothing out here to supplement our supplies."

"Why would Soon . . ."

She ignored me. "And it means the old woman is failing. Earlier today she asked me if she could talk to Laman."

"You're kidding."

"I wish I were."

I stared at her, not knowing what to say. Laman Genn had led Survival Colony 9 for twenty-five years. But like so many of his followers, he'd died a little over a week ago, just before we set out on our journey.

Died. Been killed. I tried not to think about it, but I remembered the nest, the bloody wound in his side, the creature that had torn him open.

The Skaldi.

The ones we'd been fleeing all our lives. Monsters with the ability to consume and mimic human hosts. It was hard to believe anyone could forget them. Even though we'd destroyed their nest, I kept expecting them to reappear, like a second nightmare that catches you when you think you're awake and drags you back under.

"Any more good news?" I said, trying to smile.

She didn't return the offering. "The children are failing too," she said. "Keely and Beatrice especially. If we run out of solid food . . . We forget how fragile they are. And how many of the little ones simply don't make it."

I turned to look at the kids, lying on the ground like so many dusty garlands. "What can we do?"

She didn't say anything for a long time, and her gaze left mine, drifting to the desert beyond. I thought she wasn't going to answer when her voice came again, as far away as her eyes.

"I know this area," she said. "Or at least, I did. None of the others has been here—Laman seems to have avoided it assiduously. But I was here, once upon a time. So long ago the details are fuzzy. Either that or it's . . . changed."

I glanced around us, as if I expected to see something I hadn't noticed before. "Why didn't you tell anyone?"

Her shoulders inched up in the slightest of shrugs. "I didn't want to give anyone false hope. They were excited enough about the mountains. And I wasn't sure I could find it again. I'm still not sure."

"What is it?"

She waved vaguely toward the northwest. "A sanctuary, or as much of one as we're likely to find in this world. Not mountains, but a canyon. Shaded, protected from the worst damage of the wars. The river gains strength as it flows through, nourishing what grows on its banks. If we could only reach it, there might be a chance for the most vulnerable members of the colony."

I studied her face, as still and remote as the surface of the moon. This time, though, I thought I caught something there.

"If this place is so great," I said carefully, "why did Laman stay away from it?"

Her eyes snapped to mine, and for the briefest second I imagined I saw a glimmer of fear. But it vanished so quickly I wasn't sure I'd seen it to begin with.

"I've been seeking the canyon since we left camp," she said. "But it seems my memory failed me. I thought we'd be there by now. I pushed us too hard in an effort to attain a goal I believed was within reach, and now the little ones might not have the strength for the final leg of the journey."

"Then we turn back."

She shook her head. "You've seen the terrain we passed through. They won't make it."

"So we keep pushing forward," I said. "We don't give up. I'll help. What do you need me to do?"

Doubt and relief warred in her eyes. "You've always been good with the little ones. Maybe you can find a way to . . . inspire them."

I nodded.

"But be careful, Querry. Especially with Zataias. He's sharp. We can't let him know how dire the situation is."

"We won't," I said. "I won't."

"Tyris is aware of my concerns. She checked vitals when everyone was asleep. She assures me there's no sign of . . ."

She didn't need to finish. *No sign of infection.* No evidence Skaldi had taken over people's bodies. That we might be carrying a monster with us.

"And I've spoken to Nessa about the old woman," she continued. "She's going to do what she can to help."

"Nessa?" With her random comments and sleepy green eyes, I'd always thought Nessa was kind of dense.

"She's been a help to me many times in the past," Aleka said. "Including the time we rescued Laman, as you may recall. Plus the old woman's always been fond of her. Don't be so quick to judge, Querry. There's more to people than meets the eye."

I looked down, feeling like a stupid kid who'd just been scolded by his mother. Which I pretty much had.

"But the others don't need to know the true state of affairs," Aleka finished. "I don't want anyone to get their hopes up until I'm sure of our position. So for public consumption, this journey is just business as usual."

I nodded. Secrets were one thing I'd come to expect from her.

"Good." Her face softened for a moment, and her long, thin fingers reached out to caress my cheek. "And Querry. If we get there—when we get there—I promise we can talk. Really talk."

"That's all I want," I said.

"I know," she said in almost a whisper. "And I'm sorry I haven't been able to give it to you."

Before I could say anything else, she turned and strode back to the others.

We found them resting beneath a thumb of volcanic rock. The kids hadn't budged, and Nessa was busy draping tattered blankets over them. I watched her, trying to see what Aleka saw, but when she glanced in my direction, I looked away in a hurry. The rest of the adults and teens milled around, not doing much of anything. Wali looked up and smiled wryly.

"Anything you'd like to share?"

Aleka gazed at the spot where the old woman lay, a nearly motionless bundle in the shade of a dead tree that somehow clung to its rocky perch. She snored noisily, her mouth more full of darkness than teeth.

"We could all use a break," Aleka said. "A couple of hours. Querry, can you help Soon set up camp?"

I jumped to my feet faster than I should have and started digging through my pack. Soon ambled over to join me, and when his eyes met mine, I realized he'd known all along what Aleka had managed to hide from me. I glanced at the other adults and teens, saw them going through their routines wordlessly, and I was pretty sure Aleka's schemes had come to nothing.

They all knew what we were up against. They all knew we were in a race against time, with no sure goal in sight, and with the little ones' lives at stake.

We rested in the shade of piled rock through the worst part of the afternoon, when the sun felt like a hot knife slicing through my uniform and into my skin. Aleka had said two hours, but when two turned to three and three to four, she made no effort to get us moving. I fed the kids a spoonful of concentrated mush, and they swallowed it dutifully enough, but I couldn't help noticing the vacant look in their eyes as they chewed mechanically. Trying to start a conversation with them was like tossing a handful of dust in the air. The old woman slept the whole time. Nessa sang to her, in a soft, clear voice I heard only as notes, not words. Maybe it was the same lullaby she'd sung before. Me, I couldn't remember any lullabies, and I was the only teen who'd joined Survival Colony 9 too recently to have heard the old woman sing. Hard to say if Nessa's efforts did any good. The old woman's brow never lost the pinch she'd worn when she fell asleep, but at least she did sleep.

I wondered if she was dreaming. Remembering the time before. I wondered if that was the problem.

Eventually, though, she had to wake up, and that gave Aleka her signal to get us moving again. Gauging the sun, I estimated we had enough daylight to cover three or four miles, what with the rough terrain and the twin burdens of the old woman and the little kids. Adem helped Soon with the stretcher, while the rest of us took turns giving the little ones piggybacks. There weren't enough big people to go around, so one of the kids always ended up lurching along beside me, immune to my attempts at chatter or jokes, holding a hand that dragged him more than it held him up. Zataias skipped his turn more than most. I suspected he was in on Aleka's secret too. That would be just like him, young enough to play the grown-ups' game even though he was old enough to guess its true purpose was to deceive.

We descended the slight rise where we'd set up our temporary camp and entered a flat, broad valley of stone. I'd have said the terrain looked no different from the land I remembered the past seven months, but that wouldn't have been fair to the past seven months. In fact, this area looked a lot worse. I'd grown accustomed to dust, a choking brown dust that coated every surface and rose in swirling storms when the wind blew. Out here the dust had been swept away along with everything else, exposing reddish rock that rippled like an endless series of motionless waves. If there'd ever been a human civilization in the vicinity, roads and houses and farms, it had all been leveled as completely as if a giant hand had wiped the place clean. I kept alert for possible food sources—flowering trees, river stones that could be flipped for squirming multi-legged creatures—but there truly was nothing, just an endless table of rock like an enormous tombstone.

The river struggled along by our side, cutting a slim channel through the unvarying stone. It had shrunk to a muddy trickle, and I found it hard to believe it could ever pick up steam the way Aleka had promised. Still, we hugged its eastern shore, determined not to lose this frail lifeline. We'd never been able to stay so close to water for so long—the Skaldi had always found us by the rivers, so we'd shied from the water's edge, making furtive trips to fill our canteens then veering off into the desert again. Being near water made me feel as if I was doing something wrong, something risky and disobedient. It wasn't only that I was afraid something might have survived the destruction of the Skaldi nest. It was that I didn't trust the river to last. The more we relied on it, the more we'd be lost if it ever ran dry.

It didn't, though. By late evening it had shriveled to the point where you could barely dunk your hands to the wrist, but it kept going.

We swallowed another spoonful of slop from our nearly empty cans and slept by the river's side, and when I woke, I realized what none of us had been able to tell during the dusk: the color of the stone around us had changed from rusty red to pitch black, smooth and glossy and bright in the gleam of the new day. It might have been the remains of a road if not for the fact that it was simply immense, extending as far as I could see to the east and northwest. And there was something else: stone shapes were visible all around us, not

15

just the usual ripples or rises in the ground but distinct forms dotting the land like black sculptures. Some of them were roughly the size of the stunted trees that grew in the desert, others no taller than a human being. They were blunt, misshapen, glazed blobs of rock without distinguishing features. But all of them gave me the eerie feeling that they'd once been alive, as if a thick, glassy layer of stone had flowed over and trapped whatever lay inside.

Nessa tried another of her songs, but she fell silent when the stone bounced back her voice in a hollow, mocking echo. "Maybe this is the mountains?" she suggested.

"Does this look like mountains?" Wali said.

"I was just asking."

"Try using your brain instead," he muttered.

Nessa turned on him, eyes hot, but Aleka stepped between them.

"This isn't the mountains," she said. "But it's a good sign."

I looked around at the endless desert of black stone. How it could be a good sign of anything I couldn't figure.

Aleka turned to the rest of us and gestured toward the northwest, where the expanse of black rock vanished into a gleaming haze of distance. "We're close to our destination," she said. "We came out of the desert farther east than I wanted us to be, but not so far that we can't cut across this region in a day or less. We'll need to take precautions, though. The stone gets very hot, especially at high noon."

"What's on the other side?" Wali said.

"Shelter," she replied. "Clean water. Possibly—"

"Food?" Soon interrupted.

She didn't answer. I glanced at the little ones, the pitiful thinness of their shoulders and cheeks, the eagerness glowing through the dusty veil that had descended over their eyes. I realized it wasn't only Zataias who suspected that this journey was anything but business as usual.

I think Aleka realized it too. "We'll have to wait and see," she said softly. "But we're in a much better position now. Let's break camp quickly and prepare to cover as much ground as possible before midday."

Everyone moved with new purpose. In minutes we were packed and ready to go. I rounded up the kids and made sure the littlest ones had the lightest burdens. Aleka insisted on wrapping extra cloth bandages around people's boots, tying extra head scarves to cover faces and necks. We spent precious minutes erecting a canopy over the old woman, who snoozed on. We filled our canteens with muddy water, and I saw people lick their lips at the thought of what we might find ahead.

Then we were on the move.

I turned to say a word to Aleka, but found her already at my side. She dropped her voice and spoke low enough that Keely and Zataias wouldn't overhear, but still her words gained a weird, tinny reverberation from the polished stone.

"Stay alert," she said. "We're not in the clear yet."

"What are you afraid of?" I whispered back.

She sized me up, as if gauging how much to say.

"You wanted answers, Querry," she said at last. "I hope you're prepared to get them."

2

We tramped across the plateau in double file, weaving our way through monuments of stone.

Aleka must have cautioned the other adults and teens as well, because Soon discreetly withdrew his gun and Wali his knife. Nessa stayed by the old woman's stretcher, but she didn't sing, and her eyes darted from side to side, all sleepiness gone from them. Even Zataias looked edgy, though maybe that was only from the excitement of playing an adult game.

Aleka's promise—or was it a warning?—rang in my ears like an echo off the glassy stone. There were so many things I wanted to know, so many things only she could tell me. About my past. My family. My father. Myself. I knew how a starving man felt when he saw an oasis in the desert. The only difference was, I felt like I'd been starving for seven months, and it was finally coming to an end.

All we had to do was cross the plateau of stone.

We hadn't gone more than a mile before I realized how hard that was going to be. The sun had barely cleared the horizon, and already it hammered down on us, making the air writhe with heat, the black rock sizzle like a brand. Not only that, but the stone that had seemed so smooth at first glance turned out to be sharp and broken, stabbing into the soles of my shoes with each step—though that wasn't surprising, considering my boots had been worn down not only by me but by whoever had lived and marched and died in them fifty years ago. Though the kids had started off with a burst of energy, it soon took all my coaxing and hand-holding to keep them on the move. I began to imagine that a giant fist had smashed down on the surface of the plain, shattering everything into shards and splinters of stone that sparkled like a trillion fragments of glass. Waves of heat radiated from the surface, weird ripples that made everything in the dead zone sway as if it was alive. The effects of light and sound produced by this wasteland made the journey as disorienting as it was exhausting: every time I saw one of the stone shapes rising in the distance, I caught my breath, thinking I was seeing an actual, living human being—or worse, one of the monsters that hid in human form. I wouldn't have been completely surprised if these figures had sprung to life and chased us across the plain, like shadows freed from the coal-black ground.

I touched one of the monoliths as I passed it. I'm not sure if I was testing to see if it was alive or simply checking to make sure it was really there. It burned my fingers as if I'd thrust my hand directly into a fire.

The farther we traveled across the deadly plateau, the more I began to wonder what had created this place, whether it was the result of some natural disaster or a left-over from the wars that had swept away the old civilization. Laman used to talk about the bombs that had been dropped in those days, bombs that could not only level buildings but vaporize entire cities, mimicking the power of the sun for a split second of total destruction. He'd told me that was why there were so few traces left of the old times, why everything was desert, why we so rarely stumbled across the remains of a highway or skyscraper or playground. That also explained why the sky stayed filthy and brown even after all this time, because everything that had been incinerated down here had entered the atmosphere as a permanent, oppressive cloud. What that meant was that every time you breathed, you breathed residue from the world before: houses, shop-ping malls, people. That used to give me a sick feeling, until I considered the alternative, which was not breathing at all.

But in all his stories, Laman had never told me about bombs that could turn the landscape to volcanic glass. He'd never mentioned a power that could make everything melt and then re-form into the polished, mocking shapes that surrounded me. I supposed this might have been the site of an actual volcanic eruption, the ground heaving upward and spewing out superheated rock that had cooled into these twisted, lopsided remains. If that was the case, though, I couldn't figure out what had happened to the volcano, unless one of the larger rock formations was its extinct cone. Aleka, as usual, said nothing, and no one asked her for an explanation. What could have had this effect on the landscape, short of some prehistoric monster that had scoured the land with molten fire, was beyond me.

As noon approached, a more pressing problem presented itself: water. I had carefully weighed the canteen in my hand when we set out, and I could tell that we'd drunk far more than usual as we inched across the scorching plain. The kids especially we kept dousing with water, hoping to keep their small bodies from drying up in the blaze. But we'd also discovered that the river had become completely undrinkable in its narrow channel through the rock, its depth little more than a few inches and its color the black of ash. Aleka might say that the watercourse grew again once it reached the canyon, but at the moment, pure water seemed as far off as that oasis in the desert. And like the spectral rock forms that crowded us on all sides, I was beginning to wonder whether the oasis might turn out to be a mirage.

We rested from noon until the sun neared the western horizon. Our shadows spooled out behind us like gigantic threads, but when I looked back, there was no sign of anything they might have connected us to. I could tell from Aleka's rigid posture that she hated to waste so much time, but we didn't have any choice. The kids were practically comatose from the heat, and the rest of us were sunburned, famished, and exhausted from carrying them and the old woman. As it was, we were barely able to find relief from the sun's assault. A shallow declivity was the best we could do, with blankets stretched across the rock to shelter us. Wali, I noticed, draped his own blanket over Nessa's shoulders, his peace offering I guess. She accepted with a nod and a weary smile. As I sank into a half sleep, I wondered if Aleka planned to march us through the night.

She did. As soon as the sun hit the horizon we were up, and with nothing to trap the heat, the relative cool of dusk— a few degrees cooler than day—hurried in. It was a moonless night, only a single bright star pulsing through the murk that covered our world. Without flashlights or flamethrowers to light a path, I was afraid we'd veer off course. But Aleka was determined not to stop now that her goal was within reach. And so, while the kids slept in our arms and the old woman in her hammock, we followed our leader into the endless black land.

She'd never let us down before, I kept reminding myself as we stumbled through the dark. And once we arrived, she'd not only give us what our bodies needed, but give me what my heart so desperately wanted.

As the sky brightened, I saw that we'd entered a part of the landscape where large slabs of the black rock lay jumbled and heaped on each other, looking almost like buildings that had collapsed or been bombed to the ground. Wali and

Soon clutched their weapons more tightly now that we'd come to a place that provided cover for enemies. I gripped Keely's hand, feeling the tiniest bit of relief when he returned my squeeze like he used to. Aleka tested one of the stacks of stone, and when it turned out not to be as precarious as it looked, she led us to its summit to survey the landscape.

Nessa's hands fumbled with her scarf as she retied her dirty-blond ponytail. "This isn't the mountains."

"No," Aleka said. "There are no mountains here."

No one showed the least surprise at her announcement that we'd been chasing something that didn't exist.

"What is this place?" I asked.

Aleka stared into the distance for an eternity before answering.

"A place from long ago," she said at last. "We need to be careful."

"Did it look like this before?"

She glanced at me, and I was sure she was hiding something. Then she pointed and said, "We've reached the canyon. There!"

Everyone followed her finger as if an electric bolt had shot from it. In the distance, southwest of the wilderness of stone, the black desert came abruptly to an end and the color of the land changed back to its typical drab brown. But I could see, just beyond the edge of the blackness, a dark line zigzagging through the land. It looked as slender as something drawn by a pencil, but it must have been enormous to be visible at all from where we stood. The trickling river angled straight for it, as if it was as eager as we were to get out of this dead land. It might only have been a trick of weariness and distance, but I could have sworn the light that hung over that line was softer than the angry red light of morning, a pale blue light like an exhalation of clean air and water from the canyon's mouth.

No sooner did Wali see it than he charged down the stone mound. He was followed a second later by Soon, each of them clutching a kid to their chest and leaping down the rock before pounding across the black land. Adem and Nessa were left beside the old woman's stretcher, while the rest of the kids squirmed out of their caretakers' arms and charged after their companions, pointing at the canyon and shouting words that alternated between taunts and encouragement.

"I see it!"

"Me too!"

"Beat you there!"

"In your dreams!"

"Hurry up!"

"Wait for me!"

"I need a piggyback!"

"Querry . . ."

"Keep order," Aleka shouted over the din of their voices as she raced down the hill after her colony. "Querry, watch the children. Tyris, Nekane, guard our rear. Adem . . ."

The rest of her words were drowned out by a chorus like

nothing that came from human throats: a long, ululating shriek that emanated from the piles of black rock. Up ahead, I saw Soon raise his gun then fall, the child he held rolling free as his big body hit the ground and lay still.

Aleka whirled, her own gun leveled. The next instant, the heaps of stone seemed to come alive as human figures appeared out of crevices and grabbed Nekane, Tyris, and Adem. Other dark shapes materialized from the ground, intercepting the children and hoisting them into the air, their legs kicking vainly. Wali bounded toward the captives, shouting, "Get your goddamned hands off of them!" But the strangers blocked his path to the children, and he fell beneath their weight, surrendering the child he was hold-ing—Beatrice—to their arms. I lost sight of Soon in all the bodies, but I heard Nessa scream before her voice was cut short as rough hands wrapped her mouth.

For a moment I stood frozen. Our captors looked human, men with long dark hair, faces free of beards, and lean, muscular frames stripped naked except for brown loincloths. Looking human meant nothing, though. If these were Skaldi, in less time than it took to blink they'd shake off the bodies they'd counterfeited and consume the bodies they'd cap-tured, moving from victim to victim while the skins of those they'd eaten fell in tatters to the ground.

But they didn't. They weren't Skaldi. They were people like us.

Aleka must have realized it too. Standing at the base

of the stone mound, she flourished her gun, a silver pistol. Whether she could manage a clean shot with the prisoners held tightly I couldn't tell.

"Let them go," she said in a commanding voice that rebounded across the black land. The men made no move to obey, but one of them raised his voice in a call like a scream of pain.

Aleka spun toward the sound, her weapon on the alert.

She never got a chance to use it. A dark object came hurtling from somewhere high above and struck her arm with a sickening crunch. The gun flew from her fingers and she dropped to the ground, clutching her wrist. Her right hand dangled like a limp weed.

I shook off my paralysis and leaped down the hill for her gun, but before I could reach it, a pair of powerful arms pinned me from behind and lifted me off the ground. I struggled in a grip like steel. The only members of our party who stayed free were the old woman, who lay untouched on her stretcher, and Aleka, who stayed down, her always pale face drained of every drop of color. Soon lay too far away for me to see what had happened to him, a cluster of warriors surrounding the spot where he'd fallen.

"Strangers from beyond the Shattered Lands," the man who held me spoke in a deep, oddly accented voice that I not only heard but felt vibrating against my back. I strained to look at him, but he held me fast. "By what right do you travel in our realm?"

No one spoke. One of the warriors lifted Aleka roughly to her feet, her head lolling on her thin neck.

"Release them, Archangel," a new voice issued from above. The words rolled over the scene of battle, rich and melodious but at the same time as sharp as the crack of the unknown weapon that had maimed Aleka.

The arms dropped me, the other warriors freeing their prisoners as well. I turned to face the most massive human being I'd ever seen: well over seven feet tall, brown-skinned and with a chest and shoulders bulging with muscle. He was dressed as skimpily as the others, in moccasins and loincloth, except he wore an ankle-length cloak made of the same brown material. His clean-shaven face was immobile, impassive, more like the face of a cliff than the face of a man. His black eyes traveled upward to the place where the new voice had come from.

I followed his gaze and saw a man standing on the summit we'd just descended, his skin pale against the black. He was nowhere near as huge as the one he called Archangel. In fact he was small, not much taller than me, and he seemed particularly puny compared to his lieutenant's hulking frame. Like all the men, he wore no beard, and his brown hair hung to shoulder length. But the cloak that spilled over his shoulders and hid his arms and chest was red, a glaring red that made his figure explode from the empty land like a splash of blood.

He descended his perch, traveling on a narrow trail either

carved or worn into the stone. His steps were lithe and quick, almost cocky. When he reached the level ground, he strode toward Aleka, who stood unsteadily, her broken wrist cradled in her left hand. The weapon that had done the damage, a pair of palm-size black balls connected by a foot-long cord, lay coiled at her feet. I waited for the red-cloaked man to retrieve it, but he walked past his weapon, past his victim, to the discarded gun no one had yet touched. I'd thought Wali might go for the pistol when the warriors freed him, but like everyone else in our colony, he seemed too shaken to move. Everyone except Nessa, that is, who had decided to take the opportunity to braid her hair. I turned from her, shaking my head, and followed the progress of the warriors' leader.

He bent by Aleka's gun. "Archangel," he said, and the giant left me. When he reached his captain's side, the smaller man said, "What do you make of this?"

The giant stooped, picked up the gun gingerly. He held the barrel between thumb and forefinger, dangling it as if he'd never seen anything like it before. In his huge hand, it looked as harmless as a child's toy.

"Their power lessens, to send such a trinket against us," he said at last, his deep voice rising on the final words as if he was asking a question or seeking approval.

"So it is foretold." The man nodded. "Leave it, Archangel. We will bury it with the rest, when the time comes."

Obediently the giant lowered the gun to the ground. The red-cloaked man kicked it dismissively with the toe of his moccasin, then stood and paced back to Aleka. His lieutenant shadowed his steps.

The red-cloaked man stopped before Aleka, who'd slipped down in the warrior's grasp, huddling over her injury. Close up, I saw that the leader's face, though lean and strong, was cut by scars that trailed across his forehead, down his cheeks, over his jaw to his neck and throat. If Aleka had been standing straight, she'd have been looking down at that face. Now she looked up, and her eyes widened in an expression of unmistakable terror.

"Athan," she said, her voice trembling.

The man said nothing in response. Instead, he shrugged, wiggling his shoulders in a snakelike way that threw the blood-red cloak clear of his arms.

And I saw that the wounds didn't end with his face.

His entire body was crisscrossed with shiny, long-healed scars. They were thick and broad, as if he'd been deeply gouged by a blade. There were so many of them, running in so many directions across his chest and shoulders and arms and thighs, it looked like he'd been torn apart and stitched back together. The man smiled, the scars on his face stretching his lips back to show all his teeth.

"*Aya tivah bis, shashi tivah bracha*," he said in a strange tongue. "The day of the despoilers is no more. The sun has risen on the children of the blessed."

3

The man with scars talked to his warriors in an unknown language, and they bound our hands in front of us while they stripped away our packs and searched through our possessions.

The cords they tied around our wrists seemed to be made of the same brown material as their clothes and Archangel's cloak. It felt both scratchy and sinuous, and as strong as rope. Any thoughts I had of trying to break free ended when they leveled spears at us, wooden shafts topped with evil-looking shards of black stone. But that didn't stop Wali, who struggled violently as they searched him. "Give that back to me!" he screamed, and I saw that they'd slipped a cord off his neck, something gold glinting at its end. I recognized it instantly, and I knew why he was so desperate to get it back: it was the ring Korah had given him, partner to the one that had been destroyed when fire consumed her body. I hoped they wouldn't find the red-handled pocketknife I'd inherited from Laman, the one that had belonged to his lost son, but their search was too thorough for that. They also found the book Aleka had given me just a week ago on my fifteenth birthday, a homemade book with a single charcoal portrait from when I was a baby. Wali's curses rang out against the volcanic stone as they gathered everything we owned and showed it to the scarred man.

Most of it he merely nodded at before Archangel added it to the pile that had started with Aleka's gun. The old woman's collection jar he dashed to the ground, where it shattered into a hundred fragments. But he held Wali's ring up to the sunlight for a long moment, watching it gleam as it slowly rotated on its cord. My knife too caught his attention, as he opened and closed the blades several times before handing it back to Archangel. When he came to the baby book, he seemed to freeze on the portrait, his eyes tightening in concentration. But then he cast it aside, letting it fall to the ground with the rest. As if that was some kind of signal, Archangel dumped everything else onto the pile and gestured to the warriors to lead us away, toward the canyon.

That was when I got my first good look at Soon. One of the warriors stood over him, pulling a spear from his back. It was obvious from the location of the wound and the stillness of his body that he was dead.

I turned shakily from the sight, my eyes seeking Aleka.

Her injury didn't appear to be life-threatening, but it was ugly: an unnatural bulge protruded from her forearm, blood drenching the surrounding skin. Her face had turned gray, and beads of sweat stood on her upper lip as she gritted her teeth against the pain. When Tyris saw her, she tried to muscle through the warriors to Aleka's side.

"It's a compound fracture," she said to their leader. "You have to let me set it."

"We have medicines of our own," he replied in a flat voice. "If she cannot walk we will assist her."

One of the warriors lifted the frail body of the old woman from the stretcher. Nessa started to object, but the old woman slept on in the warrior's arms, her gnarled hands twisting mechanically now that she had no jar to cuddle. When they led Aleka to the stretcher she stared at it, her eyes unfocused. I edged closer to her and reached out with bound hands to touch her shoulder.

"You should lie down," I said. "Come on. Aleka. Lie down."

She barely nodded, but she didn't resist when the warriors lowered her onto the stretcher.

We were marched toward the canyon, which was visible beyond the edge of the black rock plateau. The warriors offered their backs to the little kids, but all seven shied away—all except Zataias, who roughly shrugged off the hands they held out to him. Nessa refused to let them touch her, and walked with her head high. I tried to follow her example, but the thought of Soon's lifeless body sprawled on

33

the field of battle behind us rattled me, and I had a hard time keeping up the act. The scarred man walked at the head of the column, surefooted and jaunty in his stride, his red cloak flapping behind him. At some point, probably while they were tending to Aleka, he had retrieved his weapon. It hung at his right side, the weighted balls bouncing with each step. Another object hung at his left hip: a short staff, no more than a foot in length, bone white and polished to a high shine. Given what he'd been able to do with the ball weapon, I hoped we'd never find out what that was for.

After a half hour of silent marching, the black rock ended and we entered a narrow gorge of reddish-brown sandstone, the puny river trickling beside us. The walls of the canyon blocked some of the sunlight, so the air felt cooler than usual, cool enough that you could breathe deeply without feeling your lungs fry. At the same time, it was unnerving to be hemmed in like this, with the knobby-smooth rock rising to a height of twenty, then forty, then seventy feet on either side of us. After a few minutes, though, the gorge broadened to a width of maybe a hundred feet, and the leader called a halt. The warriors set Aleka down near the canyon wall, and Archangel didn't interfere when I went to her. Tyris joined me. I looked at my mother's pale, drawn face, her eyes closed tight in an effort to clamp down on the pain. Her right forearm was a mess of flesh and blood. I knelt by her side and took her undamaged hand in mine. I wished I could use my sleeve to pat the sweat from her forehead, but that was more than I could manage with my hands bound.

Her eyes fluttered open. "Querry," she said weakly. "This"—and she drew a sharp breath between her teeth—"hurts."

Tyris stooped beside me and placed a couple fingers on Aleka's intact wrist. "The pulse is strong," she said. "We'll get you fixed up, Aleka. Do your breathing. It'll help."

Aleka nodded and closed her eyes again. I watched her chest expand with a deep breath, her lips purse to let it out. I tried to breathe with her.

"I'm going to talk to him," I told her. "He can't just leave you like this."

"Querry," she said, her eyes flying open. "Is Soon . . . ?"

"Yes," I said.

Pain knotted her face. "Then the others will need you to—"

"I know," I said. "Don't worry. I will."

"Querry." Her voice dropped to a nearly inaudible breath. "Don't trust Athan. Don't believe him. He wants . . ."

Too many ears might be hearing this. I tried to lean closer. "You know him?"

I thought I saw a flicker of a nod. "I wanted to tell you," she said. "I'm sorry. . . ."

"It's okay," I said, though I wasn't sure what she meant. Had she known we would encounter these people? Or was it our missed conversation she was apologizing for? "Who is he?" I whispered as close to her ear as I could.

"He's . . ."

But before she could say another word, the huge shadow of Archangel fell over us, and her eyes widened with warning. Her mouth formed a word I couldn't read, and anger bubbled up in me as I looked at my mother's suffering face.

"Don't worry," I said. "I'll take care of them. I won't let anything happen to the colony." I patted her hand, awkwardly raised it for a kiss. Then, for her ears only, I whispered the word I'd never used before: "Mom."

Her eyes, normally so hard, softened and closed. I laid her hand on her chest and stood, stumbling at first without hands to balance me, and turned to look for the man who'd done this to her.

I didn't have far to look. As soon as I gained my feet, I found the scarred man standing beside Archangel, his own shadow swallowed by his giant lieutenant's.

"Her injury is grave," he said softly. Though he spoke in a stilted, formal way, I didn't hear any trace of the accent I'd detected in Archangel's words. What I did notice was the musical quality of his voice, how its rich tones conveyed a depth of compassion I wouldn't have believed even without my mother's warning. His eyes, too, seemed to melt with concern. Confronting those eyes up close, I saw that though the irises were almost black at the core, their edges held a prism of colors, brown and green and gold and gray, flickering like reflections off water. "Would you like us to heal her now?"

"I think you've done enough damage already," I said.

"The techno woman wielded a gun," the man said calmly, even soothingly. "I am required to defend my people."

"And our other man?" I said. "The one you killed? What did he do to deserve that?"

"In battle, there are unavoidable losses," he said, his voice dropping with false remorse. "The techno warrior we perceived to pose a threat, and there was no time to determine whether he deserved to live or die."

"He had a name," I said, furious that he could dismiss Soon's death so casually. "He wasn't a *techno*."

"You are all technos," he said in the same quiet, reasonable voice. "Men with machines, men of machines. You are the children of the despoilers, those who poisoned the air and land and water. Your leaders would have you believe their weapons of metal can save you. But nothing can save you now but the way of righteousness."

My heart sank at the realization that we'd been captured by a madman. I'd heard stories of people who'd lost it in the years after the wars, people who'd gone on killing sprees in their own colonies or run off by themselves to die in the desert. People driven mad by grief or guilt or despair. Laman's own son had surrendered himself to the Skaldi after a lifetime of trying to live up to his father's impossible demands. But I'd never heard of a madman who'd recruited an army of lunatics to fight his demons for him. And I'd never imagined anyone, mad or sane, who could provoke such fear from the woman I'd never known to show fear before.

"Well, I'm the leader now," I said, anger making my voice strong. "Pledged, like you, to protect my people."

His face quirked with surprise or amusement. "And how shall I address the leader of your people?"

I saw Wali make a slicing motion with his hand, but I ignored him. "My name's Querry Genn," I said. "And you're going to have to deal with me from now on."

The man's expression never changed, though I thought I saw his eyes flicker with interest. "Is it customary among your people to delegate such power to one so young?"

"It's necessary," I said. "To keep the chain of command intact."

He nodded as if that made sense to him. "We, too, train our young in the ways of wisdom. From their earliest days, they heed our word and learn to follow the true path. But what wisdom can there be in following a path that leads only to death?"

"Are you going to let us fix her wrist or not?" I said.

He smiled then, a pleasant, unforced smile, as if I'd complimented the color of his cloak or agreed with him about the chance of rain. He took one last look at Aleka's wrist, then turned and whistled sharply. A man I hadn't seen before separated himself from the cliff face and came to stand by his captain's side. Unlike the others, he held no spear, and a neat beard lined his chin.

The scarred man spoke to this new arrival in a low voice, too quiet for me to tell if he was using our language or not.

The bearded man listened silently, nodding and alert. Seeing him and his leader face to face, I became aware of something the common uniform had disguised: the two were much older than the rest. Some of the warriors, I realized, might have been Wali's age or even mine, though their stolid faces and muscular bodies made them look older. But none of them, including Archangel, was much past their early twenties, while their leader and the bearded man were easily twice the warriors' age, the skin around their eyes crinkled and dry, threads of gray woven into their hair. Everyone, including the bearded man, watched the man with scars intently. When he talked they all straightened, their concentration focused on him, their faces open as if his words filled them with a combination of fear and joy.

When the one-sided conversation ended, the bearded man knelt by Aleka's stretcher, reaching for a brown pouch that hung at his belt. Tyris and I tried to get between him and his patient, but both of us were pulled back, me by the irresistible might of Archangel's iron hands, Tyris by a tug on the cord binding her wrists. The scarred man spoke again, raising his voice loud enough for all to hear. But his shifting eyes rested only on the teens and little kids, who stood in a huddle with Nessa at their head.

"Hear me," he said, "children of the despoilers. You must know that you are ours now, and so long as you remain in the Sheltered Lands our word is law. We will heal this woman's injury, and if you allow us, we will heal that far greater injury none of you has yet imagined you bear. But if you resist us, we will cast you out, and abandon you to the power that dwells in the Shattered Lands: the Scavenger of Souls."

The name meant nothing to me, but a shiver went through me as he said it. Maybe it was the name, or maybe it was the effect of his rich, rolling voice, as mutable as the spinning prism of his eyes.

"Who are you?" Nessa said breathlessly.

His shoulders rippled in a way that made me think of squirming underground creatures, and the red cloak flared over his back, exposing again the lurid scars across his chest and arms. He raised his hands in a gesture of victory, as if he was reaching up to pull down the sky.

"I am Asunder!" he shouted, his voice turned to a symphony of voices by the canyon walls. "All who come to me are reborn, and become as little children again!"

The bearded man worked on Aleka for a good hour while the rest of us watched. Though he said nothing, he pantomimed all his motions in an exaggerated way, and Tyris's face passed from wariness to guarded approval. First he took the pouch from his belt and poured what looked like water into a clay bowl, then laid brown bandages in the water and kneaded them until they were soaked through. A pungent smell rose as he worked. Carefully he bathed Aleka's wound, wiping away the blood to expose the protruding bone. She winced but didn't flinch. Before setting the fracture, the man inserted

four long, thin needles, maybe made of bone, into her forearm above the break, and her face relaxed visibly. Then, with
a swift, expert motion, he snapped her bone into place and
wrapped another dampened bandage around her wrist. With
this temporary cast holding her arm steady, he emptied a
bundle of bright green leaves from a second bag at his side,
and after grinding them in his mouth for a couple minutes,
he spat out a lumpy green poultice and packed it evenly over
the injured arm. Another layer of the brown bandages completed the cast, and the man stood, bowed low to Asunder,
and returned his supplies to his bag. Then he vanished back
into the canyon wall, slipping through a man-size fissure I
hadn't known was there.

Aleka barely made a peep during the entire operation.
Her face calmed, and what color she possessed returned to
her cheeks. She looked up at me and Tyris with gratitude
before closing her eyes, murmuring a word I didn't know:
"Melan." In seconds her breathing took on the smooth,
steady rhythm of sleep. It happened so fast I wondered if
there was some kind of drug in the healer's potion.

But I didn't have time to think about that. No sooner did
Aleka drop off than Asunder's men approached us again, this
time holding brown cloths and gesturing toward our eyes.

At the sight of the blindfolds, Wali's anger returned. "Are
you kidding me?" he snarled. "What's with this secret-agent
crap?"

Asunder's face showed no offense, but his eyes sparkled

as he turned Wali's way. "You are in our lands now," he said simply. "And here our word is law."

"Your word is bull," Wali growled. "Why should we trust you?"

"Trust or no trust," Asunder said, "you must obey."

Wali's hands clenched, and for a second I thought he was going to launch himself at Asunder. Archangel must have sensed it too, because he stepped away from me to stand closer to his leader.

Asunder, though, didn't look worried. "Your spirit is admirable," he said in his calmest tones. "But this is a fight you cannot win."

"I'll be damned—"

"He's right," I said to Wali. "You're not helping."

Wali's anger shifted instantly to me. "I don't remember electing you leader. Just because she's out—"

"You have a better plan?" I said softly. "You want to take them all on?" Personally, I wasn't convinced we could take on Archangel alone, even if our hands were free. "What about the kids? What's going to happen to them if we get ourselves killed?"

Wali's look stabbed me. "Laman would never have put up with this."

"Yeah, well, Laman's dead." A pang shot through me as I said the words, the first time I'd said them out loud. "And so is Soon. Unless you want to join them, you'd better do what he says."

Fury reddened Wali's face, but he shut his mouth and tried to control his breathing.

"All right," he said. "But when they walk us off a cliff, don't say I didn't warn you."

"If they walk us off a cliff," I said, "I'll remember to thank you on the way down."

Asunder had stood watching us argue, an amused smile on his lips. Now he signaled for his men to put on the blindfolds. I glanced around at our group, saw the bewildered expressions on Tyris's and Nekane's faces, the terror on the kids'. The old woman slept on in the warrior's arms. Only Nessa returned my look with a steely calm. Unexpectedly, meeting her eyes strengthened my resolve. I knew that if I was going to get us out of this, I had to think like a leader. And that meant making sure we didn't lose anyone else.

The last thing I saw before the strip blocked my vision was Asunder's self-satisfied smile.

We marched in darkness, the warriors guiding us with their hands as our path sloped gradually upward. At one point the darkness became absolute and the air turned chilly, and I figured we'd entered a cavern that cut into the wall of the gorge. We banked this way and that in the dark, our footsteps taking on the echoing sound of an enclosed place, and before long I lost my bearings. When we emerged into semidarkness and the hotter air of the outside, I became convinced our detour had served no purpose except to confuse our sense of direction. But then we sheared inside the canyon wall again, and this time we didn't come out into the open. Instead, we stopped moving. I felt hands untie the blindfold, and I took my first look at the world around me in at least an hour.

For a moment it was as dark as the world inside the blindfold. Then torches sprang to light, and I blinked in the sudden brightness. When my eyes adjusted, I saw that we stood inside a tunnel, a bare gray space of solid rock no more than five feet across, with a curved ceiling that hung a mere foot above our heads. Archangel's hulking body stooped nearly double to fit in the cramped space. A strange, musky odor filled my nostrils, maybe from the smoke of the handheld torches.

Asunder took the lead once more as we started down the tunnel. The torches threw our shadows against the walls, and I realized those walls weren't as bare as I'd thought. In fact they were covered, floor to ceiling, with stick-figure drawings in faded red and brown. I picked out images of humans with animal antlers, hunters tracking four-footed creatures, dancers spinning around rough sketches of campfires. My eyes were caught by one drawing that had been rendered with more than usual detail: a solid brown shape that rose to two sharp points, with a single human figure standing between the uprights. The artwork, flickering and twisting eerily in the torchlight, sparked the word I'd been searching for to describe our captors, a word I had no memory of learning about a people I'd never imagined I had the possibility of seeing.

Cavemen. They were like cavemen.

But not dirty, hairy, backward cavemen. Archangel might be stooped, but I could tell he wasn't stupid. Like the rest of them, he was far cleaner than us, lacking the layer of accumulated grit that clung to us like a second skin. Their skimpy outfits were neat and unsoiled, and though their weapons might be primitive, they'd made ours look like pathetic toys. I wasn't sure whether Asunder and his followers were a survival colony, but they operated like a people perfectly at home in their surroundings, totally unlike the desperate, day-to-day fight to stay alive I'd known under Laman and Aleka.

We walked for maybe fifteen minutes, the drawings parading on both sides of us in an unbroken mural. If the tunnel had been built by human hands, it hadn't been built with humans Archangel's size in mind. But the giant lieutenant showed no signs of discomfort as he followed along, not even a hitch in his breath to suggest his lungs were compressed by the awkward position. I had just turned to inspect him, hoping to catch a hint of his thoughts in his broad, expressionless face, when I bumped into the warrior in front of me and realized Asunder had called a silent halt.

I looked around and saw that we stood in a spot where the tunnel branched into three. Curtains made of the same material as Archangel's cloak hung over each entrance. Asunder turned to face us, and though his eyes were only a dark flicker in the torches' glow, I had the creepy feeling they were directed at me.

"We stand within the outer circle of the Sheltered Lands," he said. "Here you will rest for the remainder of the day, while your minds are permitted time for reflection. Your blindfolds we have removed, that you might see clearly the promise we hold for all who seek the one true way. Your hands will remain bound until it is shown to us that you have chosen to accept the gifts we have to offer."

He lifted the central of the three curtains, revealing a shallow cave lit only by the tunnel's torchlight. When the warriors began to herd us toward the opening, it was obvious these were prison cells. And when they began to divide our colony into three—adults in one cell, teens in another, little kids remaining in the company of the warriors—Nessa and I jumped forward at once to prevent them from separating the children from the rest of us.

The reaction was immediate. For the first time since they'd captured us, they pointed the wicked-looking spears at our chests, surrounding me and Nessa with a palisade of lethal spikes. Before any of us could move, we were pinned by the warriors, Archangel holding Wali so tightly it was as if his body had been frozen into stone, the adults and children hemmed in by a swarm of armed men. The leader shook his head sadly, but his eyes flashed with the first sign I'd seen of anger. This time when he spoke, there was no mistaking that his words were aimed at me.

"You will find that a leader's first charge is to compel obedience from his people," he said, torchlight coloring the facets of his eyes. "For their own good, lest disaster befall them. Perhaps that is one lesson your former leaders, in their folly, neglected to impart to you. Let us hope for your sake that you discover this wisdom before it is too late." Then, with a dismissive toss of his head, he signaled his warriors to lead us into the caves.

"Great move, Commander Querry," Wali said.

The four of us were alone in one of the cells: me, Nessa, Wali, and Adem. We'd been here for hours, the only change in the monotony coming when two of Asunder's people pushed aside the screen and entered to give us brown mats to sleep on. They kept their heads down and said nothing, and it took me a second to realize they were women, long-haired like the warriors, wearing brown bands across their chests and around their throats in addition to their loincloths. When they left, Adem retreated to a dark corner, huddling against the wall, but Wali resumed the pacing he'd begun when we arrived. As he walked, his hand played with the hollow of his throat, as if he was still feeling for the ring they'd taken from him.

Now he stopped in front of me and snapped his fingers an inch from my face. "Ground control to Querry. Come in, Querry."

"I heard you," I said.

"So what's the plan, boss? We going to stick around and learn more of that bastard's ways of wisdom?"

"Quiet," Nessa said, gesturing with her eyes toward the cave opening. Light from the tunnel threw a guard's silhouette against the curtain.

With a visible effort, Wali lowered his voice. "Well?"

"Let me know your alternative," I said, keeping my voice down, "and I'd be happy to listen."

"You weren't so interested in my alternative before," he said. "But I'm sure they're petrified now that they think a scrawny kid's in charge."

"Someone has to be in charge," I said. "The last thing Aleka told me to do was take over from her. Which is exactly what I did."

"And you're doing such a brilliant job, too," Wali sneered. "You tell him your name, you let him lead us into this maze . . . What's next? You going to offer Bea and Keely as his personal slaves?"

"Did you see the women?" Nessa whispered. "It's like they actually are slaves. And don't you think it's a little suspicious that—"

"That's what I'm saying!" Wali cut her off. "The whole thing's suspicious. And Querry's working on ways to get us in so deep we'll never get out."

"I'm still waiting to hear your alternative," I said.

Wali paced to the cave's mouth. The guard's shadow didn't budge.

"I'm trying to figure out a way to get us out of here," I said. "Alive. You think I trust Asunder? You think I don't see what he's doing? But I'm not about to put everyone at risk just to show how tough I am. We've lost enough as it is."

Wali turned from the cave mouth and glared at me across the shadowy space. I stared right back. His hand clutched at his throat, like the missing string was a lifeline he was grasping for, or a noose he wanted to slip around my neck.

Nessa looked back and forth between us. Then she hooked a hand around Wali's arm and pulled him away from the curtain. When she got him in front of me, she stopped and smiled. I thought she was going to make us shake hands or something equally ridiculous, but instead, she released him and leaned over, her long braid dangling to the ground.

"Go on," she said to me. "Take it."

At first I thought she meant her hair. Then I saw, nestled securely in the strands of her braid so it was hidden when her hair hung down her back, the handle of a pocketknife.

"I can't loosen it myself," she said. "Take it."

I reached out and gripped the handle of the knife. She'd woven it so tightly between the links of the braid a few strands caught and I had to yank it free.

"Ouch," Nessa said, but when she lifted her head she was grinning.

"How did you . . . ?" Wali said.

"Well, while you boys were busy being no help at all . . ." She smiled again, a devilish smirk I'd never expected to see on her pertly pretty face.

Wali tried to hug her, but the best he could manage was a rough shove. "Did I ever tell you I love you?"

"Thankfully, no." She held her hands out to me. "The first thing a leader has to learn, Querry," she said with a wink, "is to never underestimate the deviousness of his subordinates."

I stifled a laugh, then fingered the blade open and laid it against the brown ropes binding her hands. The cords had a springy, living feel beneath the metal.

Adem had stood and joined us. Everyone in our little huddle leaned over the knife as I sliced the ropes. As I'd expected, they resisted in a rubbery way, but in a second I had Nessa's wrists free. Wali shoved his hands toward us next, and I gave Nessa the knife so she could do the honors. When all of our bonds were cut, Wali started for the curtain, but I grabbed his arm to hold him back.

"Get off of me," he said, shaking me loose. He was older and stronger, and I didn't try to fight back.

"We're staying here," I said.

"What are you talking about?" he said. "This is our chance!"

I shook my head. "You said it yourself. This place is a maze. If we try to escape now, we'll be right back where we started. Except without our one weapon and with someone like Archangel watching us. We need to wait for them to drop their guard before we make our move."

Wali paced to the curtain and stood there for a second, quivering with anger. Then he returned to me.

"So let me get this straight," he said. "You give them the green light to lead us here, where you knew we'd get lost. And now that we have our one chance to get free, you tell us we can't, because we're lost. Whose side are you on, anyway?"

"My side," Nessa said. She reached out and touched my hand, then loosened and retied her braid with the knife held securely in its links. Next she retrieved the ropes from the floor and, making sure to disguise the knots, tied them loosely around my wrists and Adem's. I did the same to hers.

Wali watched the whole procedure in silence. When Nessa reached out to retie the cords around his wrists, he flung himself away and retreated to a corner of the cave. She started to follow him, but fell back when she saw the murderous expression on his face.

I played what I thought was my trump card. "Wouldn't Laman have wanted us to stick together?"

He gave me a look of pure hate. "You don't know what Laman would have wanted. He taught me and Korah to fight. What did he teach you?"

I was trying to come up with an answer when Nessa spoke. Her voice was filled with sorrow, but her words were made of steel.

"Korah's dead, Wali," she said. "We know how much you loved her, but you can't bring her back. The question is, are you going to help us keep the others alive?"

Wali's eyes blazed, and when he spoke, the words came

out bleeding and raw. "Screw you, Nessa. You were always jealous of what me and Korah had. Why don't you and your freak boyfriend go end your miserable lives? In fact"—and he took a step toward us, hands knotted in fists—"why don't I just do it myself?"

Nessa didn't back down. Her eyes, I thought, glistened with unshed tears. But she took my arm and steered me away, while Wali hurled curses at our backs. They echoed loudly in the tiny cave. The guard outside remained motionless. Adem covered his ears and sank once again into his corner.

"Well, that went just the way I planned," I said, trying to smile.

"Give him time to grieve, Querry," Nessa said softly. "He's in so much pain right now, but he'll come around. I've known Wali forever, and I know he'll do what's right for the colony."

"If he doesn't—"

"He will," she said, putting a finger to my lips. "Now let's make our plan. Whatever happens tomorrow"—and her eyes flashed in the semidarkness—"I want us to be ready for it."

4

Asunder's men came for us in the morning.

At least, I assumed it was morning. Spending the night in an enclosure more substantial than a tent was a first for me, and where I expected sun, all I got was more gloom. But the warriors who threw aside our curtain and prodded us with the butts of their spears were obviously anxious to get going, so it seemed the day had dawned.

I'd spent a restless night. For one thing, I discovered that Adem made up for his lack of intelligible speech with a surplus of snoring. I'd never noticed it when we slept out in the open, but in the tiny cave his snorts and snuffles just about rattled my brain. More importantly, I kept turning over in my head how we were going to get out of this trap. Wali had finally relented and let Nessa retie his cords, but I still didn't trust him not to foul up our plan. And I had to admit, it wasn't much of a plan. Figuring Asunder might ease off once he'd gotten whatever he wanted from us, Nessa and I had agreed we should play along for the time being, not confront him openly. That might not win our freedom, but it might open up space for us to operate, and it was sure better than charging headfirst into a nest of armed warriors. Still, it was a pretty slim hope, and as the hours of the night marched relentlessly toward dawn, it started to feel slimmer and slimmer.

Every time I closed my eyes, Wali's question returned to haunt my thoughts. What *had* Laman taught me? Lots of things. How to tie a knot, how to hunt for food and shade, how to scout for Skaldi. He'd told me never to give up, always to keep looking toward the future. But at the moment, it felt like the most important thing he'd taught me was this: stick together. If you're going to fight for something, fight for the colony. Because in this world, nobody makes it on their own.

I didn't want just one or two of us to get out of here. And I didn't want to lose any more lives. I wanted the colony together, and free. Wali might not think I knew how to fight, but I was ready to fight for that.

I glanced at Nessa as the guards pushed us out of our cell to face their leader. She nodded and discreetly touched her braid. Knowing we were still on the same page definitely helped. Not knowing what lay in wait for us definitely didn't.

They led us down the third branch of the tunnels to a short flight of stairs carved into the rock. There Asunder met us, emerging from a recess in the wall that must have led to his sleeping quarters.

"You stand near the very heart of the Sheltered Lands," he said, speaking no louder than a whisper but with no loss of clarity or power. "In our tongue we name this place *Grava Bracha*, the Spring of the Blessed. Here you will learn our ways and partake of the gifts we have to offer. Do not doubt what you see. It has been prepared for those who wander and are lost."

With that, he ascended the stairway. At the top, he faced us once more, smiled, and threw aside a curtain of the brown material, letting a flood of brilliant light bathe our upturned faces. When he disappeared inside, the rest of us followed. One of the warriors held the curtain, and I stepped into the light.

Despite Asunder's words, I couldn't help stopping in shock.

My first thought was that I'd walked through a gateway into another world. As far as I could see, thousands of multicolored lights floated in the air a hundred feet above my head, and I had to stamp on the ground to convince myself I hadn't drifted off into space. I craned my neck and squinted at the soaring vault to try to make out what these lights were and how they hung at such a dizzying height, but they dazzled me and made it impossible to tell. Gradually I realized the light came from the ceiling and floor and distant walls of a cavern so huge I couldn't see the end of it. An array of luminescent colors spilled from the rock itself: blues far brighter than any sky I'd seen, pinks that put the healthiest of the little kids' cheeks to shame, yellows and greens and purples that shimmered like the curved bow the old woman told us used to come after a rainstorm. In the approximate center of the cavern lay a pool, its surface dotted with countless points of light, the water kept in constant motion by a bubbling fountain that seemed to harbor a pure white radiance of its own. Reflections from the water swung lazily across the room, keeping time with the soothing sound of the fountain. So much light poured all around me I half expected to look at my own hands and see them glowing with an inner fire.

And there were people seated on brown mats throughout the cavern. Lots of people. I'd been hoping the twenty or so warriors we'd seen were the total of Asunder's forces, but I counted close to a hundred more, scattered in groups of five to ten. Most of them were warriors, but some were women like the ones I'd seen last night, wearing brown wraps around their chests and brown bands around their throats. Like the warriors, they mostly appeared young, possibly no older than Nessa. But while the men lounged on their mats, talking quietly in their own language, the women worked noiselessly on one job or another, heads lowered to their tasks. Some mended mats, others stirred pots over a small fire, others washed brown garments in the fountain, wrung them out, and draped them over another fire to dry. Two women sat with a circle of children, heads lowered as if they were leading them in some sort of prayer. Studying the group more closely, I realized with shock—but also with relief—that some of the children were our own, except they'd been clothed in the cave dwellers' uniforms. Their bellies showed pale and scrawny next to the bronzed bodies of our captors. But they didn't seem distressed. In fact they seemed to have found new playmates among the children of the cave dwellers, all of whom, it appeared from their hair and clothing, were boys. Only Zataias kept a wary distance from the cave-children, and when he caught my eye he nodded slightly as if to show me he was still on my team.

I searched for the adult members of our colony, and in a moment I found Tyris and Nekane, sitting under the guard of a group of warriors. Unlike the children, whose hands had been freed, theirs remained bound. The only people missing were Aleka and the old woman, and my heart dropped at the realization.

"What have you done with the others?" I asked Asunder.

"They are well," he answered in an unconcerned voice. "Their needs are tended by our healer Melampus."

"Take us to them," Nessa demanded.

I glanced at her, but Asunder didn't appear to take offense. At a silent signal from him, two warriors broke away from one of the groups and led us to a much smaller cave that branched off from the main cavern. There we found Aleka and the old woman, resting on brown mats while the bearded man hovered over them. I couldn't tell if my mother's color looked any better, but her breathing seemed easy and her forehead didn't feel feverish. Neither she nor the old woman woke up while we were there, and our visit was all too brief, Archangel appearing at the doorway to usher us back to the main cavern. I threw a look back at my mother's pale face, hoping she'd be okay and realizing how her injury complicated any escape plans I might make.

Back at the main cavern, we found Asunder standing by the bubbling fountain, the children of his colony and ours arranged around him. A benevolent smile disguised any impatience he might have felt. When we appeared, he strode to a luminescent rock carved in the rough shape of a chair and seated himself on a cushion as red as his cloak. One woman left the fountain and hurriedly laid a circle of mats on the ground, then scampered back to her work by the pool's side. Asunder nodded, and we followed our guards' example, seating ourselves on the mats. Wali needed a sharp look from me before he would agree to lower himself in front of what was obviously meant to be a throne.

"Food is prepared," Asunder said simply. His rich voice was muted, and a kindly smile played on his lips. As we looked up at him from our seats on the ground, the gushing fountain seemed to frame his head with a halo of light.

"Thank you," I said, knowing it was what he expected. Wali glanced at me with distaste, and Asunder's smile flickered sardonically. But he nodded and turned his gaze to the women at the cooking station, who instantly brought steaming bowls and set them on the ground before us. They kept their heads lowered and didn't say a word.

The meal consisted of a thick, sloppy stew and flat, palm-size wafers, which I saw Asunder's men doubling to form a sort of cup so they could shovel the food into their mouths. The littlest members of our colony mastered the technique quickly, helped by having their hands free. I clumsily tried to do the same, the trickiest part being how to hide the knots we'd tied in our bindings. I managed to spill most of what I scooped, testing what remained with the tip of my tongue. It was hot and surprisingly tasty, unlike so much of the gag-worthy food I'd eaten in Survival Colony 9.

Asunder didn't join the feast, but his eyes roamed over us throughout our meal. The warriors chattered the whole time in their own language. At another mute signal from their leader, one of the women appeared, bringing water from the fountain in a clay pitcher. The warriors held out their hands, and when they were clean, some cupped their palms to receive a drink. My stomach felt too full for more than a small sip, but I found the water cool and refreshingly clean. When I was done, I leaned back, letting my stomach expand, and watched as the women hurried the bowls to the fountain for cleansing. Nessa, I saw out of the corner of my eye, was frowning as she watched them fulfill their menial tasks.

"My children," Asunder said warmly, snapping me out of my reverie, "we welcome the strangers to our home, and we invite them to hear the words we have to say."

He stood and stepped down from the throne. As the remaining warriors and women drifted over from every corner of the cavern and seated themselves around us, he reached for the bone-white staff at his side, laying it on the ground in the center of the circle. At the sight of it, the warriors and women bowed low, their arms outstretched and their heads touching the ground. The cave-children, I saw, did the same. They stayed like that for a long moment before sitting up again.

Asunder's eyes swept the audience, his irises as full of colors as the rock surrounding him. I tried to meet his gaze, but that was hard to do when moment by moment I seemed to be looking into a new pair of eyes.

"Our guests have traveled from afar," he began, in the rich tones that seemed to come so naturally to him. "They have crossed the desert waste, they have walked the very rim of the Shattered Lands, and now they come to us, weary in body and sick in soul. They have faced the Merciless Ones, the ones who feed on men's flesh, and they have suffered losses almost too grievous to bear. Their companions they have watched fall, and their hopes they have seen crumble into dust."

I stared at him, and he stared back, the scars on his face once again pulling his lips upward in a weird smile.

"Oh yes, we know their ways, and their woes, far better than they think," he said. "Even better, perhaps, than they know them themselves. For long years we have watched the sons of the despoilers vainly struggling for existence within the wasteland their fathers prepared for them. We have seen that they do not learn from the sins of the past, but seek to relive them: to drive their foul machines atop the ashes of their ancestors, to slaughter each other with their weapons of war, to desecrate the ground with their tools of metal. We have walked among them, and sickened at the stench of death that pursues them. And we have seen them wither before the ones sent in judgment of their crimes."

He paused, and in the silence it struck me that maybe he had once belonged to a survival colony. He was obviously talking about the Skaldi, and he sounded like someone who had witnessed their attacks. Was that what accounted for the scars across his body, the madness in his mind?

"Yet we of the Sheltered Lands have ever pursued a different course," he resumed after a moment. "We have learned to disdain those false idols that have been the despoilers' undoing. With clean hands and clean hearts, we have renewed the ground, drawing from it the poisons of the despoilers, restoring it to its former health. Working only with that which is given freely by the land—wood and water, sand and stone—we have healed the land of its sickness. And so we live in comfort and ease, delighting in all the needful things of life: food aplenty, and clean water to drink, and clothing for our bodies, and safe homes for our children. We ask for little, for we have far greater gifts than any man of olden days could claim."

His audience was nodding, so whether they understood our language or not, they must have been familiar with the theme. But with a sharp look from him, they froze as perfectly as if they'd been turned to stone.

"And so we might live forever," Asunder said in a voice quieter yet sharper than before, "enjoying what is ours to enjoy, keeping from all others those gifts our wise acts have merited. But we who are wise bear no ill will toward any other. Though we despise the deeds of the despoilers, we do not ignore their children's desperate need. And so to these forsaken ones we offer what they most sorely lack: rest from their weary struggles, an end to affliction, the comfort and safety that come only to those who follow the one true way. We offer this freely, and without begrudging any man the gifts we have to give. We ask only that they make a choice: to give up the lives they once lived and come to us as children reborn. That is all we ask. And we say to those who accept this offer, come and live with us, and live in joy abounding! But to those who reject what we have to offer, we say: let them be cast out, let them return to the waste their fathers have laid for such as them, and let them be abandoned there to meet the one who lies in wait in the Shattered Lands beyond. Let them stand upon his altar in nakedness and fear, and let them meet their judgment at his hands. Let them face him, the one we name *Nidach bar Tivah*: the Scavenger of Souls."

At the sound of these words, the cave-people bowed their

heads again, murmuring something in their own tongue. Asunder waited for their voices to ebb, then his own voice was raised again.

"This is what we ask of you, travelers from afar: to choose between the ways of death and the ways of life, the doom of all who doubt and the victory of all who truly believe. We offer this choice freely, and we ask that you make it freely. Which will you choose, my friends? Will you prefer the path of the despoilers, the path that leads to your own and your children's destruction? Or will you choose the path of salvation, the path that leads to life and joy everlasting?"

With this final word, he stooped to clutch the staff that lay at his feet. When he rose I tensed, fearing what he might do. But he merely walked through the crowd, lowering the stick to the shoulder of each of his followers, who closed their eyes and smiled as if they'd received a blessing. Men, women, and children submitted to this ritual, all except Archangel, who stood silently outside the circle, arms crossed. When the ten-minute long ceremony concluded, Asunder returned the staff to his side and his followers stood, the women moving off to their stations with the children of our colony and theirs, the warriors remaining in a circle by the throne. Then, to my surprise, one of the warriors entered the circle and began to dance.

He gyrated in a stiff, awkward way, with bent knees and bobbing torso and stamping feet, his whole body turning in a tight, slow circle. The other warriors hummed wordlessly as their fellow danced, one of them pounding out a rhythm on the cavern floor with his palms. Asunder returned to his throne and watched, a critical look on his face as if he was scrutinizing the performance. The dancer's body glistened with sweat, his flesh seeming encrusted with tiny jewels as the droplets reflected the cavern's gem-fire. All at once he stopped, and the drummer stopped too, only the humming continuing at a lowered volume.

The dancer threw his head back and shouted words in their tongue. The others responded with an unfamiliar sound when he paused for breath. I turned to Nessa. "Are we supposed to watch—?"

"Shh," she said. "I'm trying to listen."

"You understand what they're saying?" It seemed I'd never stop being surprised by what was going on behind her sleepy green eyes.

"Not really," she said. "I picked up a few words. Like *tivah*—that's 'people,' but I think it's also 'soul.' As in *Nidach bar Tivah*, Scavenger of Souls. And they kept saying *shashi* for the torches, so I assume that's 'fire,' or maybe 'light.' *Bracha* is 'water' or 'drink.' They said it when they passed around the pitcher. So *shashi tivah bracha* . . . The fire drank his soul? Or maybe his soul was washed clean by fire? I think that's what he means."

"What are the others saying?"

"No idea," she said. "It might just be a sound, not a word. And the rest of it is gibberish to me." She squeezed her eyes tight in concentration. "*Nidach asa minach* . . . I have no idea what that means."

"He says the Scavenger of Souls awaits," a voice rumbled by my ear. I jumped and found Archangel hovering over us. "The Scavenger waits to see if any will refuse to cleanse his soul with purifying fire. *Nidach asa minach*. The Scavenger awaits."

"What happens to those who refuse?" I said.

He shrugged his massive shoulders. "The Scavenger awaits those who resist us. He is tireless and all powerful. Against him there is no resistance."

Nessa jumped in. "Who is he?"

Another shrug. "The Scavenger wards the faithful, and does not suffer the sons of the despoilers to raise their hands against us. He is the one who sits in judgment, the watcher at the world's end."

I tried a new tack. "Have you ever . . . lost anyone to the Scavenger of Souls?"

He didn't answer at first. For a moment I thought I'd hit a nerve, as I saw a roiling in his almost-black eyes like currents beneath still water. But the stony expression returned to chase any turbulence away.

"There are those who have resisted us," he said simply. "Those who have doubted the rightness of our way. The Scavenger is ever mindful of those whose feet stray from the one true path."

"He is also a complete crock," Wali unexpectedly joined

the conversation. "But a really convenient way to keep a bunch of ignorant savages in line."

Archangel shrugged one final time and moved on.

The dance lasted a minute more, the dancer collapsing dramatically at the end only to spring up smiling and receive pats on the back from his companions. When it was over, Asunder nodded gravely at the company and stood.

"Through our faith and acts, we unshackle our souls from the sins of the past," he said. "*Shashi tivah bracha, aya tivah bis.* In the holy fires of renewal, our souls drink deeply, and they return wholly other than once they were. *Minach, minach tivah.* Fill, oh fill our souls! Only those who cling stubbornly to the ways of the despoilers"—and his eyes fell on Wali—"can fail to be touched by this solemn appeal."

He clapped his hands together, the sharp sound reverberating through the cavern.

"Travelers from afar," he said. "You have heard what we have to say, and listened to the rich offer we have extended to you. Now each of you has a choice to make: accept the path that is laid before you, or refuse that path and fall into the arms of the one who waits. We grant you one day and night more to reflect on this choice, and to answer of your own free will at morning's first light. But do not deceive yourselves"—and now his eyes lingered on me and Nessa—"in thinking to delay, or to wheedle, or to malinger. Do not think, as some have thought, that we waste breath on idle threats. By tomorrow, the choice must be made: life or death. No other choice is possible."

With that he exited the throne and left us, the warriors approaching to take us back to our cell. For once, Nessa seemed too stunned to keep up her composure, and she shuffled forward numbly with the warriors at her back. My head swam as I tried to process what Asunder had said. I'd thought we might have days, weeks, to play his game—time for Aleka to heal, for us to glean useful information from him, even to spot a weakness. But I realized I'd been fooling myself. Why would he wait, when he had us in his power now?

The cell was as quiet as a tomb. Wali threw himself down in the corner he'd chosen, as far from the rest of us as possible. Nessa kept touching her hair as if to assure herself the knife was still in place. We waited for what seemed like hours, and probably was, but there was no change in the twilight gloom. The guard's shadow on the curtain never moved. At last I broke the silence.

"Did you see any ways out?" I asked Nessa.

"There were lots of recesses in the main cavern," she said. "But I couldn't tell if they led to exits or just to more caves."

"What about the spring?" I said. "It has to start somewhere."

She shook her head. "Aleka and the old woman would never make it. And most of the little ones can't swim."

I nodded, trying to look as if I'd been evaluating our

67

options as thoroughly as she had. The truth was, it hadn't even occurred to me that I probably couldn't swim either.

We talked some more about the layout of the main cavern, the guards at the cell doors, the mismatch in our numbers. The kids too small to run, the members of our colony too weak to fight. The fact that even if we did get out in the open, we had nowhere to run to. The canyon belonged to Asunder. The black rock plateau wouldn't keep us alive for long. And if Asunder was to be believed, the Scavenger of Souls waited for us if we tried to find refuge there.

We talked until I knew we had nothing left to say.

Stick together. The colony is the key. As artificial day dragged into artificial night, Laman's words returned to me for the umpteenth time. Was it worth saving people's lives if it meant forfeiting their freedom?

I didn't want to say it, but finally I did.

"Maybe we need to join them. For now, until we figure out a way to free ourselves."

Wali surprised me by not saying anything. Adem surprised me even more by speaking up.

"It might not be so bad," he mumbled. "You heard what Asunder said about how they've restored the canyon. That could be a good thing. Maybe we could . . . help them. With the bioremediation."

We all stared at him. Even Nessa seemed surprised to hear that word come from his mouth.

"Bio-what?" Wali said sharply.

Back in character, Adem blushed. "Remediation. I heard about it from—from someone. Leeching toxins from the soil. Rebuilding its nutrients. So things can grow again."

I knew the *someone* Adem couldn't bring himself to name was Laman. But I'd never heard our former commander talk about repairing the land, much less on the scale Asunder had described. The only time he'd come close was the day before he lost control of the colony. He'd spent that whole day trying to rebuild the ruined compound where we'd made our camp, the whole night fighting the Skaldi that had infiltrated our defenses. The Skaldi that had killed Korah and then attacked me. By the light of morning, any hopes we'd had of resurrecting the past had been trampled into the dust with the rest of our dreams.

"I wonder how they did it," Adem continued, an unmistakable edge of excitement to his voice. "The things Asunder said. He was talking about bioremediation on a massive scale. Diverting the waste alone would take a lifetime. Plus you'd practically have to scrub the atmosphere clean for anything to grow." He looked at us eagerly, blushing when no one said anything. "I just don't see how they could do all that with the technology they have."

"How'd you become such an authority?" Wali asked.

The blush deepened. "Someone told me."

Wali laughed bitterly. "So the Stick agrees with our fearless leader that we should stay and help these lunatics out. I say that's what cowards do."

Adem's face crumpled. Nessa laid a hand on his arm, which didn't improve his color one bit.

"I say we've had enough of trying to make nice with these nutjobs," Wali continued. "I say we make our break tonight."

"And leave the kids?" I said. "And Aleka?"

"And return for them later," he said. "When we can come for them with numbers."

"And where are we supposed to find those?" I was aware that I was practically yelling, that the guard could surely hear me, but I couldn't seem to stop myself. "Admit it, Wali. If you leave, you're not coming back. You're leaving everyone else here to rot."

He shoved me, the sloppy knots around his wrists snapping with the force. I fell against the wall, remembering how much stronger he was than me. But I faced him anyway. I was too angry to hold back.

"You're the coward!" I said. "You're the one who wants to ditch everyone else to save your own neck!"

"And you're the one who wants to kowtow to his majesty!" Wali screamed. "I've let you run the show for two days, and in the meantime he's got Aleka practically in a coma, and the kids walking around like little savages, and you're still in here talking about appeasing him, not fighting him. The next thing you know—"

"The next thing you know he'll be putting one of those collars around my neck!" Nessa shouted. I'd been so focused on Wali I'd practically forgotten she was there. Now she stood between us, her face suffused with fury. "Did you ever stop to think of that? You act like you're so smart, Wali. You haven't even noticed the way Asunder looks at me."

Wali and I fell silent, staring at her in shock. I was mortified to realize I hadn't noticed either. "Do you think he—"

"There's nothing I think he wouldn't do," she said. "You've seen the way they treat their women. They're not Asunder's children. They're barely even human. They're his *wives*."

I tried to say something, but couldn't.

"You boys can argue all you want about whether we should stay or go," Nessa said. "But it's not the same for you. The worst that can happen to you is death. The worst that can happen to me and Beatrice is *life*—as that monster's slave."

She faced us, cheeks flushed, eyes on fire. The cell seemed even quieter after all the shouting. Wali flung himself away and retreated to his corner, Adem stumbling to his own. Nessa tore her bonds free, wrapped her arms around her chest, and turned away.

I tried to approach her, but she wouldn't look at me. My hand started to inch toward hers before my head had the sense to make it stop. I racked my brain for the right thing to say, to show her I understood. To tell her I knew what it was like to have your life taken away from you. To tell her I would fight for her.

I wanted to tell her, but I never got the chance. Wali

returned from his corner of the cave, and I tensed for another face-off. But he went up to Nessa instead and looked at her, his eyes feverish and wild.

"I'll help you," he said to her. "I won't let that bastard touch you."

She scoffed. "And how are you going to do that?"

Wali said nothing more, returning to his corner and stretching out on the mat.

For the second straight night, sleep laughed in my face. I tormented myself over the choice I'd made, the way I'd failed Nessa and Aleka and everyone. I wished I'd fought with Asunder, refused to go along with him, let Wali take the knife. At least that way, the worst that would have happened to us was death.

Deep into the night I heard Nessa murmuring to herself.

"Minach," I heard her say, turning the word over and over like a stone she was trying to peer beneath. *"Minach, minach tivah."*

I woke from dreams I couldn't remember to find Nessa shaking my shoulder, speaking my name. Her dusky outline rose before me in the never-changing gloom of our prison cell.

"Querry," she whispered sharply. "It's gone."

"What is?"

"My knife," she said. "It's gone."

"They took it?"

"I don't know," she said. "But it's gone."

I sat up straight, the fog of sleep clearing at her words. In the dimness of the cave I saw her shape, one hand clutching her braid as if she could make the knife reappear. Then a look of horrified recognition stole across her face, and we both turned to the corner where Wali slept.

His mat was empty.

"He can't have gotten far," I said. We stood and moved to the curtain that blocked the cave mouth.

All was quiet beyond. No shadow broke the torchlight from the tunnel. My stomach dropped when I realized what that meant.

Hesitantly I pulled the screen aside. The light spilled over me like a chill sun.

In its glow, I saw the guard stretched on the floor, his eyes like mica, his throat a red gash. Blood pooled beneath his head, smeared by his killer's footprints. Wali had taken the man's spear, too, but he'd used Nessa's knife to carve a parting message in the stone.

Its letters were crude streaks flecked with the guard's blood, but I could read them clearly, lighter scratches against the tunnel wall's light.

He'd written three words: *metal cuts better.*

5

Nessa, Adem, and I tried to follow the bloody trail of foot-prints, but we didn't get far.

We were met by Archangel at the head of a group of war-riors, who forced us back to the cave. They stared in horror at the body on the floor, only Archangel's expression remaining unchanged. Then they retied our bonds securely and led us to Asunder.

The leader was awake, standing in the throne room with a terrible smile on his scarred face.

Nessa threw herself at him too fast for the guards to stop her. He made no move to defend himself as she spat violently in his face.

"You knew!" she screamed. "You knew this would hap-pen! You *meant* for it to happen!"

Asunder said nothing as Archangel restrained Nessa. She struggled, tried to bite the giant's hands. When Archangel held her in his unyielding grip at last, Asunder lifted his voice so that it rang across the cavern.

"The sons of the despoilers have defiled our sanctuary, spilled the blood of those who offered them priceless gifts!" he boomed. "What punishment befits such a crime?"

"Behal!" the warriors thundered in a single voice. "Behal Nidach bar Tivah!"

Asunder smiled cruelly. "Feed them," he said softly, as if to himself. "Feed them to the Scavenger of Souls. It is just, my children. It is our way." Raising his arms above his head, he called out to the company, "The Scavenger awaits! Take them to his altar, and there let them be bound to meet their fate!"

He nodded at Archangel, who half prodded, half dragged me and Nessa across the cavern. Nessa needed a lot more dragging than prodding. Asunder took the lead, and twenty or more warriors flooded after us. I turned to see Adem, Tyris, and Nekane bound and struggling to keep up with their captors' mad rush. The children of Survival Colony 9 had joined the crowd too, though their hands remained unbound. Their faces looked strangely empty, and though I couldn't be sure as I was jostled and shoved, it seemed to me they shied from eye contact, all except Zataias. At the very rear of the throng, I glimpsed a stretcher bearing a single pale form, the still-unconscious body of my mother.

Nessa's voice was in my ear, speaking in a hushed tone. "He used us, Querry. He used Wali to cement his hold over his people. That's what this was about all along. The Scavenger of Souls, all the rest of it—it was all a lie to justify a lynching."

"You think they killed their own man?"

Her lip curled. "I wouldn't be surprised. But Wali was desperate enough to do anything. I wish I'd seen it, I wish I'd said something to him. . . ."

"It's not your fault," I said. "I let you all down. I let them do this to you."

Nessa sighed. "It's no good playing the blame game, Querry," she said. "What we've got to do now is look for a way out. We wanted them to free us from this place." Her smile didn't soften the determination in her eyes. "It looks like we're about to get our wish."

She was right. We stampeded to the cavern's far end, where two warriors with spears blocked another exit. They sprang aside as if Asunder's eyes had physically repelled them. The new tunnel we charged down was much broader than the one from two days ago, though the lack of torches suggested it wasn't used much. In a few minutes I saw what looked like daylight patterning the stone, and moments later we reached the tunnel's end, two more armed warriors stepping out of our way as we burst into the outside world.

I blinked in sunlight every bit as bright but nowhere near as dazzling as the gem-fire of *Grava Bracha*. From the ledge where we stood, I saw that we remained within the canyon, but farther north than where we'd been captured, with the western wall rearing hundreds of feet across the open space and the clear-flowing river unfurling below. I had no time to take in the view before the crowd surged forward again, carrying us up a steep trail that clung to the canyon's eastern face. The sun hammered down on us, and though a wind tousled the cave dwellers' hair, it was the hot, stifling wind I'd known all my life. I gasped on the dusty air, felt my skin prickle under the beating sun. It was as if this trail marked a dividing point, an invisible boundary between the island they claimed as their own and the surrounding waste they had worked to keep at bay.

The crowd forced us upward at an almost inhuman pace. I tried to catch a glimpse of Aleka and the little kids, but Archangel's unbreakable grip prevented me. All I could see were spears and bare bodies, and all I could hear were pounding feet and the angry muttering of the mob. Asunder's cloak flamed ahead of me. The heat of the day and the heat of the warriors pressing around me made me feel light-headed and dizzy, and I wondered if, in the end, what they called the Scavenger of Souls was only a euphemism for pitching their enemies headfirst over the cliff to be splattered on the canyon floor.

Finally we stopped. The warriors grew instantly silent, their rumbling replaced by the moan of the wind. A combination of wonder and dread twisted my stomach.

We stood at the highest point of the canyon. At this height the gorge had divided like an opened scar, the western side hazy with distance. The trailhead offered enough room for everyone, but I leaned away from the drop, a feeling of vertigo taking hold. Asunder stood where the trail cleared the rim of the canyon, his arms crossed over his scarred chest. But he didn't need to point for my eyes to find what he wanted us to see.

The table of black rock we'd walked two days ago stretched out to the east, its lifeless expanse gleaming in the sun. Nothing moved in that inky waste, no speck of dust stirring in the hot wind. None of the rock formations or mounds we'd seen farther south blocked our view. But a mile or so away, a single shape bulged out of the dead land: a towering heap of night-black stone, a hundred feet tall at least, topped with twin spikes like horns. Seeing it through the blur of heat and glaring light, I realized I was seeing the peculiar illustration from the first tunnel, painstakingly reproduced to mirror the real: the rough, irregular outline, the tapering peak, the perfect symmetry of the horns. It stood too far away for me to tell if it had been shaped by human hands. But it reminded me enough of the Skaldi nest that a shiver ran through me despite the pounding heat of the late morning sun.

I knew without asking, without even thinking, what this place was.

The altar of the Scavenger of Souls.

Asunder stood silent for a moment, his cloak snapping in the wind, his brilliant eyes piercing the molten air. Then, in a voice that echoed across the empty land like the crack of a whip, he began to speak.

"My children!" he said. "In this place, as we have done

since the days of our first becoming, we gather to cast the unrighteous from our midst. We have spoken to the darkness, we have relinquished to the void those tricks and traps of the despoilers that would poison our hearts and enslave our minds. We have glimpsed a new life, the life of the faithful. *Aya tivah bis, shashi tivah bracha.* We have vowed to pursue the way of the righteous, that the wickedness of those who came before might perish utterly from the land."

His black eyes roved the crowd. His followers nodded fiercely at his words, or maybe at his commanding tone. I saw little Bea's head nodding too, though I couldn't believe she accepted or even understood half of what he said.

"In the days of old," Asunder continued, "the despoilers laid claim to this land, and in those days the land sickened and failed, and the skies darkened, and the great many perished in fire and ash. *Shashi bis, tivah bracha.* And yet there was one"—and his voice rose to an exalted pitch—"one man who resisted the despoilers' ways, and who did not suffer their sentence. This man took himself out into the waste, to pray and to be healed, and there he wrestled with a demon of the pit, and lo! though his body was broken he heard a voice speaking through the purified vessel of his soul. And this man traveled the land, gathering those who would heed his word, and he foretold that the children of the despoilers would bow down before the children of the light. And in the fullness of time these accursed sons of accursed fathers would be marked for all the world to see, and bound to the altar of the Shattered Lands, a fit sacrifice for the one we name *Nidach bar Tivah*. The malice-striker, the one who tears at flesh. The scourge of the unbeliever: the Scavenger of Souls."

The wind had picked up in intensity, whipping around us. Asunder's voice creaked and whined as it poured over the glassy surface of the Shattered Lands. His people began to sway, their eyes closed, their fists clenched on their chests. A low chant arose from their throats, a mutter like wind or water or blood throbbing through secret veins. Asunder listened to the murmur as it rose and fell, then cut it off with a glance. It died as abruptly as if a single giant creature had let out a grateful sigh.

"Bring them," he said.

Leaving Nessa in the hands of two warriors, Archangel stepped onto the black rock, forcing me ahead of him. Two additional warriors followed, bearing the prone form of Aleka in her stretcher. Getting my first good look at her since yesterday, I thought her face appeared thinner, the hollows around her eyes deeper than ever before.

Then, to my utter amazement, a final warrior detached himself from the throng, bearing the bound form of Wali.

He was naked to the waist, his uniform pants torn off at the knees to resemble the cave dwellers' costumes. Blood, whether his own or the dead guard's, streaked his chest and face, matted his hair. Though his eyes were open, he looked at me without seeing. As if in ridicule, they'd hung the ring they'd stolen from him around his neck, where it gleamed against the bloody stripes that crossed his chest.

The guard threw him at Asunder's feet. Wali crashed to the ground, then struggled into a kneeling position. But his head hung to his chest, and he seemed too exhausted or battered to rise.

Out of the corner of my eye, I saw Nessa fighting to free herself. Asunder looked straight at her and smiled, then reached for the white staff at his side. Eyes ablaze, he pointed it at Wali like a flayed bone. The warriors on the trailhead fell back, covering their faces with their hands as the staff touched Wali's forehead.

His head snapped back as if he'd received a stunning blow. For a second he remained on his knees, the ring around his neck wobbling as his body swayed. Then he went limp, chin lolling onto his chest, body collapsing to the stone. In the instant before his eyes closed, I saw something I'd never expected to see there. Not confusion, or surprise, or shock. Not even dismay.

What I saw was fear.

Asunder covered the ground to where Aleka lay and repeated the performance. At the touch of the staff, her body arched upward so violently she fell from the stretcher and thrashed against the stone, her injured arm snapping beneath her. I struggled to overcome Archangel's crushing strength, but he held me fast. Yet somehow Nessa wrenched free of her captors' hold, and I saw that she'd sliced the bonds around her wrists, maybe using one of the warrior's own spearpoints when we were surrounded by them. She leaped toward Archangel and pounded on the giant's back, but she might as well have been hammering the trunk of a tree. Another warrior grabbed at her, but she spun, ramming the heel of her hand into his nose, and he fell in a spray of blood. Then a group of warriors from the trail swarmed her, and she went down. The next instant Archangel lifted my feet from the ground and rocked me forward, bringing me within reach of Asunder's staff.

He smiled. I saw myself reflected in his eyes, my face fractured in their black depths like a kaleidoscope. I felt the staff touch my forehead.

I had a momentary sensation of cold, freezing cold, then searing pain coursed through me.

It felt as if I was being torn apart by hundreds of razor-sharp teeth. They punctured me, penetrated me. They filled my mind, blotting everything from my thoughts. I couldn't tell if I was conscious or not, if Archangel still held me, if my feet rested on the ground or my body had been cast into space. I couldn't remember my own name, the touch of the little kids' hands, the sound of Nessa's voice. I had felt the pain of the Skaldi when they attacked me at their nest, felt as if everything inside me was being sucked away to fill their empty shells. This was worse. With the Skaldi, I'd had only one body for them to torture. Now it felt like I had a million bodies, and every one of them was being eaten alive.

I thought I heard Nessa scream. I thought I saw Asunder's

staff grow veins and muscle and flesh until it was no longer a staff but an arm, no longer one arm but two. Then I thought I saw the arms being torn from a child's body and blood exploding all around me. Then I thought nothing more.

I woke with my back against rock, my head a knot of pain.

My hands remained bound, but my shirt had been removed and my pants sliced like Wali's, leaving my skin to bake on the black stone. The figures of my companions surrounded me, all of them half-stripped like the cave dwellers. Asunder and Archangel were nowhere to be seen, but the rest of the warriors stood guard in a circle around us. The sky had turned the color of a day-old bruise, reducing the glow of the black desert to a dull gleam like burnished metal. I tried to stand, but found my feet bound too.

I counted my colony, and was relieved to find that of those who'd left the cave, only Wali was missing. But Nessa was tightly bound and gagged, Adem and the little kids under heavy guard. And when I saw Aleka, my heart froze.

She lay on her stretcher with eyes open but sightless, and for a second I thought she was dead. Then I saw her chest move beneath what was left of her uniform jacket, sharp and shallow breaths like a kid caught in a nightmare. Her face had turned a chalky gray that reminded me of nothing so much as the Skaldi's skin. The angle hid her injured arm, but I could see the blood that had soaked into her tattered uniform and the canvas of the stretcher.

I looked around frantically for a sign of Asunder and Archangel, and realized we'd been moved. At the time of the attack, the black mountain had been a blotch on the horizon. Now it loomed over our heads, gleaming like obsidian, its steep sides cut into sharp facets. At its base stood an assortment of stone shapes that looked like grotesque, twisted mockeries of human beings. As my eyes adjusted to the altar's solid blackness, I saw a rough stairway carved into the monolith, a series of narrow, uneven steps that spiraled to the top like a spinal column. The twin horns stood too high for me to be sure, but it seemed the stairs ended right between them.

I turned my attention to the cords knotting my wrists, but gave up trying to untie them when one of the guards leveled his spear in my direction. I cursed myself for not thinking to use one of their blades to free myself like Nessa had. I cursed myself even more for not using Nessa's own blade when I'd had the chance.

"Querry."

I rolled over and saw Tyris, lying on the ground facing me, wrinkled and thin in her torn uniform. One side of her face was so badly swollen her eye was sealed shut, and blood crusted her nose.

"I tried to get to Aleka," she explained. "They didn't like that very much."

"How is she?"

"The fracture has reopened," she said. "And the mistreatment she's suffered has made it far worse. She appears to be in shock. Blood loss, maybe, or . . ."

I shuddered, remembering the staff. "Did he touch you, too?"

She shook her head. "I've never seen anything like it, Querry. It seems to be no more than a length of bone, but its touch—it's like a severe electric shock." She gestured with her one good eye toward the mountain. "Archangel took Wali to the summit. None of the other warriors would come near him. It's as if they believe he's carrying some terrible disease."

I rolled over again and struggled into a sitting position. My sunburned body ached, and the sharp stone scratched my exposed skin. The guard watched me but didn't raise his spear. I peered through the semidarkness at Aleka, and thought I saw a red mark on her forehead where she'd been touched by the staff, a perfect circle the size of a curled thumb and index finger. It was impossible to tell in the bad light, but I could have sworn that, with every hidden beat of her heart, the redness was spreading. I reached up to touch my own forehead and felt the flesh drumming like a second heart.

Then footsteps sounded behind me, and Tyris's one eye widened in warning. I turned, my head throbbing as if it remembered the touch of the staff. Asunder stood there, his giant lieutenant looming in the twilight, brother to the stone mountain.

"Nidach asa minach," Asunder spoke. "The Scavenger

awaits. Take them to the altar, and there let them be fed to the power that rules this land. Let them be clasped in his merciless jaws, and stripped of flesh, and harrowed for all eternity in the empty waste. Let them cry out for mercy, but receive none, and let them welter in their own blood and tears from now until the end of time."

Two warriors approached me, their hands tightening on my arms, and I was dragged to the steps of the altar. I fought the best I could, but my bare feet slipped against the glassy stone. Nessa and the others remained under guard at the altar's base, but Aleka was lifted from the stretcher by Archangel, her ravaged body looking as frail as the old woman's in his oversize arms. Tyris shouted, her voice joined by Nekane's and Adem's cries. Zataias tried to grab a spear, but a thicket of lances forced him and the others back. I was first to reach the monolith, the warriors shoving me forward until my feet touched the stairs.

I stumbled on the stone. It cut my feet like glass.

We had no sooner started up the staircase than a strange sound filled the air, a buzz, a pulse. I felt a momentary shudder like a shock of static. At first I thought the noise and sensation had come from contact with the black stone, but then the warriors holding me fell back, their hands flying to their heads, their bodies hitting the ground. Without support, I pitched forward onto the stairs, narrowly missing a sharp protrusion of stone. When I looked back to see what had happened to my captors, I saw the strangest thing: a cocoon of pale yellow light surrounded their bodies, a force field of some kind that held them in place even as it tortured them. They rolled under its light, blood flying where the black stone cut them. Angry red welts appeared on their bodies, and in seconds they stopped their anguished thrashing. The smell of cooked flesh filled the air.

The other warriors had broken and run when the beam hit their companions. Some made it only a few steps before the glow surrounded them, and their mouths opened in a silent scream before their charred bodies fell and lay still. Most of them, though, vanished into the encroaching dark, carrying prisoners with them. I watched helplessly as warriors scooped up Bea and Keely, Nekane and most of the other children. Only Zataias held his ground, fighting like a mad-man with someone twice his size. Adem came charging to his aid, a spear held in his bound hands like a club. Archangel was headed in their direction when Asunder shouted some-thing I couldn't make out and ran off, his red cloak flapping violently behind him. The giant dropped Aleka's limp body and stooped to lift Nessa instead. I pushed myself to my feet in an effort to make my way to her, but the cords tripped me and I landed on the bodies of the men who'd burned by the stairs.

Archangel slung Nessa over his shoulder. She was tied too tightly to move and gagged too securely to scream, but I saw the terror in her eyes. Her captor seemed about to run too when something caught his attention.

I followed his gaze and made out an unmistakable object: the barrel of a rifle, protruding from behind the base of the altar and trained on the ground at Archangel's feet. The buzzing sounded in my ears, and a short burst of yellow light like a glowing thread emerged from the muzzle, striking the stone with a sizzling noise. The gunman stepped from behind the altar, and I saw that he belonged to a survival colony, with the customary boots, olive-drab fatigues, and short-brimmed hats we'd worn before Asunder's warriors had stripped us down for the sacrifice. He stood no taller than me, but he carried himself with authority, his shoulders squared and his stride nearly a strut.

He and Archangel faced each other for a long moment, the giant's expression clouding with the first hint of surprise or doubt I'd seen him show. The gunman took a step toward him. For a second I thought they were going to speak.

But then the giant turned and sprinted toward the canyon with Nessa hanging over his shoulder, his long strides carrying him away like a rocket. The gunman didn't shoot, but took off after him and soon disappeared into the dark.

I disentangled myself from the dead warriors and found a point of stone to slice the bonds around my wrists. With my hands freed, I was able to attack the knots around my ankles and pull the clinging strands loose. I ran to where Aleka lay, and my stomach lurched when I saw the shards of bone sticking from her arm like teeth.

Tyris knelt by her side. "Don't touch her," she said to me.

She tore a strip of cloth from her threadbare jacket, tried to tie a tourniquet around Aleka's arm. There was barely enough arm for the knot to hold. "The stretcher! Bring it here!"

Adem and Zataias appeared out of the dusk, carrying the bloody stretcher. Tyris gestured urgently and they set it down beside Aleka.

"Hold her head," Tyris said to me. "Carefully. Adem, you take her shoulders. Zataias, the feet. We all lift together. On my count. One, two, *three.*"

We lifted her the few inches onto the stretcher. I couldn't help feeling I was lifting a corpse.

"It's going to take all of us," Tyris said. "Me and Querry in front, Adem and Zataias in the rear. Try not to jostle her."

"Where are we going?" I asked.

Tyris looked grim. "Anywhere but here. She'll die if I can't get the bleeding to stop. Plus I don't think she'll last long in this heat."

"What about the kids? And Nessa and Wali?"

"Wali must be dead by now," Tyris said. "And we'll never catch the others. We have to try to save who we can."

We hurriedly gathered the few things that had been left on the field of battle: the dead warriors' spears, the scarf that had fallen or been torn from Nessa's hair, which Tyris had slightly better success using as a tourniquet. We had just hoisted the stretcher and taken our first step toward the south when a new voice froze us in our spot.

"Hold it right there."

I turned and saw that the gunman had returned. Carelessly kicking one of the dead bodies out of the way, he advanced, his strange weapon pointed straight at us.

"Step away," he said. "Hands on your head."

Listening to his words, I realized that he wasn't a he. The voice was female, and the small, cocky man was revealed as a teenage girl, dark-skinned and with black curls cropped short, her black eyes aimed at me with the same deadly intent as her weapon.

I took a step toward her, my hands held out. The rifle jerked up, locking on my chest.

"She's dying!" I said. "We have to get her out of here."

"The only thing you have to do," the girl said, "is put your goddamn hands where I told you."

"Please," Tyris said. "She needs medical attention. Right away."

The girl took her eyes off me for a second to glance at Aleka, and following an impulse I couldn't remember forming, I chose that moment to leap at her and grab for the rifle. I got my hands on it, tried to wrestle it away from her, but she swung the stock sharply, catching me across the forehead. I fell, too dazed to protect myself against the black rock rushing up to meet my face.

"Goddamn it!" the girl shouted. Through blurred vision I watched her spin violently, her weapon leveled at the others. "I just knew this was one of his traps!"

She marched up to Tyris and Adem and Zataias, making them lie down on the rock with their hands behind their heads. When she'd patted them down and made sure they had nothing on them, she removed the couple spears we'd laid on the stretcher and snapped the shafts across her knee, throwing the pieces to the ground. Then she came back and knelt beside me, jerking my face up to hers by the hair.

"I've been itching all day for an excuse to kill people," she hissed in my face. "Looks like you just gave me what I was looking for."

PART TWO

WRATH

6

The girl marched us back to her camp at gunpoint.

She let the others walk ahead with the stretcher, Zataias staggering under its weight. Tyris had begged her to help Aleka, and the girl had chewed her lip in thought, finally jerking her head toward the east. She'd even allowed us a moment to wrap our feet in strips torn from the remains of our uniforms, which did practically nothing to cushion our soles from the punishment of the black rock. But she forced me to walk directly in front of her, hands behind my head.

Which I thought was a bit excessive. I was unarmed, exhausted, bruised, and battered. My head swam from Asunder's staff and the butt of the girl's rifle. Not exactly what you'd think of as a threat.

But she ignored my discomfort. Or that wasn't entirely true. She seemed to revel in it. Any time I lagged or tried to look at her, she jammed the rifle into the small of my back, which was so chafed and sunburned it hurt as much as the rest of me. From the few glimpses I caught of her night-black eyes, I got the feeling she wouldn't appreciate me asking her to be more careful, much less batting the rifle away. She hadn't repeated her threat to kill me, and I figured if she was bothering to take us to her camp she must have reconsidered. But that didn't change the fact that for the second time in less than a week, I was a complete stranger's prisoner. And this time, every step I took toward her destination was a step I took away from Nessa and the children.

"You can't do this," I said. "Take the others to your base, but let me go so I can find the rest of my colony."

"You'd like that, wouldn't you?" she growled, sticking the rifle in my back. "I'm sure you'd love to bring your *colony* swarming after me."

"That's not what I meant—"

"Save it," she snapped. "I'm getting the hell out of here before his whole army shows up. And you should consider yourself lucky I don't fry your skinny butt right now."

And that was it for that conversation.

We marched for hours in silence. Tyris tried to engage the girl more than once, but she was no more successful than me. I lost track of time, lost the ability to do anything but put one foot in front of the other. The moon had long since come and gone, and my aching body felt on the verge of collapse when we finally reached her camp.

Such as it was. I'd wondered if there might be others

with her, but the campsite was nothing but a camo tent propped up in the middle of the darkness. No stove, no fire, no supplies except small plastic bottles of water. Nothing for Aleka that I could tell. I'd hoped there might be something to transport her, but there was no vehicle, either. I tried to see that as a good sign. Unless the girl lived out here, which I couldn't believe, we must be close to whatever place she counted as home base.

Tyris busied herself with Aleka's shattered arm. She'd had some luck stanching the blood on our way here, but I could tell from her face that the damage was too severe for her to repair. After she'd done as much as she could, she turned to cleaning and rewrapping Zataias's chewed-up feet. He winced and tried not to cry as she removed slivers of glassy stone from his soles. I tried to inch over to check on her patients, but the girl's rifle jerked to my chest the moment I made a move. She sat on a stone formation and handed a water bottle to Tyris, keeping the rifle trained on me. It seemed like a week since I'd tasted water, but my parched throat found nothing to swallow but burning air. At last, when the others had taken a drink, the girl tossed a bottle in my direction. My hands were so stiff and sore I could barely unscrew the cap, which I suspected she'd fastened extra tight. I finally got it off, resisted the impulse to pour water over my hair and face and instead let a trickle drip down my throat, too grateful for the relief it offered to care that the girl was sizing me up the way you'd look at a snake coiled to strike.

"Thank you," I said when my throat felt supple enough to produce words.

The silence that radiated from her was as poisonous as her stare.

"Is your base nearby?" I tried.

Still nothing. Her hand went to her left arm and rubbed rhythmically as if it was itching her, but she kept the rifle leveled at me, as steady as her laser-sharp eyes.

"Look," I said. "I'm asking you one more time. Take them to your base, but let me go."

"Piss off," she said. "You're not going anywhere. And we're only staying here long enough to give the little boy a break."

I thought that was going to be the end of it, but then, with an edge in her flat voice that might have been curiosity or might have been simple disdain, she added: "So that's the plan now, huh? Fake a sacrifice then jump us when our guard's down?"

"Does her arm look fake?" I said, pointing to Aleka. "They were about to kill us. I assumed that's why you stopped them. I assume that's why you're helping us now."

A string of curses met my ears. I'd lived with soldiers as long as I could remember, but none swore as constantly or as creatively as she did. "I stopped them because every one of them I take down today is one less I have to take down tomorrow," she said when she'd exhausted the possibilities. "And if you think I'm planning to *help* you, just wait until you see what Udain has in store for you."

With that, she went back to staring me down. And though I tried to get her to explain what she meant, she wouldn't say anything more.

The others settled down beside the stretcher, Zataias giving in to sleep so quickly he let Tyris wrap her arms around him and lay his head on her chest. I tried to fight off the urge to close my eyes, but with nighttime hastening to a close and my hopes of getting away pretty much vanished, I realized how utterly exhausted I was. "You going to sleep?" I asked the girl through a yawn.

She sniffed. "Fat chance."

"Well, I am." My words sounded hollow and far away. "Am I going to wake up?"

Her shoulders lifted in a slow, careless shrug.

"Fine," I said. "But you're making a terrible mistake."

That was all I had left before my eyes closed. My final image before I fell asleep was of the girl's hands still gripping the stock of her rifle.

I woke to the glare of daylight off black rock. I could tell from the position of the sun that I hadn't slept long, but the fact that I'd woken at all gave me hope. When I rose and stretched my sore body, made even sorer by the jagged stone that had been my only bed, I realized two things: my strength had returned during my short sleep, and the girl hadn't budged from her spot. It seemed as if her rifle hadn't moved an inch from its target on my chest, though she'd packed her tent before I woke. She showed no signs of tiredness as she stood and reached into her pocket, coming out with a small, oblong shape covered in what looked like tin. She threw it at my feet, and I realized it must be food, wrapped in some kind of metallic paper. I bit the wrapper and tugged at it with my teeth, but it wouldn't open.

She sniffed, almost a laugh. "Here."

Rifle still aimed at my chest, she pinched the wrapper and tore it open. The food inside, a crumbly brown bar, tasted like dirt, but it revived me an amazing amount after more than a day on empty. Tyris and the others, I noticed from the wrappers sprinkled around their feet, had already eaten. They resumed their places at each end of Aleka's stretcher and hefted her from the ground. This time, the girl gave me a brief moment to check on Aleka, whose waxy face and mutilated arm looked neither better nor worse than the night before. Then she dug her rifle into my back, said, "Let's go," and continued to march us east across the stone wasteland.

All attempts at conversation failed this time. We marched until midday, when I was relieved to discover she was human enough to stop and rest in the relative shade of a large stone. We sat through the worst of the day, the whole time spent with the rifle lined up on my heart and her right hand straying periodically to stroke her left arm. We drank when she offered us a fresh water bottle, ate another of the bars when she handed it to us or, in my case, shoved it under my nose. She showed no overt hostility to Tyris or the others, watching silently while our healer went through the ritual of dressing Aleka's wound. But me she continued to regard with anger and distrust. I looked for opportunities to open a conversation, but there were none, much less any chance of distracting her so I could get away. When we resumed our march, I tried repeatedly to catch her eye, without success.

Evening had come again when a black wall of polished stone blocked our way. The girl signaled with the rifle and led us around the wall. Only then did she say curtly, her first word since morning, "Stop."

We did. We stood on a margin where the black rock came to an abrupt halt, the glassy surface giving way in a perfect arc to the familiar dusty landscape of the desert. The wall of volcanic stone at our backs cast feeble evening shadows down the slope, but they were blotted out before they reached the valley floor by something so bright it took my eyes a second to figure out what it was. When I finally did, I drew in a breath and blinked in wonder.

Nothing I'd seen or heard prepared me for the sight of the fenced compound that spread out before us. Pale yellow light poured from a palisade of metal posts at least twenty feet high, the same light that had defeated Asunder's warriors except on an immeasurably larger scale. It wasn't torch or lamplight, wasn't even, from what I could tell, like the electric lights that had beamed from Survival Colony 9's trucks, back when we had trucks. It seemed to be a field of energy that either enclosed or was emitted by the fence, as if the metal was a body and the light its blood flow. Within the fence, white spotlights illuminated every inch of the compound's perimeter, spilling over squat white buildings, blinking from a guard tower double the height of the surrounding palisade. The compound was small, probably no more than a mile square, but I was convinced no city from the time before could have been this imposing. Together with the rhythmic pulse that emanated from the whole, the glowing compound seemed so otherworldly I could do nothing but stand and stare.

The girl nudged me in the back. "Move."

I took a step, stumbled as my maimed feet touched soft, hot desert sand. She laughed, the same short sniff from breakfast.

"Athan's getting sloppy," she said derisively. "Sending a pipsqueak like you on one of his precious missionary runs."

Athan. The name Aleka had given Asunder. "Who's Athan?"

The girl didn't answer for a long time, and I figured her one outburst was going to be her last. Then she swore under her breath. "I beg your pardon. *Asunder.* The king of—what's he call it?—the Shut-In Lands?"

"I've been trying to tell you," I said. "I'm not one of them."

"No?" she said. "You're sure as hell not one of us."

Her voice sounded so furious I almost felt sorry for her. But I'd had enough.

"Listen." I stopped and turned, holding my hands in

front of me. "For the last time: I'm not what you think."

The rifle dug into my stomach. "Keep moving."

"I'm not going anywhere," I said. "At least not as your prisoner. We've got the same enemy, all right? Athan, Asunder, whatever you want to call him. I get it. He's raided your colony too. Now he's stolen half of mine. If you won't let me go so I can find them, maybe you'll work with me to put him out of business."

She grunted, her eyes never leaving mine. I had the uncomfortable feeling she was deciding whether to pull the trigger.

But at last her gun relaxed ever so slightly, dipping toward the desert floor.

"All right," she said. "But I swear to God, if this is another of his tricks, you're going to pay."

"It isn't," I said. "Trust me."

"I don't trust anybody who tries to take my gun," she said. "Speaking of which, I can't very well walk you into camp without it. If you know so much about the survival colonies, you have to know that."

I nodded.

"After we get your friends taken care of, I'll talk to the commander," she said. "Tell him what you told me. That's the best I can offer."

"Fair enough."

"Don't get your hopes up," she said. "I'm not exactly on his good side."

"All right," I said. "But can you tell me one more thing?"

"We're persistent, aren't we?"

"Your name," I said. "If you're going to help us out, I'd like to know who to thank." I held out my hand. "I'm Querry. From Survival Colony Nine."

She ignored the hand, but a look of surprise crossed her face. It was followed by the first hint of a smile I'd seen. "Mercy," she said, her black eyes gleaming wickedly in the compound's glow. "But don't get the wrong idea about me from that."

We marched down the slope to the desert floor. Mercy let me relieve Zataias at the stretcher, which was a good thing, because he was dead on his feet. As promised, she held her rifle at the ready but refrained from nudging me in the back.

The front gate of the compound rose before us, bathed in the eerie yellow light. Two guards in camouflage uniforms stood before the gate. Both appeared young, not much older than me. They held weapons identical to Mercy's, which looked similar to the rifles we'd once owned in Survival Colony 9. I wondered how they'd been doctored to produce the energy beam.

The guards raised their rifles as we approached. Then one whose cheeks and forehead were scarred with pimples let out a laugh. "Well, look who's back."

"What's the matter, Mercy?" the other taunted. "The giant scare you away?"

Mercy marched straight up to them, ignoring their gibes. "Delivery for Udain," she said. "Found them in the impact zone."

"Doing what?" the pimply-faced guard laughed. "Taking a walk with their mommy?"

"Stick it, Geller."

The guard's eyes widened in fake alarm, then he and his partner gave in to laughter. "He one of them?" the second guard asked between snorts, pointing his rifle at me.

"That's for Udain to decide."

"What about Athan? You bring that little bastard in too?"

She paused, and for a second I thought she was going to tell them the whole story. "He got away."

"What?" The guard named Geller was laughing so hard he could barely control his voice. "Whatever happened to, *I'm gonna waste that ugly son of a bitch if it's the last thing I do*?"

Mercy gritted her teeth. "You letting us in?"

Still chuckling, Geller waved us through. The gate swung noiselessly open, then closed behind us with the barest clang.

Mercy led us across the paved courtyard. I could hear the guards laughing behind us, but she stared straight ahead, her face composed and flat.

We approached one of the squat white buildings. Nothing marked it on the outside, but I hoped Mercy was true to her word and that it was the infirmary. She tapped a code into a keypad beside the door, and a minute later, a crackling voice made me jump. Mercy leaned close to a mesh circle embedded beside the door and spoke a few words, then the door slid open and a man dressed in a spotless white uniform appeared. His eyes went wide when he got a look at Aleka. He ushered us into a room as white as his clothes, and after a few minutes' consultation with Tyris, he led us to a back room where we laid my mother in a bed with sheets the same perfect white. I leaned over her, avoiding the sight of her arm, silently willing her eyes to blink or her breathing to return to normal. When nothing happened, I touched her cheek, stroked her hair. Then the man shooed all of us except Tyris out of the room and closed the door behind us. We were left standing with Mercy in the main room. Though it struck me as a hopeful sign that she'd been willing to go behind her commander's back to aid someone she didn't know, I couldn't help wondering if I would ever see my mother again.

But there was no time to think about that. Leaving Adem and Zataias under the watch of another teenage guard at the infirmary—Zataias wanted to come with me, but for once Adem muttered a couple words to hold him back—Mercy and I left and headed for the commander's quarters.

I took my first good look around the compound, tried to make conversation. "Pretty impressive."

"What is?"

"Everything." I nodded vaguely, embarrassed by my own words. "Everything's so—so perfect. So clean."

Mercy sniffed. "Yeah. And there's an ice cream social every Saturday."

I looked at her, trying to see if she was joking. There was no telling in her black eyes, and I had no idea what an ice cream social was, so I left it alone. "With all this tech, why don't you just storm Asunder's base? March into the canyon and flush him out?"

She stopped walking. "You can't be serious."

I shook my head, more in confusion than answer. "I just . . ."

"Do you think we're complete idiots?" I could read her expression now, and it was back to being furious. "Udain tried your suggestion already. Athan's goons ambushed them at the rock city. Most of his troops didn't get out of there alive."

The rock city, I guessed, was the place where we'd been ambushed as well. "But at the altar . . ."

"I got lucky," she said. "They were in the open and I had the element of surprise. And even so, I could have gotten a spear in the eye if I wasn't careful." She looked at me, a sneer curling her lip. "I thought you were some big survival colony expert. You never heard about home field advantage?"

I started to explain myself, but before I got a word out she cut me off. "The hell with it. You're either the biggest fool I've ever met or the biggest fool that's ever lived. Either way, you better get your head screwed on straight if you want to survive Udain." She jerked a thumb. "Now move."

I headed in the direction she'd indicated. My head

buzzed from the constant light and vibration of the compound. Either that, or from what she'd just said. I had no doubt from our encounter with Asunder—and my personal encounter with his staff—that he was powerful. But I'd had no idea how powerful he was. There must have been hundreds of warriors I hadn't seen in the canyon, enough to overwhelm her commander's forces despite the fact that they were using Stone Age weapons against high-tech energy beams. What hope did I have of freeing Nessa and the kids from that kind of army? And what did it say about Mercy that even knowing what Asunder was capable of, she'd set off by herself toward his domain, intent on a confrontation?

We turned the corner of one of the compound's buildings and I pulled up short, staring at the shape that sat in the center of the concrete yard.

"So you can't fight Asunder," I said once I caught my breath. "But you can fight *that*?"

Mercy said nothing. She didn't have to.

I was looking at a cage. The moment I saw it, I knew it was where she would have put me—and maybe the others—if I hadn't convinced her to appeal to her commander first. It consisted of the same metal stakes as the perimeter fence, though it stood only half the fence's height and only four or five yards across. The energy flow washed it in pale yellow light, and a hum issued from it. Standing stark and alone in the expanse of cement, it drew my eyes to the thing huddled inside.

It was a Skaldi.

Not a Skaldi in human form. A Skaldi as they existed without a body to mimic, a Skaldi as I'd seen them the night I'd discovered their nest. Scrawny frame stripped of flesh, featureless face staring blindly into the night, open gash running the length of the torso, flat paddlelike tail instead of legs. It lay on its side, one arm extended above its head, seeming too exhausted to rise or move. But it was still alive, if *alive* was the right word for Skaldi. Its head bobbed and swayed rhythmically, and the edges of its scar waved as if stirred by a breath.

I sought Mercy's eyes. She stared back without blinking. "You keep them caged?"

"Just this one," she said. "But it's enough."

"But how?"

She shrugged. "That's Athan's department. Or was." She paused, sizing me up in the yellow glow. "This little devil comes in handy in case one of his missionaries decides to pay us a visit. But don't think for a minute I won't feed your sorry ass to it if you so much as look at me the wrong way."

"Thanks for the warning," I said. "Is there a right way?"

She smiled without humor. Then she nodded toward the building across the square, and with the rifle held relaxed at her waist, she walked me past the cage. The Skaldi raised itself a few inches from the ground as we strode by, and I felt the hairs on my neck prickle as its blank face swung to follow us toward the building.

As with the infirmary, the door had no knob or handle,

but it slid to the side when Mercy punched a code into the adjacent keypad. We entered a room brightly lit by long glowing tubes that hung overhead, emitting a harsh white glow. They hummed like everything else in the compound. Two guards stood by a single door in the empty room. Like the guards at the gate and the infirmary, both of them seemed to be about my or Mercy's age.

"What the hell is this?" one demanded.

"I'm bringing him to Udain."

The guard shook his head. "Goddamn it, Mercy. You can't just disappear for a week then barge into the commander's office dragging one of Athan's rejects. I don't care who you are."

"This one's different," she said. "He . . ." She took a deep breath. "I think he might be one of Laman's."

The guard reacted with astonishment, but it couldn't have been greater than mine. I remembered Aleka telling me that Laman had steered clear of the place Mercy called the impact zone, but I couldn't believe he would have kept a safe haven like this secret if he had known about it. I had no chance to ask, because the head guard marched the two of us to a pair of metal chairs and told us to sit, his companion keeping watch.

"Wait here," the guard said. "I'll talk to Udain."

He pressed a button and spoke into one of the wire-mesh circles, then leaned close to listen to the reply. All I heard was a staticky rumble. It took a while, but eventually the interior door slid open and the guard entered. I sat beside Mercy and tried to ignore the other guard, who stared at me as if I was a ghost. Once or twice he opened his mouth as if to say something, but Mercy cut him off with a glare. In the absence of other sound, the buzzing lights made me feel like the bones of my skull were vibrating, and I was about to talk just to break the monotone when the door finally reopened and the guard signaled us to enter.

"He's in a pissy mood," he whispered to Mercy.

"Him and me both," she said, before elbowing me through the door.

The interior room was as bright and empty as the one we'd left, except for a long table at which a man sat. He rose from his chair when we entered, and my first thought was that Mercy had tricked me and led me back to Archangel. The man stood over seven feet tall, the muscles of his chest and arms evident through his immaculate uniform. But he was much older than Asunder's lieutenant, with pure white hair falling in twin braids down his uniform front and a long white beard to match. When we approached, I saw how lined his face was, but I also saw no marks of frailty in his dark eyes, strong brow, and hooked nose. His entire body radiated strength and power, and even before he spoke I sensed this was someone used to having his word obeyed, someone who wouldn't take kindly to deviations from the plan.

Then he did speak, confirming my hunch. "I should throw both of you in the cage," he said, his gravelly voice low and menacing. "Maybe that's what it would take for you to follow my orders."

To my surprise, Mercy replied in a firm voice. "You want to get rid of me, go ahead. But I'm thinking that might not be such a great idea right now."

"Mercy," he sighed. "Are you intent on forcing me to make an example of you?"

She shrugged. I couldn't tell if this was a show of bravado or if she really didn't care what this titan did to her.

"You've been AWOL for a week," Udain continued. "More than enough time for me to decide to lock the gate and leave you to your own devices."

"You didn't, though," she said, and again I noticed her rubbing the biceps of her left arm.

"I was sorely tempted."

"But you didn't," she repeated. "Why can't you let me go, Udain?"

He said nothing, and she sidled closer to him, looking into his face without fear. If this was a show, it was a convincing one.

"You knew I was out there," she said. "And you knew what I was up to. You could have come to get me anytime you wanted. But you didn't do that either. Why is that, Udain?"

His eyes flashed, and he lifted a strong, lined hand. A metal cuff on his wrist caught the room's icy light. Mercy faced him squarely, while he stared at her as if she was an impossible child he'd never managed to reform. Her face lit again with the humorless smile.

"So here I am," she said. "And I brought you a present. The question is, are you going to open it?"

He shook his head. "One more of Athan's primitives wandering the impact zone means nothing."

"I told Ramos, this one's different. He's—"

Udain silenced her with a hand. Circling the table, he stood before us, seeming to fill the room. His eyes were as dark as hers, and I saw nothing in their inspection to give me hope.

"So this is the boy," he said to her, his eyes remaining on me, "you claim is one of Laman's."

Mercy nodded.

"And I should take a chance on your word alone," he said. "I should let this jackal loose in my camp, and allow him to work his will on my troops. Is that what you're advising?"

She said nothing.

"Laman's people are gone," Udain said, turning from us. "Lost to time and memory. Take this filth to the cage, and let him meet his god that way."

"They're not gone!" I burst out. "Not all of us. If you won't listen to her, maybe you'll listen to me."

Udain paused. I saw the tension in his broad back, and I was afraid he was about to level me, but I kept going.

"Laman's dead," I said. "I'm his—I was his—I was with him when he died. He gave me his name. I'm Querry Genn."

Udain half turned, showing me his profile. "You saw him die?"

I nodded. "In a battle with the Skaldi. We destroyed their nest, but he died the next day. There are only"—Soon's and Wali's faces flashed before my eyes—"fourteen of us left. We were captured by Asunder's—by Athan's colony. Our commander, Aleka—"

At the mention of her name Udain turned fully to face me. "You've seen Aleka? Where is she?"

"She was wounded in the ambush," I said, too surprised by everything that had happened in the past hour to register additional surprise that he knew her name.

Udain turned to Mercy. "You knew about this?"

"I had no idea who she was," she said, sounding defensive for the first time.

"Take me to her," Udain growled.

"No point," Mercy said. "She's a mess, and it looks like Athan got her with the staff. That woman's not talking to anyone anytime soon."

Udain paced to the door as if he was about to go check for himself. Then he turned back to me. "I have little patience with those I suspect of sharing Athan's philosophy," he said. "So speak fast. What do you want from us?"

"I need help," I said. "The rest of my colony is gone. Stolen by . . . Athan. He's killed two of us already, and he's taken . . ." My last glimpse of Nessa, carried away in bonds by Archangel, returned to me. "If you won't help me, then send me away. Just don't keep me here. I'm running out of time. I've got to find someone. . . ."

"There is no one," Udain said, yet his voice had lost some of its edge. He sounded weary, spent and old. "No one with the strength to raise a force against Athan. All of the colonies north and east of the impact zone have been raided by him, and too few are left to contest him in his stronghold. Those who try are slain by—"

"The Scavenger of Souls," I said.

For the first time since I'd entered the room, Udain looked rattled. "The Scavenger of Souls is a myth," he said. "Or a hallucination, induced by the power of Athan's staff. But his warriors are very real, and those who enter his domain don't return. They're either found dead on his altar or disappear altogether, and the hunters"—he nodded at Mercy— "always return empty-handed."

"I didn't exactly come empty-handed," Mercy mumbled, sounding very much like a petulant child.

Udain raised an eyebrow, but ignored her. "The canyon is impregnable. Ever since we installed our hostage, there"—he tossed his head, presumably in the direction of the caged Skaldi—"few of his disciples have been foolish enough to assail us. But we're always watchful for new modes of attack"—his dark eyes settled on me—"and we're not inclined to be merciful to wolves in sheep's clothing."

The room fell silent, except for the buzzing lights. A feeling built in my chest, a feeling of nervousness or dread mingled with determination. If Aleka had been awake, she might have been able to vouch for me, but that wasn't an option. I knew I would have to prove my innocence another way. I just wasn't sure I would survive the trial.

"Athan's followers," I said. "You feed them to that creature out there."

Udain nodded. "When we can catch them."

"But I'm not one of his followers," I said. "And I can prove it."

Udain and Mercy exchanged glances. "How?" he said.

I took a step until I stood directly in front of him. I had to crane my neck to meet his black eyes, but when I did, I saw something there I hadn't expected to see. Something hidden, buried beneath the strength and certainty. Something that looked an awful lot like pain.

"Take me to the cage," I said. "And I'll show you."

7

Udain and Mercy walked me to the cage, followed by a
trickle of curious guards.

The one named Geller was in the lead, a sardonic smile
on his pimpled face. Like him, none of the guards had
reached adulthood. Given the size of the compound, it struck
me how few of them there were.

Asunder had been busy in Udain's territory.

The Skaldi rose on skeletal forearms as we approached,
its colorless body a sickly yellow in the camp's cold light. Its
blank face couldn't show emotion, but whatever senses it
possessed to detect the presence of prey set the air prickling
between us. I'd survived Skaldi attacks before, the first person anyone knew who'd done so. The first time, the attack
had left me without a memory. The second, at their nest,
I'd fended off a whole army of the things. Laman believed I
had some special power, something born or bred in me, that

made me immune to the monsters that threatened everyone else. He had no idea what that power might be, and neither did Tyris. Whether Aleka agreed with them I'd never had a chance to ask. Whether Udain would be impressed enough to trust my word I had no way of knowing.

Mercy watched me intently. "If this is some kind of macho thing," she said, "don't do it on my account."

"Don't worry," I said. "I won't."

"Then why the dramatics?"

I didn't answer her. "It's going to attack me," I said. "And it's going to look like it's winning. Just . . . don't do anything. Let it come. It'll lose power soon enough, and then you can let me out."

"Once the beam's off, you know you're on your own."

"Yeah," I said. "I got that."

"So what makes you so cocky?"

I smiled. "Trade secret."

"Your funeral," she said.

Udain gestured toward the cage, then tapped a code into the metal cuff around his wrist. The enclosure whined like a motor shutting down, and the yellow light blinked off. He pressed one more button and the cage door released with a hiss. I looked at him before entering, but his expression was nearly as blank as the Skaldi's. As far as he was concerned, I guess it didn't matter which way I chose to die.

The Skaldi's blunt, empty face swiveled toward me. Its body quivered with anticipation. I wondered how long it had gone without a meal. The lips of its scar waved sickeningly, like tongues tasting the air.

I had a moment to glimpse Mercy edging up to the cage, then the creature threw itself across the space between us and crashed into my arms.

And I was back at the nest, and nothing had changed.

Pain. Gut-wrenching pain. My insides twisting, my head a fog. Claws raking me, the scar peeling back to reveal the emptiness inside.

Deep within me, something responded to that emptiness, something tore loose. Something was dragged free. Something was no longer mine.

Something.

My name. My life. My past.

Something.

It drifted upward, catching briefly in my throat, then exiting my mouth like a spent breath. It hovered in the air between us.

The creature's scar opened fully, and I saw an endless emptiness before me, a black pit far deeper and darker than its physical shape could hold. I clutched at the thing that had come loose from my insides—my memory, my life—but I couldn't hold on. It was dragged inexorably toward the pit, and I was dragged with it.

I was no longer *I*. I was it.

I was lost.

A voice. "Querry!"

A bright light.

The thing tugged. Pulled. Tore. Won.

A blurred shape moved against the brightness.

Then the light and the sound and the feeling died, and black night replaced them all.

I came to in a pure white room, staring up at banks of buzzing lights. My head throbbed, my throat ached like I'd been screaming for hours. I felt emptied. I knew my name, and that was about all I knew. But that was something, that and the sound of my heart beating again in my ears.

"What a damn fool thing to do," a voice rumbled above me, and I lifted my head to see the old man. For a moment I blanked, but then I remembered his name.

Udain.

He sat in a chair by my bed—I was lying in a bed, its sheets stiff and clean—and seeing him there brought back other pieces of the past. The Skaldi. The cage. The interrogation room. Mercy. The altar.

Wali. Nessa. Aleka. Soon.

Everything.

The past seven months were still there, intact. The time before, though, remained gone.

I tried to rise, but he laid a hand on my chest, and I found I didn't have the strength to resist.

"Steady," he said. "That little performance nearly got you killed."

"What happened?"

"Mercy brought you out. Against my orders, I might add."

"Is she okay?"

"It never laid a hand on her. Which is more than I can promise, if I ever catch her pulling a stunt like that again." His mustache lifted in what might have been a smile. "I will say this for her, though. She's almost managed to convince me you are what you claim to be. Or at least, that you're not one of Athan's infernal raiders."

"I guess I owe her for that, too," I said. "Where is she?"

"On duty. Or serving time, as she might put it. She seems to favor those old-world expressions, for some reason."

I watched his eyes, intense and black yet lit with affection for the girl who did nothing but torment him. I remembered her eyes, black as his. With the stark difference in their skin—hers brown, his pale—I hadn't noticed the resemblance before, but I saw it now.

"She's your granddaughter."

He nodded. "The only one left."

"And Laman?"

"My son," he said. "Mercy's uncle. Born three years before the wars of destruction. His brother Athan came after, with no memory of the time before. It may explain why they saw the future so differently. Why they followed such different paths."

I sat, the room spinning for a moment until his hand gripped my arm. I saw that they'd had the decency to clothe me in a new uniform, spotless and as crisp as the sheets. A few deep breaths restored my balance, and he let me go.

"My field is engineering," he said. "Nuclear engineering. I worked for the government, taught at the university level. That might not mean much to you. It meant nothing to Laman."

"He didn't think much of engineers," I said delicately.

"What you mean is that he blamed us for the world's destruction," Udain said. "Saw us as the enemy. *We* had built the bombs. *We* had poisoned the land. *We* had hidden the truth from the people until it was too late. And then, after it happened, *we* were the ones who profited from the wreckage of the old world."

He spoke with bitterness, but I couldn't tell if it was directed at his lost son or himself.

"What he could never stomach was that we were also the ones who organized the survival colonies. We were the ones who perceived the seriousness of the Skaldi threat and who saw the need for new, more flexible forms of organization to meet it. Not the politicians, who were too busy scrambling for the few scraps of power that remained. Not the so-called common man, who was too terrified to crawl out of whatever bombed-out hole he was hiding in. Not the preachers, screaming of doomsday and urging the race to give in to despair. It was *us*. We were the ones who saved humanity. And our thanks for it . . ."

His voice had grown angry as he talked, but now it trailed

off, and he shook his head. I got the feeling he'd delivered the same speech many times before. And that Laman had tuned him out more and more each time he delivered it.

"I was at the forefront of the movement to gather the ones who remained," he continued after a pause. "The experts, the leaders in their fields. Everyone from geneticists to metallurgists to astrophysicists, I wanted them. There were so few of us left, and we were scattered and unable to communicate. But mobile companies of a hundred or fewer, I believed, could best scour the ruins while evading the Skaldi. The survival colonies arose out of that."

"As search-and-rescue teams."

"We called them RUs," he said. "Recovery Units. Eventually they became somewhat more, living communities, a new system of social order. As much as you can call this *living*. Or *order*." He laughed, a deeper version of his granddaughter's humorless sniff. "But from the start my objective was to defeat the Skaldi, not elude them. To use our collective willpower to reclaim this planet from the ones who stole it from us."

"You sound like," I began, but changed my mind in midsentence. He might not want to hear me tell him how much he sounded like his older son. "You make it sound like the Skaldi aren't from this planet."

He stared at me as if *I* wasn't from this planet. But he answered.

"It began in the years before the wars of destruction,"

he said. "Military scientists working in the desert found the remains of the creatures that would come to be known as Skaldi. With the advantage of hindsight, we believe they arrived through a rift in space-time opened by the weapons of that era. The first specimens were thought to be dead, until the scientists discovered—to their ruin—the creatures' ability to reawaken when life-energy was near."

"So they're not really alive?"

"Nor are they truly dead," he said. "The Skaldi are parasites—vampires, the superstitious used to call them. I prefer the clinical term *biophages*. Life eaters. They feed off energy—in our case, organic energy. Similar to bacteria we've discovered, such as *Shewanella* and *Geobacter*, that consume electrons directly, without the intervening medium of sugars. In another respect they resemble conventional viruses, in that their structures are metabolically inert. They mimic life only by appropriating the metabolic activity of their victims."

I tried not to look as lost as I felt. "So when they attack someone . . ."

"They use his own cellular energy to overwhelm his body," he clarified. "They drain their victim, then deploy that stolen power to colonize the host's cells. It happens, as you know, with incredible speed. In essence, they convert human cells to Skaldi cells within seconds. Absorb our life force and turn it against us, making our bodies do their bidding."

"What about our minds?" I said. "When they take over, do they turn our minds to—I guess—Skaldi minds?"

He looked at me strangely, but nodded. "One would assume so."

I mulled that over. It made sense, fit with what I'd already begun to figure out on my own. It explained not only how they mimicked us so perfectly but how the one that had attacked me seven months ago had stolen my memory. "How much did Laman know about this?"

"He preferred not to know," Udain said, the bitterness returning to his voice.

"So he wouldn't have known why the Skaldi fail when they attack me."

"It's doubtful," he said. "We know that a significant enough 'burst' of energy—from fire, say, or an atomic blast—can overwhelm them, outstripping their capacity to absorb it. The human body doesn't generate that kind of concentrated power, so there's nothing to stop them from feeding on us. What makes the beam that powers this compound unique is that, rather than destroying them outright, it holds them in a sort of stasis. Returns their bodies to an inert state, incapable of further energy absorption. You may have noticed they resist fire far longer than a human being would."

I wasn't sure I'd noticed, but I nodded anyway.

"That's because of their innate ability to absorb energy," he said. "In the case of the beam, to render it effective against Skaldi we had to set it at a high enough intensity that it burns human beings on contact. Were we to ratchet the signal down to make it less hazardous to our own kind, the Skaldi would be free to feed. Were we to turn it up," he concluded darkly, "they'd burn too."

I searched his eyes, looking for the thing he wasn't willing to say. "So you think I'm . . . You think I have the power to . . ."

He returned my inspection with a piercing gaze I hadn't seen since my last conversation with his older son. But then the deep, mirthless chuckle issued from his chest, and he laid a hand on my shoulder.

"One thing at a time," he said. "I always have to remind Mercy of that. One thing at a time."

He walked to the room's single window, which covered nearly half an entire wall. It surprised me to see the light of day pouring through, turning the window a solid gray white. How long had I been out? Then he beckoned for me, and I slipped from the bed, testing my legs in my sturdy new boots to make sure they'd hold me before joining him.

I peered outside, only to discover there was no outside.

The rectangle wasn't a window. Instead, it was an opaque screen of some shiny off-white material. I couldn't see my reflection, only the play of wavy colors across its ten-foot length. To the side of the screen sat another keypad, this one containing not only numbers but buttons imprinted with arrows, boxes, dots, and other symbols.

"This is a *protograph*," Udain said. "One of my son Athan's inventions. Loosely translated, it means 'past recording.' He felt that 'video screen' or 'television' were too mundane. He wanted something with flair. Something for the new world we were building."

He touched the cuff on his wrist, and the surface of the protograph swam like an image blurred by a rainstorm. From its depths emerged light, motion, and sound, but no color: everything was a grainy white or gray, giving the figures that formed there the appearance of faded charcoal sketches. But the figures moved as if they were alive, and when their mouths opened I heard their voices. I leaned close to hear, when unexpectedly the scene froze, the people stopping in the midst of an action, their words ending as abruptly as if they'd been cut off by a slammed door. Udain smiled again and removed his finger from the cuff, and the figures jumped to life once more.

"The past," he said. "Preserved like a specimen in a jar, like dry bones stirred and risen from the grave."

"This really happened?"

"Exactly as you see it."

"How many times have you watched?"

"More than I can count," he said. "But I can't seem to get it to change."

I turned my attention to the monitor. It revealed a room that was little more than a bombed-out shell, skeletal frame visible beneath crumbling walls. I shivered, remembering the compound where Survival Colony 9 had hidden from the Skaldi, only to lose Korah and five others in a single night, Laman's leadership the next day. On the screen, a group of people sat in a ring of canvas chairs, all of them wearing the spotless uniforms of Udain's camp. Udain himself presided in the center, his size and long braids unmistakable though his hair and beard were dark. To each side of him sat a much smaller man, one of them looking like a child beside his huge commander. This one's hair was long and wavy, and though his face was free of scars I had no trouble recognizing him as a younger version of the man they called Athan, the man who called himself Asunder.

The man on the other side of Udain was small too, though not as small as his younger brother. His dark hair was cropped short, and no trace of the tangled beard that would sprout in later life hid his cheeks. But his gaunt face, hooked nose, and brooding eyes, set deep beneath a prominent brow, hadn't changed. When he spoke, it was like hearing the voice of a ghost, one we'd buried little more than a week ago, who'd hurried back into the past to reappear in a body not yet ravaged by time and loss.

Laman Genn.

"It's foolishness," this younger Laman said. "And pride. We don't have anywhere near the resources we'd need to build your device. Much less the time to ensure its safety."

"The beam will keep the Skaldi at bay," Athan responded. "And construction will be completed in six months at most."

"Six months!" Laman scoffed. "Is that another of your miracle gadgets, brother? A time machine? If you've got one of those, why not send us all back to the time before?"

The words of the dead man chilled me, but I kept my eyes focused on the screen.

"We need a permanent settlement if we're to continue our work," his younger brother replied. "Father"—and he gestured at the silent, hulking man between them—"agrees with me. You would too, if you weren't too stubborn to see the truth."

Laman gritted his teeth and spoke in the low voice I now knew he'd inherited from his father. "The truth," he said, "is that the past is gone. It's not stubbornness to admit that."

"The past," Athan said, "but not the future."

Again Laman laughed. "I've had my say. We can cling to an impossible dream, or face the ugly reality. The Skaldi don't care either way. But which way will save us, Athan? The human race has tried your way before. It's what brought us here."

The Athan figure raised an arm in protest, but Udain silenced him with a wave of his powerful hand.

"Your brother has spoken, Athan," he said. "He hasn't changed his position since our work began, and I don't expect him to change it now. I might ask what his alternative is, what hope he thinks there is in wandering the desert until the Skaldi destroy us all. But luckily"—and his teeth gleamed white beneath his dark mustache—"I don't have to ask, and he doesn't have to answer. This is no democracy, Laman. We *will* build according to your brother's design. All that remains in doubt is whether you'll be here when we're finished."

The room fell silent, and I felt myself holding my breath as my eyes traveled the circle looking for someone to come to Laman's support. No one did. Athan's smile turned smug. His older brother stood, his uniform as immaculate in the protograph as his father's still was. By the time I knew Laman Genn, his uniform would be ragged, soiled, no less than the man who wore it. But his face showed no compromise as he spoke across his father to the boy who'd defeated him.

"You'll build your settlement," he said. "And your machine. But it won't save you. The power to kill can't save. Remember that, brother, when I'm gone."

In the unsparing lens of the protograph, he started for the missing door of the room, until his father stopped him with a touch of the button on his cuff.

"Did you ever see him again?" I said.

Udain shook his head. He touched another button, and the Laman on the screen wobbled unnaturally and began to walk backward, his mouth movements producing no sound, sitting down as he'd stood, the brothers and their father wordlessly speaking their parts in reverse. Udain's thick finger moved to the first button, and I watched Laman stand again, heard him pronounce his final words. Back and forth, the buttons were pushed, the figures moved through time, flexible but fixed. And always the father stopped the image before his son exited the room, before he lost him forever.

"You built your camp here," I said.

"Twenty-eight years ago," he answered. "We'd found the

remains of a military base, and we used it as the foundation of our own compound. It took three years to rebuild, another ten to perfect Athan's device. We lost some few to Skaldi, but the beam held. In the meantime we heard rumors of a smaller survival colony in the vicinity, one numbered nine. I knew my son must have joined them, either that or perished in the desert. In time our scouts reported that he'd taken command of the camp, married, fathered a son. But he never returned, and I never saw his boy. My grandchild."

"His name was Matay," I said. Then, as gently as I could: "He died."

Udain nodded, and touched a new button on the wrist cuff. The screen went blank, and though I could see nothing, I heard a whirr like vehicles passing at top speed in the distance. I watched Udain's impassive face, his black eyes fixed on the protograph screen as if he could plumb its white emptiness.

"My sons," he said softly, "have not been fortunate men."

Then he released the button.

A new scene rose from the protograph. A huddle of at least a hundred soldiers stood outside the perimeter fence, the compound visible behind them, Udain as always towering above his followers. His hair had grayed in the time that had passed. The energy field that kept the camp safe from Skaldi radiated along the fence posts, shimmering like desert heat. The ground that stretched before the encampment was desert dust, gray in the protograph's colorless slate. But the world that lay beyond the valley bore no resemblance to the plateau I'd walked with Mercy only a day before. The gleaming volcanic rock was missing, as were the man-size formations of sharp-edged stone. The land I saw was all desert, a continuous expanse of flat, sandy terrain. Whatever had produced the impact zone, the protograph didn't know it yet.

And neither did the people who stood watching.

My eyes scanned the crowd. Most of the onlookers were strangers to me, soldiers in identical uniforms, grown men and women instead of the boys I'd met in Udain's camp. Beside Udain stood his remaining son, more than ten years older than he'd been when he'd bested his older brother, his dark hair falling to his shoulders, his face showing the calm confidence he'd displayed in the meeting room. By his side, a woman with rich dark skin and a proud lift to her head gripped a little girl's hand. Two other children stood behind Athan and the woman, a boy and a girl. Both were lighter skinned than the woman, darker than the pale Athan. But the remarkable thing about the boy was his size: though he had the face of a child, he stood a foot taller than the diminutive man.

Taller, I realized, than his own father.

"Archangel," I murmured.

"Ardan was his name," the old man returned. "They say gigantism sometimes skips a generation." He froze the image and gestured at the other children. "Ardan came first, then Beryl, and of course you know Mercy"—pointing at the little girl holding the woman's hand. I squinted to see her face, but I saw none of the anger that would settle over it as she grew. The screen of the protograph seemed to crackle, and I held my breath, waiting to learn what had put the anger there.

Udain's finger moved to his wrist cuff's motion button.

"Wait—" I said.

I leaned close to the protograph, staring at a woman's face I'd glimpsed at the back of the crowd, beside a man who might have been the doctor from Udain's compound. I almost didn't recognize her, she was so much younger than the last time I'd seen her. Her hair was long, not the cropped, silvering cut I knew. But the face the long hair framed was sharp and lean, carrying an intensity I'd never forget. Beside that face floated the face of a small boy, blond like his mother, his little hands caught in the act of playing with the strands of her hair.

For the first time since we'd started watching, I wanted to tell Udain not to advance the protograph, not to let the fate it captured play itself out. I almost believed, for that frozen second, that if he let the image linger forever on the screen, none of them would have to die.

But I also knew that if time stopped right there, I would never have a chance to live.

I was looking at the face of my mother.

"Aleka Reza came to us two years before Athan's device was ready," Udain said, following my eyes. "Her colony, numbered fifteen, had been destroyed by Skaldi, and her

133

husband—that little boy's father—had died. She gave birth to the boy just days after she joined us. He and Mercy were play-mates for a time, until my granddaughter scared him off." He smiled again, though the smile looked more like a scowl. "And then, a couple of months after the day you're watching, Aleka vanished, she and her little one. We never heard word of them again, not until you showed up yesterday."

"He's dead," I said. "Her son. Yov." And then, because I couldn't bear to go into the details: "Skaldi."

He nodded, sighed. "I always thought she spoiled that boy. Though I understood. He was all she had left."

All, I thought, until she had me.

But that meant Yov and I didn't share the same father. We were half brothers. And my own father was still a complete mystery.

I couldn't understand why Aleka hadn't told me. Why she'd led me to believe Yov's father was mine. Why she'd lied to Laman when she and her two sons joined Survival Colony 9, telling him Yov's father had died when Yov was a child. There was so much she hadn't told me, so much I'd longed to learn. Important things. Little things. Her last name. *My* last name. The conversation we were supposed to have when we reached the canyon held even more secrets than I'd imagined.

And now she was lying in the infirmary, her body broken and her mind missing, and she might never come back to me.

"Shall I continue?" Udain said.

I shook myself from my thoughts. "What was the device?" I said. "The one Athan was trying to build?"

"It was a variation on the beam," he said. "We had known for some time that the Skaldi couldn't withstand the beam's energy. Our firearms first proved that, and the compound confirmed its power. Athan's hypothesis was that a strong enough signal, applied at the proper coordinates, could neutralize the Skaldi on a regional scale. And, if successful at that level, additional devices of the same kind could be utilized around the globe, immobilizing Skaldi for survival teams to hunt down and eradicate."

"Which would mean . . ."

"The end of our persecution," he said. "The recovery of our planet. A new world, if not a paradise then at least a chance to wipe the slate clean. Laman, as you saw, believed the project was too ambitious. Aleka, on the other hand, was taken by the idea, and she teamed with Athan to complete the device, learning as she worked."

Yet another secret. "She never told me."

"She must have had her reasons," he said. "But it wouldn't have mattered in any event. Your colony had no means to utilize such knowledge."

"But you did."

"We'd found a way," he said evasively. "Laman, though he barely understood our work, warned us that any such attempt was perilous. But Athan didn't listen, and by the time Aleka joined us, Laman was long gone. My younger son was a brilliant man, a genius really, when you consider what he had to work with. We were all blinded by"—and he laughed, a harsh laugh like a shout of pain—"the light."

His finger flexed on the wrist cuff, and I had a moment to study the faces in the crowd: Udain's commanding and remorseless, his son's enflamed with enthusiasm, Aleka's stern and composed, Mercy's unhardened by the events that were about to unfold. Yov played with our mother's hair, clutching the long strands in his fists and pulling, laughing as she held him in her arms. Mercy's face turned upward as if to feel the sun.

Then I flinched as the screen filled with a terrible light, bright enough in its recorded form to sear my eyes. On the protograph the light shone white, but in reality I knew it had been bright yellow. It washed away the faces, the bodies, the smiles and held hands, washed away the buildings, the fence, the ground they stood on, the sky above. It was accompanied by a hum that grew to a roar, a roar that was swallowed by a silence. The screen hadn't frozen, it was still advancing, but there was nothing there, no image or sound, until at last out of the deadly white void there came a voice, the voice of a child crying in terror and pain:

"*Daddy!*"

Then the cry ended in a scream, and I couldn't tell whose voice it was anymore, whether the child had screamed or others had answered with an anguish of their own. I looked at Udain, but his eyes remained fixed on the nothing that filled the screen. If that craggy face had been capable of tears, I felt sure they'd be flowing down his lined cheeks and into his long white beard now.

A crackling noise made me jump. Udain's hand moved to pause the empty protrograph, then snatched the walkie-talkie from his belt. I noticed that, however faintly, the radio glowed with the universal energy of the camp.

"What now, Mercy?" he said gruffly.

"I think you'd better get out here."

"We're busy." With an odd, crooked smile, he added, "I've been giving Querry history lessons."

"That can wait," her voice emerged, impertinent even through the crackle on the line. "This can't."

"What is it?"

"Trust me," she said. "You're not going to want to miss this."

8

Mercy met us at the door to Udain's quarters, and we walked out into the desert dawn.

The day wore its typical colors of dusty gray and brown. But those colors seemed surreal after the unnatural glare of the impact zone and the flat, sterile white of the protograph. The sun hadn't yet crested the buildings, but its aura was strong enough to bleach the force field protecting the compound to near invisibility. Without a word or a look at me or her grandfather, Mercy marched us straight to the cage, where something colorless and unmoving wrestled to emerge from the shadows.

When I saw what it was, I stopped dead. So did Udain.

"When did this happen?" he asked.

"Must have been overnight," she answered. "I found it like this when I came out to check the cage this morning."

"And you're sure no one tampered with the beam?" Udain marveled.

"As if they could," Mercy said in reply, but her eyes locked on mine. I moved closer to the cage, staring in disbelief at the thing inside.

It was the Skaldi. Or what was left of it. Which wasn't much. A lump of scorched, discolored matter, maybe half a skeletal arm. On the cement surrounding it, a roughly circular mark radiated streaks like the rays of a small black sun.

Mercy saw me staring. "That's all that's left of your dance partner from yesterday. I guess it wanted to tango just a moment too long."

"I did that?"

"Evidently," she drawled. "Geller told me it was acting agitated all evening, pacing the cage and opening its mouth over and over like it wanted to puke something up. And"— her eyes darted toward Udain before returning to mine—"he swore he saw sparks deep inside it. Yellow sparks."

"Like the beam," I said stupidly.

"Like the beam," she repeated. "Care to explain that?"

I shook my head, feeling disoriented and dizzy. At the nest, I'd discovered that the Skaldi couldn't stand to touch me—that their skin burned when they tried. But I'd never incinerated one before. And it didn't make sense to me, if I could do that, that it had taken all night before the combustion occurred.

Udain moved closer to the cage, the low-lying sun casting his huge shadow over the pale mess inside. "We can discuss Querry's talents later," he rumbled. "I'd say our first priority is to determine how we're going to keep Athan's minions from visiting us until we find a replacement."

"That's *your* first priority," Mercy snapped. She pointed an accusatory finger at me. "I'm beginning to wonder why *he* visited us."

"How can you ask that?" I said. "I wanted to leave. You were the one—"

"Save it." Her gaze drilled into me. "After fifteen years, a mystery man claiming to be Laman Genn's long lost foster child saunters out of the impact zone with the power to fricassee Skaldi, and this after spending an all-expenses-paid vacation with Athan Genn. And I'm supposed to believe you're on some kind of humanitarian mission?"

"So, what, you still think I'm Athan's spy?"

"I don't know what the hell you are!"

"Neither do I." It struck me with fresh force how little I knew. I didn't know my past, my present, my future. I didn't know if my colony was alive or dead. I had just learned my own mother's name, and I still didn't know my own father's face. "All I know is, I'm not in league with Asunder *or* the Skaldi. You can believe me if you want to."

"There's one way to find out," she snarled, and without warning she swung her rifle at me.

The current rattled my teeth and knocked me to the ground, my shoulder smacking the pavement hard. "Mercy!" Udain roared. He leaped at her, moving with unexpected speed for one his age and size. Instantly she shouldered her weapon, the stream of sparks rocketing into the sky for a second before she shut it off. She didn't resist when Udain disarmed her. But what amazed me even more was her face, which no longer wore the hardened look of the soldier. It was as if someone had reversed the protograph, and what I was seeing was the child she'd been the day her father set fire to the world.

I wondered if it was her voice I'd heard screaming.

I rolled to a sitting position. My eyes watered and my tongue buzzed, but I didn't feel hurt. Mercy looked at me for a second, her eyes grieving, before she turned and ran. Udain watched her disappear behind his headquarters, then he grasped my hand and pulled me to my feet with a strength matching his giant grandson's.

"We'll take you to the infirmary," he said. "Though you look none the worse for wear." The expression in his dark eyes made me distinctly uneasy.

"Will she be all right?"

"She has her moments," he said. "The best thing to do when they come is to let her be."

He gripped my arm and steered me toward the infirmary. Though he didn't squeeze anywhere near as hard as I knew he could, the message came through loud and clear: he wasn't letting go. I chided myself for how quickly I'd let my guard down, forgetting that I was his prisoner. What had he and Mercy discussed last night, while I was sleeping off the Skaldi attack? What further tests had they designed for me? And for what purpose?

I realized I'd been right about Udain the first day. He might act like a kindly grandfather when it suited him, but he was Athan and Laman Genn's father. Whatever had convinced him to show me the protograph and tell me his life story, it hadn't been out of concern for me.

He led me to the small white infirmary building, its door opening at a touch of his wrist cuff. The pressure of his hand guided me inside, gentle but unyielding.

"Udain," I said. "What did Mercy see that day?"

His expression didn't change, but the hint of pain floated back to the surface of his eyes. "I think," he said, "you should ask her that yourself."

The doctor who checked me out—the same man who'd treated Aleka, and the only adult I'd seen in the compound other than Udain—found nothing wrong with me. My shoulder was red and sensitive beneath his probing fingers, that's all. I couldn't remember feeling pain from Mercy's assault, only a shock, a buzzing, the same thing I'd felt when her beam hit me and my captors at the base of the altar. I remembered the warriors writhing on the rock, the Skaldi cowering in its cage. What Mercy had been trying to prove I wasn't sure. If I'd succumbed like the warriors, she'd have known I was human, and if I'd been drained of power like the Skaldi she'd have known . . . what? But whatever she was thinking, the fact that I'd barely been affected at all had obviously surprised her, and maybe Udain as well.

It had certainly surprised me. But what it meant, I had no idea.

Udain and the doctor talked privately after the exam, then Udain disappeared. I asked the doctor if I could see Aleka, and after a moment's hesitation he consented, leading me to the back room of the infirmary, where Tyris sat by her bedside. A sharp smell, not unpleasant but not natural, permeated the room. My mother lay in bed, clear tubes running into her left arm from plastic bags on a metal rack. Her color still seemed bad to me, but I felt hopeful when I saw that the red mark on her forehead had vanished and that her breathing had softened and her eyes closed in something like real sleep. Her right arm, though, was packed so tightly in a bundle of gauze I couldn't tell its condition. Tyris, haggard with lack of sleep, her own wounds turning ugly shades of yellow and green, whispered to me: "Doctor Siva plans to operate. You should come by tomorrow." I leaned over and kissed Aleka's forehead, feeling the flush of heat beneath her skin. "Get better, Mom," I said. I thought her eyelids fluttered when I said that, but I couldn't be sure.

Zataias needed to get out and move around, so he and Adem joined me when I left the infirmary to take a look around the base. The first thing I noticed was that the teenage guards who casually roamed the square never let me out of their sight. Geller in particular, his pimple-scarred face easy to spot, seemed always to be trailing us, though every time I looked his way he acted like he was doing something else.

Once I stopped paying attention to him, I was able to take in how truly impressive the compound was. It was all lines and right angles, the buildings and lanes laid out in a perfect grid. Nothing seemed in disrepair, not a single bulb or girder missing or askew. I could hardly believe this had once been the broken-down base I'd seen in the protograph. We wandered past glass structures whose misted windows showed rows of plants growing, fans of water bursting from the ceiling to keep them moist. "Hydroponics," Adem said, surprising me once again with the kind of word he saved up for days to say. Zataias proved a somewhat better companion—he didn't talk any more than Adem, but he stared appreciatively as I traced the network of pipes that sprang from buildings and that dived beneath the pavement to tap an underground aquifer, or maybe to connect with a distant water source, another river. He gaped at the blinking lights and soaring guard tower and buzzing gadgets, and his eyes absolutely bugged out of his head at the vehicle we found parked behind Udain's headquarters, something that looked like a truck stripped down to its frame and wheels. The metal chassis was as spotless as everything else in the compound, showing no signs of the rust that coated every piece of machinery we'd owned in Survival Colony 9. Zataias nearly danced in his eagerness to climb aboard, but I got the feeling Udain wouldn't like that, so I took his hand and pulled him away.

With each moment that passed, each shining feature we saw, the genius of Athan Genn became more and more evident. His older brother's colony had saved or scavenged plenty of junk from the ruins of the old world, but no one had been able to bring any of that stuff back to its original life, much less refashion it for new purposes. Mercy's father had done just that, raising a futuristic fortress out of a scrap heap. In order to work that miracle, it occurred to me, he needed one additional ingredient—something people had possessed in the past, but something that had totally eluded us all my days in Survival Colony 9.

A power source.

I found where they kept that during our self-guided tour. One low, locked structure, more like a shed than a housing unit, stood at the compound's rear, humming with energy. Even the pavement shook when we neared it. Thick cables sheathed in hard rubber ran down its sides, plunging into the concrete. The building didn't glow, but I could easily imagine it as the origin of the glow that powered everything else. I guessed that the guns and walkie-talkies held miniature versions of it, battery cells of some kind. What it was I couldn't imagine—Laman had told me about the old world's addiction to fossil fuels, their belated efforts to shift to wind and geothermal and solar, but he'd never said anything about the kind of power that seemed to run this place. Maybe, if his father was to be believed, he'd never understood it. But whatever it was, I knew it was something both necessary and dangerous—the same source that had warped the desert as well as its own inventor. And it was also the compound's best-kept secret, with six armed guards stationed outside the building, one at each corner and two at a panel in front. They eyed us as we approached and didn't stop staring until we moved away. Even Geller, I noticed, hung back from the power supply, keeping a much safer distance from us than he had the rest of the day.

We left the power plant and roamed back to the perimeter fence. The circle of desert dust sloped upward to the row of twisted rock formations that divided rusty soil from obsidian stone. The late day sun turned the place they called the impact zone into a single sheet of fiery glass. I squinted at it, wondering if we'd ever be allowed to leave in search of our kidnapped friends. It occurred to me that Udain Genn's compound wasn't only a fortress, an armed defense against his mad son's raids. It was also a prison, one the commander had decreed for his followers on that day fifteen years ago when . . .

"Fifteen years," I said to myself.

The meaning of Mercy's words struck me for the first time.

Fifteen years. My own age.

I couldn't believe I hadn't connected the dots before. According to Udain, Yov had been born when Aleka joined his colony, making him about two in the protograph. That matched what I knew: he was approaching his eighteenth birthday when he died. About three years older than me.

But that meant the Aleka I'd seen in the protograph . . .

The solid cement swam beneath my feet. Hesitantly, while Adem and Zataias watched in open-mouthed silence, I reached for one of the fence's metal struts. With the full light of day, the force field had faded to almost nothing, but I knew it was there, a buzzing I didn't so much hear as feel in the bones of my hand. As my fingers got near the fence, the buzzing grew stronger, bathing my flesh in a dull warmth. It didn't hurt, in fact it was the opposite of hurting, making my hand tingle as if I'd slept on it wrong. The tingling grew so strong I was about to snatch my hand away when something else happened that made me jump back in shock.

A pale yellow spark shot from my fingers, and my hand jerked away involuntarily.

I flexed the hand, balled it into a fist. The tingling had vanished, and the skin looked fine except for a little redness. I reached for the fence again, with the same result. Buzzing, tingling, then the spark and my hand flying off just before contact. My companions said nothing, and I tried to convince myself all I was seeing was the crackling of the energy field. But after three tries I couldn't deny it anymore. The energy beam that wrapped the fence called out a defensive energy of my own.

I knew now why Mercy's gun hadn't hurt me.

It hadn't touched me.

"*That's* why I don't trust you," came a voice from behind us. I turned to find Mercy, rifle slung over her shoulder, black eyes reflecting the glow I couldn't otherwise see.

She came to stand beside us. A single glare from her was enough to turn Adem bright red and convince him to grab Zataias's hand and make a run for it. I watched the two of them disappear behind the empty cage before I turned my attention back to Mercy.

"The beam is hot as hell," she said, nodding as if in satisfaction at scaring the others off. "Not hot that you can feel, but hot. Put your hand in it for ten seconds and your skin peels off. But here you are, pawing at it like a kid eager to take his first pony ride."

"Pony?"

"Ever hear of horses?"

"I've heard of them."

"Same thing. Only smaller."

She waved her hand a foot or so from the fence, then stuck her finger straight through the nearly invisible force field and touched the metal for a second before pulling back. I looked at her, startled, expecting to see pain in her face, but I saw only her usual angry calm. When she showed me the finger, though, I noticed a bright red spot blooming on the tip.

"I feel nothing," she said. I took it as an answer to the question in my eyes. "But it'll blister. You, on the other hand, don't seem to be hurt by it at all. You react to it, but not with pain. With . . . power."

"Was it that obvious?"

"Udain's eyes aren't as sharp as they used to be," she

said. "I saw what happened when I shot you." She said the words *shot you* the way you might talk about giving someone a playful punch in the arm. "You lit up like a jack-o'-lantern. You—"

"A what?"

"Can I finish, please?" she snapped. "We'll discuss your woeful ignorance at a later time."

I waited.

"As I was saying," she went on. "When the beam hit you, you lit up. Just for a second, but long enough. It was weird. Like your—I don't know, like your bones were on fire. I *felt* it too, like a shock wave had passed over me for a second. I've been looking extra close ever since to see if you glow."

"And?"

"The jury's still out. I'm waiting for nightfall to make sure."

Without warning, she laid a hand on my cheek. I pulled away, but her hand followed, and as its warmth adjusted to mine, I relaxed. She held it there for a long minute before removing it and inspecting her palm.

"Nothing," she said, sounding almost disappointed. "Whatever you do that makes you the scourge of Skaldi worldwide, it's not on the surface. Or you don't emit it, at least not until you need to. Has anyone close to you ever died of radiation sickness?"

A hole yawned in my gut at the thought of Keely, and Nessa, and Aleka. But they were fine, I told myself. Or if not fine, at least undamaged by me. Or if not that, at least undamaged by anything my body had done.

"What happened?" I asked her. "The day your dad's device malfunctioned?"

Her face flinched at the memory, or at the word *dad*. But she answered. "The pulse was too strong. Either that or it wasn't properly contained. Something about the binding energy. Grandpa's the nuclear physicist." It was the first time, I realized, I'd heard her call Udain that. "It fused the desert sand, turned it to a substance like glass or stone. It probably would've destroyed the whole compound if something hadn't absorbed its force."

"Something?"

"Or someone." Her eyes flicked toward the wall of rock that corralled the impact zone. "The guards' bodies were trapped in the fused glass and stone. Or parts of them *became* stone, it's hard to say which. The ones who weren't affected tried to free them, but the rock was too strong." She shrugged, the motion somehow savage. "In the end they begged the others to shoot them."

"You remember this?"

She stared off into the distance, over the impact zone. "Sometimes it's all I can remember."

"And your family?"

Her eyes snapped back to mine, as hard and jagged as the stone. "Beryl got scared by the light and ran. By the time my mother caught up to her it was too late. All she could do was cover Beryl's body with her own. When it was over my father—*Athan*—tried to pull them free. Their hands came away in"—her teeth clenched—"pieces."

I started to say something, but the look on her face stopped me.

"He left the next day," she said. "We found Mom and Beryl dead, what was left of them. The rest was pulverized to shards of glass. The last thing he did must have been to take a sledgehammer to them. Which was also the last unselfish thing he did, because by nightfall their skin had started to blacken and bubble where it wasn't turned to stone." She drew a deep breath before continuing. "Grandpa took me and Ardan to live with him. I wasn't even three years old, but something told me I'd never see my father again. And I was right."

Abruptly she pulled away from the fence and stalked toward one of the smaller buildings, a new one I'd never visited. Without a word, I followed. I didn't need her grandfather's advice to know this was one of those times it was best to keep quiet.

She stabbed the code to enter the building and then the back room, not slowing for a second to find out if anyone was there. Overhead lights flickered on automatically, and I saw that we stood in a tiny, plain room with a single metal bed and chair. A protograph screen, half the size of the one in Udain's quarters, hung from one of the walls. It hummed to life without her touching a button. I guessed it was calibrated to her eyes or movements, but I couldn't shake the feeling that she'd *thought* it on. As if the lifeless machine was trying to make up for what its creator had done to her.

"Grab some popcorn," Mercy said. "And enjoy the show."

We sat in front of the screen. It showed nothing for a minute, but I heard the sound of it searching. Then Mercy nodded ever so slightly, and the flat screen filled with the oversize face of a man.

I recognized Athan from the earlier images in Udain's protograph: lean cheeks, long hair, dark eyes. But now scars ran down his cheeks, over his brow, into the flesh at the corner of his lips. And every feature had become exaggerated, the cheeks not just lean but emaciated, the hair not just long but unruly, the eyes not just intense but insane. They rolled and spun in his gaunt face, colorless like everything else in the protograph but radiating a kaleidoscopic pattern. They seemed to be seeking something only he could find.

"I thought you never saw him again," I said to Mercy.

"I didn't," she said. "That's not my father."

"We believed you had died," a voice spoke from the protograph screen.

"I did not die," the mouth of her father said. His words came out cold and unshakable. "I was reborn."

"Yet you returned."

"*Aya tivah bis,*" Asunder spoke. "*Shashi tivah bracha.*"

There was a pause while the invisible interrogator took in these strange words.

"You have come to stand trial for your crimes?"

"I have come with a message for the unbelievers," Asunder said. "I have given my flesh to the all-powerful one, that I might warn the infidels of the fate that is prepared for them."

"Do you deny what you have done?"

"I deny nothing," he said. "I have been reborn."

Without transition, the image widened to reveal Asunder's whole body, seated rigidly in a metal chair.

But his body wasn't whole.

He wore only a loincloth, one that seemed to be cut from his camouflage uniform, so there was nothing to hide the terrible gashes that ran across his chest, his arms, his legs. The flesh was ragged as a Skaldi's scar, the wounds unhealed, dark with dried blood. But something about the way his eyes leaped eagerly to the ruin of his own body made me question whether these were Skaldi bites or whether he had done this to himself. I looked for the bone-white staff, but it wasn't there.

"You will be tried by our courts," the interrogator said, and I realized the voice belonged to Udain. "That is the only power you need fear. But they may be merciful."

At that Asunder smiled, a cold smile that did nothing to chase the deadly calm from his face. "There is no mercy among men," he said. "There is only judgment."

"Athan—"

"All will bow before the Scavenger of Souls on the day of his coming," the son's voice spoke. "The men of metal and machines as well as the purified ones. Else they will meet their doom."

The figure of the interrogator moved into the frame, and I saw that it was Udain, his body towering over the ruined shape of his younger son. But before I could watch his response to Asunder's latest threat, Mercy blinked twice, and the screen went blank.

"Mercy—"

"There is no mercy among men," she said. "There is only judgment."

"When did he come back?"

She shrugged. "A week, two maybe. I was only three years old."

"Did you see him?"

She nodded.

"Did you talk to him?"

"He scared me," she said softly. "He had the face of my father, but his body . . ." She shivered. "Before Beryl and my mom died, I went out to—to be with them. To touch them. They were broken too. Their bodies had turned partly to stone, and those parts had crumbled away when he tried to free them. But they still held me. In the embrace of the stone. I felt their warmth, their hearts beating. They were still *alive*." She nodded at the empty screen. "Not him. He was dead. His body still moved, his mouth still spoke, but he was dead."

"But he came back," I said. "Why?"

"How the hell do I know?" she said. "To convert everyone

to his loony cult, apparently. He was sentenced to banish-
ment, but he kept coming back. For years. Only now he had
that staff, and he started holding meetings out in the impact
zone, and the people who went to them came back acting
crazy. They babbled about the evil they'd done, and how
they'd been purified with fire, and how all our sins would be
washed away if we joined their lord Asunder. Half the time
they didn't even talk in a real language. Eventually they tried
to blow up the whole camp. They were sentenced to death,
but right before they were executed Athan showed up with
a bunch of warriors and stole them away. And when Udain
tracked them to the canyon to put an end to it, they killed
almost everyone, and captured the ones who didn't die."

"And Archangel?" I said. "Ardan? What happened to
him?"

"You ask a lot of questions, Beam Boy," she said. "Maybe
it's none of your goddamn business."

"You don't believe that," I said. "You know I'm part of
this. You knew right away, and that's why you took me to see
Udain. You knew I could help you get at Asunder."

She regarded me warily. "You seem to have it all figured
out. So how exactly *are* you going to help us tiptoe past his
defenses?"

"Because I know something about him you don't," I said.
"Something about him even he doesn't."

"Which is . . . ?"

I took a deep breath before answering. I wasn't sure why

it was so hard to utter the words, whether I was worried about giving away my advantage or didn't want to admit it to myself. But it was the truth. Knowing it now, seeing it in the protograph, it seemed I'd known it from the moment I'd met him in the black rock desert. I'd just never realized what it meant.

"He's an amnesiac," I said. "His past was stolen from him by Skaldi. Like mine. He doesn't remember who he is."

I told Mercy everything.

Or everything I could. I told her about the Skaldi attack, now seven months ago, that had robbed me of my memory and destroyed Survival Colony 27, the colony I'd shared with Aleka and my half brother. I told her about my short time in Survival Colony 9, my life with her uncle Laman and her childhood playmate Yov, the details of their deaths. I finished that part of the story by telling her about the Skaldi nest, the monsters' inability to kill me. Next I told her about Aleka's attempt to reach the canyon, our capture by Asunder's colony, our abortive escape, the murder of the guard. I told her how her father had attacked Aleka and Wali and me with his staff, and her eyes simmered. When I told her the part her brother Ardan—Archangel—had played in our imprisonment, the simmer turned to a boil.

"So Athan touched you with the staff too?" she said.

I nodded.

"And yet you're still basically compos mentis," she mused. "So it seems that's another thing you're immune to."

"He uses it on his own people," I said, remembering the ritual in *Grava Bracha*. "But all it seems to do is make them forget. It's more powerful when he wants to kill someone. Like a"—and Tyris's words returned to me—"like an electric shock to the system."

"But he never touched Ardan with it?" she said anxiously.

"Not that I saw."

She mulled that over. "Ardan saw me," she said. "At the altar. He must have known who I was. But he wouldn't talk to me." Her mouth turned down. "If he's not under the staff's power, why's he agreeing to do everything Pops says?"

I had no answer for her.

She told me about the early years of Asunder's reign. How the raids had been intense at first, with many of Udain's colonists lost to the prophet and his growing army of disciples. Some people, she said, went willingly, people who felt responsible for what had happened that day. Parents who'd lost their kids, kids who'd lost their parents. Ardan was less than ten years old when he followed his father into the desert. Other people Athan targeted for kidnapping: women and children especially, as well as members of Udain's team with specialized expertise in things like horticulture and toxicology. His prize recruit was a geneticist named Melan, who'd been Athan's right-hand man in the trials that produced the device. He'd joined Asunder voluntarily, leaving behind the bodies of a son and daughter frozen in the rock.

"Melampus," I said.

Mercy told me that her father had tried to abduct her, too, but her grandfather had kept her hidden. And Asunder had stolen lots of tech as well, though from what she understood he'd taken most of it only to destroy it. It was obvious to me, though, that some of it—the living tech, like the toxin-resistant seeds she told me Melan had invented—had been used to build their civilization and bioengineer their canyon home. Within a few years of the attack at rock city, Mercy said, Udain's scouts counted hundreds of warriors in the southern end of the canyon. And they reported seeing little kids trailing after the older members of Asunder's colony, all of them with the long brown hair and dark eyes of their leader.

"So you think . . ." I began.

"That Daddy got busy, yeah. And I think that's why he wanted that bimbo of yours."

"Nessa," I said, but she was no longer listening.

She told me that after Asunder's victory over his father's forces, his tactics had changed: rather than appearing at the compound himself, he started sending emissaries to stir up trouble. A few of Udain's people were convinced by these preachers to join Asunder—though those were the ones, Udain later discovered, who ended up sacrificed as warnings to the rest. But in some ways the missionary runs were worse than the full-scale assaults, because the people who showed up at camp sometimes posed as refugees from Athan, and that made it hard for Udain to keep them at bay. Finally he got the idea to use his son's technology to cage the Skaldi, and he decreed that anyone from outside would be fed to it. For years there'd been no more attacks, and Udain thought his son might finally have called a truce. Then, a half year ago, the missionary runs started again.

"It was right around the time you keep talking about. The time"—she nodded at me—"you had your first date with the Skaldi."

"You think there's a connection?"

"The timing fits," she said. "Just when you join Laman's colony, Athan starts recruiting again. Maybe he learned his big brother was a daddy too, and was getting ready to pluck some fruit from him."

"Laman's son died," I said. "His name was Matay. He would have been your cousin."

"Most of my life is would-have-been," she sighed. "But I guess I'm not alone."

"No," I said.

And then, finally, I told her about my mother. Aleka. Who, if my numbers were right, had been pregnant with me the day Athan's device devoured the desert, killing Mercy's mother and sister, driving its creator insane.

We sat silent for a long time. Mercy stared at nothing, her lips moving occasionally without making a sound. In the buzzing quiet I tried to total my own list of would-have-beens. I quickly lost count.

"And so you think—what?" she said at last. "That the explosion turned you into some kind of mutant killing machine?"

"I think its power went into me, yes," I said. "It's the only thing that explains why the Skaldi can't touch me. When they try, it calls out the power of the beam. Except the reaction's so strong it doesn't just paralyze them—it burns. I think the one in the cage must have pulled even more power than usual, and that's why it ignited."

She stared at me intently, as if she could spot mutation in my eyes. Then she laughed, but her laugh carried a manic edge. "Oh, man, this is too much. Here I am, plotting revenge with the original human glow stick. But it doesn't really help us get into that canyon, does it? Your remarkable powers only work against Skaldi."

"But Asunder *is* Skaldi," I said. "Or at least, the product of Skaldi. Don't you see, Mercy? The memory loss is the key. Right before he used the staff on me, he said something about fleeing into the desert and wrestling with a demon. He must have meant the Skaldi. Somehow, the creature that stole his memory fifteen years ago must still be living off his body. Using him to make others forget too. Through the power of his staff."

"The staff," she said, and I could see in her eyes that she was trying to believe me but not really succeeding.

"The staff," I repeated. "It's a bone, right? Could it be from someone the Skaldi killed?"

"Skaldi don't leave bones."

"I know." I struggled to think what it could be. When the staff touched me, I saw a child's arms being torn from its body. But I couldn't tell who it was, or how it had happened. What could have given a dead piece of bone that kind of power?

"It doesn't matter," I said finally, only half convinced by my own words. "All that matters is that I can help you fight him. On his home turf. He won't—he shouldn't be able to kill me. If I can focus the energy against him, he'll be powerless. And then you and Udain—"

She shook her head forcefully. "I'm not dragging Grandpa into this. He'd never believe me in the first place. If we go, we go alone."

"Two of us. Against his whole colony."

"I thought you were the one who was so confident," she said. "Look, it's not like Udain has a bunch of commandoes at his disposal. You think Geller's going to take a spear for you? And a small force stands a better chance of sneaking into the canyon anyway. The only thing we were lacking before was firepower. Which we now have, thanks to you." When I still hesitated, she went on. "You want that floozy and those kids back, right? And I want my father—"

"Dead."

"My father *is* dead," she hissed. "He took everything

from me. Not only Beryl and my mom, but Ardan, too. The least I can do is try to save the only brother I have left."

I weighed her offer. I didn't like our chances. Mercy was good at what she did, I knew that. Give her the right opportunity, and she'd be the one who turned into some kind of killing machine. But she was also unstable, someone I couldn't trust not to go rogue at the wrong moment. I didn't like the idea of leaving Aleka and the others behind. I didn't know enough about Asunder's powers to be sure we could overcome them. And I didn't know enough about my own power to be sure I could call on it when I needed it. Everything *seemed* to fit, but I'd been wrong before. If I was wrong this time . . .

I didn't know what would happen. I only knew what would happen if I did nothing. The thought of Nessa giving birth to one of Asunder's carbon-copy children clinched it. I held out my hand, and this time Mercy gripped it and shook firmly.

"That's that, then," she said. "Better go recharge your blood-beam. Tonight, we blow this popsicle stand."

Blowing this popsicle stand, I discovered, was easier said than done. And not only because I had no clue what a popsicle stand was.

I'd been right that Udain's camp was a prison. But I hadn't realized how right I was. Not only was the front—and only— gate locked and guarded around the clock, but everyone in the compound, with the possible exception of its commander, had a tracking device implanted under the skin of their upper arm. Mercy rolled up her left sleeve and showed me the place on her biceps, a bump and a scar. "Another of Athan's brilliant inventions," she said. "It itches." The tracking device, like everything else in the compound, connected to the control cuff around Udain's wrist, and it sent a distress signal after it passed beyond a certain range. Mercy wasn't sure what the range was—apparently her grandfather could adjust it depending on whim or circumstances—but it was certainly less than the distance it would take us to cross the impact zone and enter Asunder's canyon. The signals of those he'd stolen away had beeped frantically at first but long since fallen dead.

Still, if it had been Mercy leaving by herself, she probably could have managed it without much fuss. Udain tolerated her random comings and goings, her moods, her need for space. In fact, the way she told it, he'd been more than willing to let her expand her self-directed patrols of the impact zone. Geller would give her a hard time just to tick her off, but even he wouldn't bat an eye if she decided to take a midnight stroll into the stone desert. By the time Udain realized her tracker had gone AWOL, she'd be past the point of no return.

With me, though, our chances of escape dropped to near zero. I wasn't tagged—Mercy checked to make sure Doctor Siva hadn't performed the surgery after my adventure with the caged Skaldi—but I was still a marked man. When I was alone, all the guards watched me. When I was with Mercy, all the guards pretended not to watch me—which meant they were watching me even closer. Whatever Udain wanted with me, and Mercy swore she didn't know what it was, there was no way they'd let me out of camp, no matter what whopper she came up with. Short of taking on the twenty or so guards with her single weapon—the same weapon they were armed with—I couldn't figure out how we were going to break through the compound's defenses.

"What about the car?" I asked, nodding at the strange vehicle parked by her grandpa's headquarters.

"The moon buggy?" she snorted. "It goes about two miles an hour. I heard we used to have a hot-rod version, but someone took it for a joy ride out into the desert. But never fear"—and she smiled wickedly—"I have a plan."

We waited until Udain retired for the night, then marched to the power station. With the spotlights that came on at dusk and the constant glow of the beam, the compound seemed even brighter than during the day. Stealth wasn't a concern, though. The generator, Mercy explained, doubled as a charging station for their weapons, walkie-talkies, and anything else that ran off the beam, which meant pretty much everything. The guards were accustomed to people stopping by throughout the day and night, so our presence wouldn't attract a crowd. And what she had in mind would take no longer than a routine recharging, so we'd be well clear of the station before anyone realized what she'd done.

At the moment, anyway, we had the run of the place. The guards, as she'd anticipated, gave her no more than a bored nod as we came within sight. They did their usual bad job of pretending to ignore me, but I figured I was safe so long as I acted like I was just along for the ride. Now that I'd gotten used to the hum of the beam, the place felt almost eerily quiet. More to break the silence than to hear the answer, I whispered the first question that came to mind.

"What is the power source?"

"Something Athan synthesized," she answered, not whispering. Her voice sounded unnaturally loud in the stillness of the night. "It's one of the things Grandpa's really closemouthed about. Like he's got this idea of patenting it," she cackled.

"Patenting?"

"Never mind."

The power of the generator vibrated through the heavy soles of my boots. My whole body quivered to its pulse. The thought that something similar might be lurking inside me—in my blood, my bones, my brain—gave me a sick, clammy feeling. Whatever Athan's energy source was, unleashing it had destroyed the land in a twenty-mile radius from the point of impact. If that same power lay inside me, did it make me what Mercy said I was—a mutant killing machine?

"You sure this will work?" I asked, unable to keep myself from whispering.

"Udain taught me the codes," she replied. "In case any-thing happens to him."

"He trusts you?"

"Trust has nothing to do with it," she said. "You saw the tracker in my arm. But the man's pushing ninety."

She sidled up to the power station, where one of the ever-present keypads rested in the wall. The guards eyed her lazily before turning away. This keypad was far more complex than the others: it bristled with unnumbered buttons, as if whoever had designed it—Athan—wanted the codes to be not only unbreakable but unreadable. A single green light flashed in the center, a sign I took to mean either "safe" or "ready." But as I watched Mercy's finger fly over the key-pad, I couldn't help thinking of that light as a blinking eye, couldn't help wondering if Udain was sitting in front of the protograph screen in his headquarters, monitoring his grand-daughter as she sabotaged his compound's power source.

If he was, the first thing he heard was her swearing. "What the—?"

She punched the code again, stabbing the buttons swiftly but firmly. The green light continued to blink. The guards turned their attention back to her. Mercy regarded them for a second before spinning and striding away from the generator.

"I should have known," she said. "Goddamn it, the old man never misses a trick."

"What's wrong?"

"Grandpa switched the codes," she said. "If I enter one more error in the front gate's shut-down sequence, the system's wired to sound an alarm." She was already halfway to the gate.

"How often does he switch the codes?" I said, catching up to her.

"All the damn time," she said. "But never without telling me."

She kept up her march, her strides rapid and jittery. No alarm sounded, no guards appeared. But I had the feeling that dozens of protograph lenses had been planted everywhere around the compound, in the corners of buildings, on the fence posts, on top of the observation tower, all of them targeted at us. I also had the feeling that Mercy had come too far to let this hitch in the plan slow her down.

I was right. "Get ready to run," she muttered as the gate rose into view. Her rifle remained strapped to her back, but she'd removed a pistol from its holster and started punching the miniature keys on its handle as she walked.

"Is this a good idea?" I tried.

"You got a better one?"

But then she stopped. We'd drawn level with the cage, the black scorch mark standing out in the brightness like a pool of dried blood. Mercy shook her pistol, furiously punched the buttons again, then drew her arm back as if to throw her weapon at the bars. "God*damn* it!" she shouted. She spun to take in the compound, her eyes snapping from building to building. Maybe she'd felt the same presence of silent, spying eyes that I had.

"What now?"

"He jammed my gun," she fumed. "He actually jammed my gun. I didn't even know he could *do* that."

She shoved the pistol into its holster, ripped the rifle from her back, tried to bring it to life. When it failed to respond, she gripped it by the barrel and flung it far into the air, where it flashed in the compound's blinding strobes before falling with a clatter out of sight.

"*Goddamn it!*" she screamed.

"The code . . . ?"

"Doesn't bloody work. Everything's out. The protograph!" she said, realization dawning. "He must have spied on us through it."

Hearing my suspicions confirmed didn't help the knot in my gut. "What do we do now?"

"We bust out of this insane asylum!" she said, looking around frantically. "We blow the goddamn gate to hell and leave him to pick up the pieces!"

"But your grandfather—"

"Locked me in a goddamn cage!" she said. "All my life. For my own *protection*. To keep me *safe*." From her mouth, the words sounded worse than curses. "Ever since I was a little girl, staring at that screen he installed in my room, going out on his pointless patrols only to have him reel me back in. You don't think he'll do the same to you? You don't think he already has? He's using you, Querry, now that he knows what you can do. Using you, like he used me, and my father, and my—oh, *God*!" Her words ended in a cry, and she aimed her useless pistol into the night, as if she could blast a hole in the darkness to free herself from the glowing cage.

"Maybe we can convince him," I said softly. I reached for her arm, but she jerked away. "If he already knows about me, maybe he'll come with us. He wants to stop Asunder as much as you do."

"Does he?" Her voice rose, and for a second I thought I saw her father's madness in her gold-lit eyes. "Without Asunder, how could he keep us in his prison? You don't know what it's like here, Querry. You don't know what it's like to have to live *his* life every single moment instead of mine."

By *his*, I didn't know if she meant her father's or her grandfather's. Maybe both. But I tried to reason with her.

"Let me talk to Udain," I said. "It's our only chance. We're obviously not getting out of here without his permission."

Her face froze as if I'd slapped her. Then she laughed, the high-pitched laugh I'd heard earlier in the day. She pointed the dead gun at her head and pulled the trigger, made the sound of the explosion.

"Better talk fast," she laughed.

I lifted my eyes from hers, and saw the guards approaching.

All six of them from the power station, plus Geller from the front gate, with Udain at their head. As always, the commander dwarfed those around him. In the compound's harsh light his white hair bled a bright energy painful to my eyes. For the first time, I felt I was seeing him as his older son had seen him all those years ago. And I realized why the commander of Survival Colony 9 had deserted his base and his family, why he'd never returned, why he'd never brought his new colony close to the compound in all their years of wandering. Not only because he was angry that his younger brother had found favor in his father's eyes. Not only because he doubted the technology his brother had created.

But also because he was afraid.

"Mercy," Udain said, drawing up in front of us, his guards silently forming a circle to block all chance of escape. "I am sorry this was necessary."

She said nothing, only slumped before him, her breathing heavy and her eyes dull. Udain reached for her gun, and she handed it to him obediently.

"Your friend is too dangerous to let slip away," he said, sliding Mercy's pistol into his belt. "I'm thankful to you for bringing him here. And thankful to Geller for keeping tabs on him this past day."

Mercy didn't even look up as Geller's pimpled face smiled in victory.

"You merely suspect what this boy is," Udain continued, laying a huge hand on my shoulder. "But I know. He is the final piece of the puzzle, the answer we've sought all these years."

"Laman said the same thing," I muttered.

Udain shook his head, and despite his imposing frame and calm mien, I was sure I saw fresh pain in his eyes. "Laman never understood," he said. "The risks we took, the losses we suffered. The sacrifices we made. To him, you would have been nothing but a mystery, a freakish chance."

"He treated me like a son," I said.

"He had no right!" Udain roared, and I flinched from the fury in his face. For the second time in as many days, I was afraid this Goliath was about to strike me down. But then his voice returned to its usual level, a rumble like a shaking beneath the ground's crust.

"Laman failed in his vigilance," he said. "He had you in his keeping, but he didn't know what he had. It falls to me to atone for his errors. And his brother's."

With that, he gestured to his guards, and two of them detached themselves from the circle to approach me. Their rifles prodded me in the back as their leader grabbed my arm and pulled me toward the power station. No gentleness this time: he dragged me with all the strength in his giant frame. I looked over my shoulder once, saw Mercy surrounded by the remaining guards. Geller's face beamed with malicious glee, while hers appeared drained and lifeless in the compound's remorseless light. In that glimpse, I could imagine what she'd witnessed so many years ago at the foot of the impact zone.

Udain punched the generator's code into the cuff around his wrist. The front door panel hissed as it swung open, revealing stairs that led down into dimly glowing depths. He entered, ducking beneath the low ceiling, the guards pushing me down the stairs behind him. The body of the camp's commander filled the stairwell, blocking my view of what lay below.

At the bottom of the short flight, we entered a cramped room lit by an angry golden glare.

Cables ran down the concrete walls to a series of metal boxes, each of them roughly the size of a fuel transfer tank. The yellow light came from one of them. Udain stood staring at the boxes, veins of gold lining his face. Then he turned to me.

"My younger son," he said, "was a genius. Everything he did, he did for the future of this world. You need to understand that."

He tapped a code into the cuff on his wrist, and the front panel of the single glowing box slid open.

I shielded my eyes from the light. A form resolved itself, a figure that burned with bright golden energy as if its blood and bones were on fire.

A living figure. A human figure.

It was no larger than a child.

I stared, unbelieving. The figure's eyes stared back. It wasn't entirely human, its head far too big and its limbs far too scrawny. I would have called it Skaldi if not for the suffering in its puckered face. Its chest heaved convulsively, and I thought I could hear its heart beating, in time with the pulse of its burning blood. Other than that, it stood motionless, locked into its casket with metal bands, cables erupting from its head and shoulders and chest. Udain allowed me one more torturous look before entering another code and sealing the figure in its cell once again.

My eyes met his. Tears sparkled on his cheeks like jewels, fierce and bright.

"Biosynthesis," he said. "On a scale that dwarfs the imagination. Living energy from cell metabolism, generated and stored to operate this compound for a thousand years. My son did this. At my command."

"Udain," I whispered. "How could you?"

"It was my charge," he said. "It was what gave rise to the survival colonies. For years after the aliens' discovery, our government studied the creatures, seeking to tap their abilities. Here was an organism, to all appearances without life, but capable of draining life-energy from others. And yet the alien cells, unable to store the energy they'd stolen, deteriorated rapidly after colonizing another body. What might the potential be if the aliens' genetic material could be mated to normal cells, healthy cells—human cells?"

He drew a heavy breath. "It was known as the Kenos Project, from a very ancient word meaning 'to empty' or 'to drain.' Its full name—the Strategic Kenos Living Defense Initiative—gave birth to the code name SKLDI, from which we were bequeathed the word *Skaldi*. It sought two objectives: to spawn supersoldiers, and to breed human bombs." His voice and eyes never wavered, but I thought his eighty-plus years had accumulated on his frame in a single instant. "I was its head in the years immediately preceding the wars of destruction."

"The wars," I said. "Is that what caused them?"

"The wars were both product and impetus of the Kenos trials," he answered. "The drones"—and his arm swept the row of sealed boxes—"represented some of our first successes. What we didn't know was that the energy stored in their bodies, when released with explosive force, would draw the Skaldi in even greater numbers. Drone after drone was detonated in an effort to terminate the threat, but with each new blast, more and more of the creatures poured through the gateway. There are those who believe the Skaldi infiltrated the project in its early stages, forcing us to turn our world's resources to their ends. Knowing the creatures' methods, that wouldn't surprise me. But I've witnessed enough destruction among my own kind to think we needed no such prompting from another world."

I could see it now, reflected in Udain's mournful eyes: the Skaldi's power bred in living hosts, the world bombed and broken, turned to a lifeless desert. "What do you want from me?" I asked.

"An end," he said. "An end to all this ruin and waste. I pushed my son to continue the Kenos trials, believing that if we could refine the drones, we could use them to defeat the Skaldi at last. Build a weapon that would drain them of power rather than feeding them more. A weapon that would neutralize them without damage to us."

His face flickered in the light of his son's creation.

"But I was wrong," he said. "His weapon failed too, and you've seen the result. This final drone is all that remains of his handiwork. For years he's been seeking to recover it, for purposes I think I can guess. He would destroy everything that remains in the name of his mad theology, and only I stand in his way. That's why you can never leave this compound. And why my granddaughter's impetuosity had to be curbed."

"You think I'm like that . . . that thing?"

"I think your own theory of origins is fundamentally sound," he said. "Through a process I don't fully grasp, you bear the drone's power within you. Its power—and its danger. I know you and Mercy intend to confront my son. But you're dabbling in forces you don't understand. If that power should again be unleashed . . ." He shook his head. "The consequences are beyond anything you can imagine."

"Udain," I said, as gently as I could. "My friends are out there. Your son has them, and he plans to kill them, or—or worse."

"My son's mind is closed to me," he said tonelessly. "It's possible he wishes to provoke a confrontation to further his ends. I regret the loss of your colony, but I can't risk an attack. Not anymore. All I can do is remain here and protect what he so desperately seeks to possess."

He stepped closer. The room grew even smaller, the guards crowding my back while his giant frame trapped me.

I expected him to catch hold of me again, but instead he tapped a code into his wrist cuff, and another cell slid open, a larger one.

An empty one.

"Don't you see," he said in a voice turned soft, "that this is the only way?"

I stared at the empty cell, letting his words sink in.

"It's not," I said. "I'm sorry, Udain. I'm leaving."

He backed off, glaring at me. "Even if you could leave," he said, "even if you could save the rest, I hold the one you care for most. Aleka. Your mother."

I fought down panic at his words, though it no longer surprised me that he knew. He'd known all along, connected the dots far faster than I had. Whether through the eyes of his hidden lenses or through his own eyes, he knew everything that took place in his compound.

"If you touch her," I said, trying to meet the imposing man's gaze, "if you touch any of them . . ."

Unexpectedly, he laughed. It boomed in my ears, and the light blinked as if the walls of the underground prison were about to collapse.

"Boy," he said, his face still shaking with mirthless laughter. "I've led armies, fought monsters in their dens. Who are you to threaten me?"

He reached for my arm, and I braced myself against the wall of the tiny room.

"Actually, Udain," I said. "So have I."

Without stopping to think what I was doing, I leaped for the pistol tucked in the giant commander's belt.

Udain shouted a warning, but it came too late. The buzz of the guards' rifles hit me, jarred me, but didn't hurt me. The pulse Mercy had felt when she shot me was so strong this time it knocked them against the cement walls, their rifles clattering to the floor. Before they could regroup, I sprang for the stairs. I feared that Udain might have closed the door at the top, but I shouldn't have worried. The moment I touched it, a buzzing sensation ripped through my body and the door snapped from one of its hinges, freeing me from the building that would have been my tomb.

I ran for the gate. Mercy's guards hadn't moved from the spot where we'd left them. They'd tightened their ring around her, Geller leading them in taunts and laughter, while Mercy stood silent, her face expressionless.

They saw me at the same time she did. But she reacted faster.

In the seconds it took me to reach her, she had Geller down and, from what I could tell, out. The rest backed away from the rifle she'd taken from their felled ringleader. They hesitated for a second, fingering their own weapons—but though they outnumbered her, it only took them a second to make up their minds and run. I was too far away to see her eyes, but I wouldn't have wanted to face her at that moment either.

"Head for the gate!" I shouted as I came up to her. "We're getting out of here!"

"But what about Grandpa—"

I grabbed her hand and pulled her toward the gate. She was as strong as me, probably stronger, but she didn't resist. Her fingers clenched mine so hard the nails bit into my skin. I heard heavy feet pounding across the cement courtyard, but in the quick glance I could risk, I couldn't tell who it was.

The gate bled yellow light into a sky as dark as tar. Only one guard stood there, Geller's companion from the night we'd arrived. Up close, I saw how exhausted he looked, and I wondered if the guards ever changed shifts, or even slept. He raised his rifle as we pulled up to the gate. "No way, Mercy."

"Yes way," she said. Her rifle rose a fraction, his mirroring the movement. In her eyes, I saw she was about to pull the trigger.

Again I acted without thinking. I threw myself at him, saw his rifle swing toward me and the energy beam erupt from its muzzle. But then the rebounding pulse wrapped him, and he fell to the concrete, moaning. I smelled burning hair, and I hoped the burst had been brief enough that he'd survive.

Mercy was staring at me in shock. Her eyes widened even further when I gripped the bars of the gate.

This one hurt.

So much energy flowed through the gate, I could barely hold on. But I leaned into the force, letting it hammer against me, knowing something would have to give. I just prayed it would be the gate and not me.

A jolt, the hardest I'd felt by far, blasted through my

body, and with a silent concussion, the gate sprang open. The compound was plunged into darkness. When I rested my hands against the bars again, I felt nothing, no force, no repulsion. The beam was dead.

I'd shorted the system.

Backup lights glowed weakly from the four corners of the compound, too dim to show anything but the outlines of what happened below. The two guards from the power station had appeared, their commander a looming shadow behind them. I stood between them and Mercy, daring them to shoot, hoping they wouldn't. They froze, as still as the statues that had been carved into the impact zone fifteen years ago. I wished I could return to the infirmary, check on Zataias and Adem, make sure my mother was recovering from her surgery. I feared what Udain might do to her in my absence. But I knew if I hesitated even a moment he would catch me, and shackle me in the drone room, and then not only my life but the lives of everyone I loved would be over. Shouldering the fallen guard's rifle, I grabbed my companion's hand and backed out the open gate.

Udain stepped in front of the guards, his hair crowned a ghostly white. He held a hand toward Mercy, and even in the dim light I could see the pleading expression on his face. For a moment I thought she was about to give in.

But she didn't. The impact zone lay ahead of us, and she squeezed my hand as we turned and fled into the night. In a minute we'd passed behind the row of stone guards, and the compound's weak glow vanished as if it had been snuffed out by a breath.

"Will they follow us?" I asked.

"It'll take a while to get the beam back online," she answered. "But heck yeah, they'll follow us."

"Then we'd better hurry."

We raced into the night, not looking back.

"So this was your plan?" Mercy said. She smiled, and for the first time since I'd met her, her smile didn't look like she was about to take a bite out of me. "No offense, but it seems almost like you made it up as you went along, you know?"

Mercy and I ran for hours, the black land a solid darkness
around us.

We must have covered ten miles before we finally
slowed down, but I didn't feel the least bit tired. Neither
did she. Her strides were steady and strong, her eyes shining
with the same determination that gripped me. As soon as
we were out in the impact zone I brought her up to speed
about my conversation with Udain, though I left out the
goriest details of what I'd seen in the power station. She'd
been less angry than I anticipated when I told her Udain's
true reasons for not attacking the canyon. But now I put
everything out of my mind as our feet moved in tandem,
each step bringing us closer to the canyon and whatever lay
in wait for us there.

Long past midnight the moon struggled free of its cloud
cover, and the impact zone gleamed a liquid silver in its

path. With the landscape's peaks and ridges, fathomless craters and shining pools of stone, the plateau looked like a mirror moon, spread out for us to explore. Though I knew the shapes in the rock were the bodies of people long dead, fossilized by the catastrophe that had claimed Mercy's family, they held a weird and peaceful beauty in the moonlight, a stillness like natural sleep settled to stone. I wondered, as I watched Mercy surveying the land, if she could find beauty here too. And I wondered why the little bits of beauty left in this world—the glass desert by night, Mercy's smile—had to come at such a terrible cost.

Mercy kept her inspection brief. "We should get going. Udain will be after us before we know it."

I nodded. "Mercy, I—about Udain—"

"Nothing to say," she cut me off. "He made his choice. We made ours. And it was about time, too."

I spoke the thing that was gnawing at me. "Do you think he'll do anything to my colony? Zataias and . . . the others?"

She shook her head. "He's not stupid. He knows if he hurts them, he loses his hold over you." Nodding to the west, she said, "Now let's get cracking. There's a canyon with our name written all over it."

She held out her hand. I took it, and we headed due west, running as if we'd never known tiredness before. The moon paced us, slipping through the sky like a comet. After a time it fell below the horizon, and we continued in complete darkness. Still I didn't doubt a step. Mercy squeezed my hand, and a laugh bubbled from her, choked at first, then pealing high into the night.

"Not bad for a pipsqueak," she said breathlessly. "You sure there's not something you're not telling me?"

We ran on, and Mercy's laugh lit what the moon no longer showed.

We rested once more for a drink and an energy bar, and by the time we were done with our skimpy meal, dawn had sliced the sky at our backs. The altar stood on the far western horizon, its deeper darkness bulked against the pale darkness of the impact zone, only its twin horns tipped with morning fire. Mercy, better at distances than me, estimated it to be less than five miles away. I looked out over the empty landscape, trying to penetrate the gloom. Now that I had time to think, all the doubts I'd held at bay during our midnight run came swarming back.

Mercy must have seen it in my eyes. "Having second thoughts?"

"No," I lied. "Or I don't know. I think I'm going completely crazy."

"Well, opposites attract, right?" She squinted at the distant altar. "Anything I can do to help you make up your alleged mind?"

You've already helped more than you know, I wanted to say. "Mercy, look. You don't have to—when I go into the canyon, you don't have to—"

"Stay here and look for bunny rabbits in the clouds?" she

said. "Of course I don't. I'd much rather go with you."

"But what if I . . ."

She drew close, squeezed my arm. "Did anyone ever tell you you think too much? Sometimes you just have to go for it."

I looked at her dark eyes, her smile. For a second I was reminded of Korah's smile, lost what seemed years ago. Facing whatever lay in wait for me up ahead seemed a little less awful thanks to Mercy's smile, and a lot less confusing than trying to answer it.

"All right," I said. "But can I ask you one more question?"

"Fire away. Metaphorically, of course."

"If it gets too rough in there. If they're killing me. I just want to make sure you'll save yourself—"

"That's not a question," she said. "But for what it's worth, the answer is no freaking way."

I took a deep breath. Mercy smiled in the dawn light. And the black lands led nowhere but on.

"All right, then," I said. "Let's go."

We marched west. With every step closer to Asunder's realm, a mixture of nerves and resolve tangled in my chest. I felt as if every muscle in my body had been drawn tight, the fiery rock and fiery sky pulling me between. I thought about my days of indecision in the canyon, the foolish hopes I'd clung to, the failure of everything I'd tried to do. Mercy was right, I decided. I didn't know how strong the power in me was.

But the grown-ups in our lives had screwed up plenty, starting with what they'd done to the world before either of us was born. It was about time we found out what we could do.

Mercy and I had reviewed our plan after breakfast. It amounted to little more than getting close to Asunder and shooting first. We'd decided to approach the canyon via the northern route, avoiding the rock city where the terrain made an ambush more likely. She'd tested our two rifles against the black rock, discovering that Udain either hadn't jammed them or couldn't from this distance. She gave me a crash course on how to operate mine, including how to increase the energy output, though she warned me that would expend the charge quickly. If all else failed, she suggested, she could always shoot me instead. "You obviously amplify the beam," she said. "So why not?" I couldn't tell in her dark eyes if she was joking. All I knew was that when it came, and I was sure it was coming, my trial by fire would be against a human being. I could tell myself he was Skaldi-infested, but like all Skaldi, he looked an awful lot like me.

"Down!" Mercy's voice broke into my thoughts, and instinctively I dropped to the black stone.

I had no time to thank her for the warning. The spear that had been launched at us missed, embedding itself in a rock formation where our heads had been. The weapon was followed by its owner, one of the anonymous warriors who'd lain in wait behind another jutting boulder. In the second it took him to leap across the space, I realized what his presence out here meant: we were expected, had been watched, our progress reported to Asunder. The next second, the man's body crashed into Mercy, who'd sprung to her feet the moment the spear flew past, her rifle aimed at his chest. But the warrior had the advantage of size and strength, and the force of his leap knocked the weapon from her hands and carried her against the stone outcropping, where she was pinned by his weight.

A stone knife appeared in his hand. Mercy brought a knee into his crotch, but he twisted to avoid the force of the blow. She dodged the knife's descent, caught his hand in both of hers. But her hasty grip was too awkward to hold him for long.

I scrambled to my feet and threw myself at the man, all thoughts of Skaldi or internal firepower erased from my mind. I only knew I had to get him off her before the knife came down again.

I landed on the man's back, my arms snaking around his neck. My weight threw him off-balance, giving Mercy the leverage to push him away. He staggered with me wrapped around him, stumbled backward. Something in the rock beneath his feet gave way with a sound like shattering glass. The man bucked, wobbled, nearly fell. I glanced over my shoulder and saw a crevice too deep to find bottom, felt my head spin as the warrior's feet scrambled on the broken stone—

—and then we were sailing toward Mercy, as if a silent

explosion had thrown us through space. We landed heavily, the man on top of me, his weight entirely limp where a moment ago it had been all straining muscle. I pushed him from me, felt him roll to the ground. His eyes stared blankly at the sky, and where his teeth were bared I saw shreds of bright yellow fire. The stench of cooked flesh filled my nostrils.

The man twitched once then lay still.

Mercy knelt beside him, then looked at me, shaking her head curtly. Without a word, she relieved the man of the knife clutched rigidly in his fingers. A final spark leaped from the blade, crackling as she pulled it free.

"I'd say the experiment was successful," she announced. "This loser would appear to be toast."

I looked at my hands. They shook with a power all their own, crescents of yellow light dancing across my fingertips. I realized this was the first time I'd emitted the energy without any outside force to provoke it. Fear alone had done what it had taken Skaldi or energy rifles to do before.

"Did you know him?" I said. "Was he one of yours?"

Mercy reached out and pulled me to my feet. She winced at my touch, but no sooner did we make contact than the sparks died. Ignoring the dead warrior, she turned and yanked his spear from the black rock. Then she placed a hand on my shoulder and stared intently into my eyes.

"I was only a kid when Asunder took this one," she said. "We all were."

I looked at the man on the ground, tried to think of him as a former Keely or Zataias or Mercy, tried not to think of him that way.

"We march straight on," she continued. "We don't kill anyone we don't need to. But we don't spare anyone we do."

"How will we know the difference?"

She looked at me hard. Her black eyes gleamed, echoing the dull glare of the wasteland at our feet.

"For years after my sister died," she said, "I had a nightmare. I'd be out in the courtyard, playing with her. Dolls and things. Then the sky would go solid yellow, and we'd both look up, and the light would shower down on us like rain. Beryl would laugh and open her mouth to drink it in. But then she'd look at me, and her face would turn black and crumble away, and where I held her, her hands would dissolve into black powder, and I'd scream and wake up. Every night, the same dream. You know how to get nightmares like that to stop?"

I shook my head.

"That's too bad," she said. "I was kind of hoping someone would."

She shouldered the spear, tucked the knife in her belt, and, avoiding the fissure in the stone, picked up our trail west. I glanced one last time at the lifeless form spread-eagled on the ground, then hurried after her. My legs quivered with the aftereffects of the energy discharge, and my heart raced.

"I didn't mean to kill him," I said.

"Yeah, well, he sure as hell meant to kill me," she answered, not turning her head. "So take your pick."

"That's the thing," I said. "I think I just did."

She stopped, and this time she looked at me. Her smile, weary and sad, reminded me of her uncle Laman's. "And I'd like to thank you for that. For choosing me over him."

Without another word she turned, and we continued on our way.

Mercy and I had plenty more opportunities to thank each other after that.

But we didn't waste breath on thank-yous. There wasn't time, and she wasn't the sentimental type anyway.

My suspicion about the first man turned out to be right. It seemed Asunder had sent him to test us, to see what he was up against. How he knew I was headed back to the canyon I couldn't be sure, but the Skaldi always seemed to know more about me than I knew myself. Maybe it had something to do with the part of them living in his staff. Or maybe the discharge of my power had triggered something deep inside him, so he no longer held back his forces.

He sent them against us in waves. And we responded with fire.

We passed a larger-than-usual rock formation and found our path bristling with spears. If the warriors had thrown their weapons right away like the first man had, there was no telling what might have happened. Instead, they formed a phalanx to stop us, which didn't stop us for a second. Mercy and I exchanged glances, then we raised our rifles and fired a series of quick, short bursts, disabling the men in front. When several of the uninjured warriors cocked their arms for a volley, Mercy switched tactics, training her rifle on me. I had a split second to be amazed she was actually doing it before the beam hit.

At its touch, angry power burst from me like a searing wind. It scattered the warriors, flung them against the rock, snapped spears and bones like twigs. Once they were down, Mercy turned her rifle back on them, firing one precision shot per man, the energy from her gun filling the air with a burning smell. I hefted my own rifle and laid down a stream of fire the way she'd taught me. After a couple minutes, I stopped trying to keep track of which victims were hers and which were mine. Mercy's rule didn't seem very useful once we'd entered the battle: all of the warriors posed a threat, and none of them showed any sign of retreat or surrender. What I told myself, while I watched human bodies slam against the stone or take flight in a stream of amber fire, was that I'd made my choice. I didn't want to kill anyone, much less people whose sorrow and grief and despair Asunder had warped into madness. Deep down, I wanted to believe what Laman had said in the protograph: *The power to kill can't save.* I knew I couldn't cauterize guilt with fire. But I wasn't the one who'd started this war. I wasn't the one who'd stolen people from their homes and enslaved their minds.

The warriors met me without a trace of fear in their blank faces, even when their companions fell before my and Mercy's fire. Maybe death was welcome to them. Maybe they didn't want to remember the lives they'd lost.

Within minutes the plateau had been cleared, the few surviving warriors so bruised and burned they could barely crawl. My body trembled with the energy I'd expended, but I didn't feel like it was ready to burn out. In fact, I felt like I was just getting started.

Mercy stooped to recover an extra knife, then we were on our way again.

"Now you see what I meant by firepower," she said.

"You actually had to try it?" I asked. "You actually had to shoot me?"

"Would I be me if I hadn't?" she said.

The next ambush went pretty much the same. Six or eight armed warriors dropped from a ledge, but Mercy shouted a warning and the power ripped through me, producing a shield of energy that scorched them as they fell. Seeing their bodies streak through the yellow light was like watching some bizarre meteor shower. They hit the ground still alive, though with patches of charred skin glowing ember red on their tanned chests and shoulders. This time the ones who could stand hurled their spears, but they were too weak to aim straight, and the points bounced off the rock like pebbles. The few who were able to run did, and though Mercy was all for shooting them in the back, I managed to restrain her. The burned and battered warriors who remained, feebly creeping on the black rock, took the butt of her spear to the head and didn't rise again.

"Never a good idea to let the enemy get away," she grumbled. "Or was it part of your brilliant plan to let Asunder know what he's up against?"

"He already knows," I said. "I don't think anything happens here that he doesn't know."

"I wonder if he knows the party's over."

We shared a smile, and walked on.

We met no other warriors on our way across the plain. I found my hands prickling, my heart racing. It felt like the nervous energy that comes from staying up too many nights in a row, that feeling of hypersensitivity all along your scalp and pressure building behind your eyeballs. I almost would have welcomed another confrontation, if only to bleed some of the energy worming through my fingers. I figured, though, the confrontation would come soon enough, whether I wanted it or not.

Mercy laid a hand on my arm. The power must have been contained, because she didn't flinch.

"News flash," she said. "We're not going to the canyon."

I looked at her, confused.

"Over there," she said with a jerk of her head. "I think that's our welcome party."

I turned my attention to the altar, its horns poised like fangs to take a bite out of the sky. I'd totally forgotten about it in the heat of battle, but it dominated the vast and barren plateau, its peak crowned in the gold of daylight but its sides drenched in red like fresh blood. Now that I knew what had put it there, I saw its history carved into the shape of the stone: if an explosion could be frozen in place, this was what it would look like. It seemed to me figures clustered at the top, too high up to tell who or how many. But at the base, right at the foot of the stairway, I could clearly make out a single human form. I had no idea who it was—they all looked so similar in their caveperson outfits—but I breathed a sigh of relief when I realized it wasn't the giant Archangel. I'd been worried about facing him, and not only because of his size and strength. On the protograph, I'd seen Mercy lose most of her family. I couldn't stand the thought of her losing her brother at my hands. I wondered whether, if it came down to it, she'd consider Ardan another enemy we had to kill.

"Why just one?" I said. "Unless this is some kind of trap."

"No *unless* about it," she said back. "The only question is what kind."

We stood still for a moment, Mercy scanning the plateau, me wondering what the range of our rifles was. It seemed crazy to stop at the sight of a single warrior, but Mercy was right: Asunder had something planned, and I didn't want to walk right into it.

"Any cover?" I asked.

"Waste of time," she said. "I'm sure they've spotted us already."

"So what do we do?"

Her face broke into an evil grin. "We find out the old-fashioned way."

And she walked right into it.

I joined her. No spears rained down on us, no warriors materialized to back up the one at the altar's base. The man himself seemed unconcerned by our approach, standing stiffly with arms at his sides, his gaze, from what I could tell, fixed not on us but on the sky over our heads. When we got within several hundred feet, I saw that he held no spear.

And that's not all I saw. Mercy saw it too, at the same time as me.

"Peculiar," she said. "I didn't think he allowed his women out in the impact zone."

"Maybe he had no choice. Maybe he ran out of reinforcements."

"Much as I appreciate the vote of confidence in my gender," she said, "I don't think a solitary woman's going to be able to stand up to the kind of heat we're packing."

We kept walking. The woman showed no reaction, her gaze fixed and her long blond hair whipping carelessly across her face.

"I hate to say this"—Mercy nudged me—"but we're going to have to take her down."

"She's defenseless."

"And my dear old dad is anything but," she said. "So let's stop being such a wimp, okay?"

I looked at my partner, saw the anger threatening to rise back to the surface of her eyes, but also the plea that lay even deeper in those black wells. I felt the power building in me, straining for release. I might not know what our rifles' range was, but I was pretty sure I knew my own.

At the last second, I clamped down on the power, letting it die. Mercy's eyes snapped to mine.

"What's the problem?" she whispered harshly. "Take her down!"

"I can't."

"If this is your idea of a chivalrous gesture," she said, "I'd advise you to get the hell over it. We're running out of time."

She rolled up her left sleeve, placed my fingers on the tracker. Faintly, like a heartbeat, I felt it pulsing.

"Udain's on his way," she said. "So unless you want to tangle with him on top of Asunder, it's now or never."

"I'm sorry, Mercy," I said, my heart sinking as I said it. "I just can't."

"Why the hell not?"

"Because . . ." I pointed to the motionless figure at the foot of the stairs, the blond girl dressed as one of Asunder's brides. Then I raised my hands above my head in surrender. "Because that's Nessa."

When Asunder saw me and Mercy drop our rifles, he descended the stairs of the altar, his giant son shadowing his steps.

But Archangel wasn't the only one who came with him. Surrounding him and clinging to the hem of his blood-red cloak were his own children, a cluster of kids with brown hair and black eyes. I could barely tell one vacant face from another. The children of Survival Colony 9 came next, dressed in identical cave-dweller costumes and looking far better fed than they'd been less than a week ago. Like Asunder's children, their faces were so empty they might have been robotic. They nestled against his body, seeming content and safe in his embrace. They formed such a tight ring around their new father, I knew we'd never be able to hit him without scorching them as well.

Nekane was nowhere to be found. Neither was the old

woman. But Nessa's face was as blank as the children's. As if to prove his complete victory, Asunder tilted his head, and she fell to her knees at his feet. I watched her slim hands pick up the staff he'd let drop and mutely offer it to him.

He fastened the staff to his belt. His smile stretched so wide it seemed like the scar of the Skaldi.

"At last you learn the truth, Querry Genn," he said. "None may resist the power of the Scavenger of Souls."

"It's great to see you too, Dad," Mercy remarked.

Asunder's eyes passed over her face with no more interest than they would have shown a complete stranger, or a fresh slave. Then he shook his shoulders until the cape settled over his scarred body.

"Bind their hands," he said, and a company of warriors stepped from behind the altar, holding the brown ropes. Nessa herself tightened the bands around my wrists. The careless touch of her fingers froze my blood.

Asunder strode to the head of the stairs, where he turned to face his followers. Nessa joined him, her golden head bowed.

"Querry Genn," Asunder said with a smile. "I welcome you once again to my lands. And yet it strikes me that your coming today is not as it was before. I find there are scores to be settled between us."

"More than you know," Mercy muttered.

Again her father ignored her. "My warriors you have slain, their bodies left to waste away under a cruel sun," he said, his voice modulating to convey the impression of sorrow. "You have come bearing the weapons of the despoilers, desecrating with unholy fire the valley of the blessed. What punishment befits such a crime?"

"Step away from the kids for a second," I said, "and you'll find out."

His smile never wavered. "But these young ones are mine. And your presence here poses a grave threat to their safety. Those other deaths I might forgive, but never the deaths of ones so innocent as these. So again it behooves us to ask: what punishment should we mete out to an intruder who so threatens our way of life?"

"Feed him, father," Bea sang sleepily. In her cave-dweller clothes, her tiny figure looked less like a girl than a girl's doll. "Feed him to the Scavenger of Souls."

Asunder gazed affectionately at her. Yet when he spoke, his hand strayed to the staff of bone, caressing it as if he was stroking a child's hair.

"It is just, my daughter," he said softly. "It is the way of our people."

"You tried that once before," I said. "What makes you think it'll work any better now?"

At that, Asunder's fingers fell from the staff, his eyes springing to mine. Behind their feverish lenses I glimpsed a fragment of pain, some small part of what he'd felt when his real daughter's body had shattered under his hands. Remembering the same look in his father's eyes, I wondered if there was any struggle left in him, any part of him the Skaldi hadn't claimed. But then the look vanished, and he sent his voice booming across the waste.

"We will rest here till nightfall, then feed the traitors to the almighty one," he announced, his voice echoing from stone to stone. "With the death of Querry Genn, none will remain to stand in our way. His destruction will mark the dawn of a new era, one in which the blessings of the chosen people will be fulfilled for all time."

Mercy took a step toward her father, but she didn't get any closer than that. Archangel's hands descended on us with a grip of steel and dragged us away.

We sat by the base of the altar, waiting for night to come. Our jailer stood within view, a silent sentinel as massive, and as motionless, as one of the desert's basalt forms. Asunder's warriors had disappeared up the stairs to prepare the ritual of our sacrifice. Faint sounds of revelry—chanting, drumming—floated down from above. Their leader had retreated a short distance into the black rock desert, supposedly to pray. The children from our combined colonies had stayed behind, watched by the girl I'd once known. She stared into the falling sun as if she no longer felt its piercing rays.

Mercy glanced at her, then turned to me. "So that's Nessa."

"What about her?"

"No, she's cute," she said. "When she's not, like, groveling at Asunder's feet and licking the ground clean."

"That's not her," I said. "That's the power of the staff."

"Still, you'd think she'd have a little more dignity," she yawned. "But actually, you're wrong about her. She knows exactly what she's doing."

"What are you talking about?"

"Let's see if I can explain this in simple terms," she said. "Look, if she was completely under his power, his wish would be her command, right? No coercion necessary. In which case she wouldn't need the knife."

My heart jumped. "I didn't see a knife."

"That's because you were too busy moping about Goldilocks and the big bad wolf. But she's got one, all right. And she's keeping it where she can get to it fast."

"Where?"

"A lady doesn't tell," she snorted. "But trust me, if he tries anything ungentlemanly, he'll find himself getting a nasty little paper cut."

For the first time since I'd seen Nessa at the altar stairs, hope flared in my chest. "I wouldn't put it past her. When we were in the canyon, she—"

"Yeah, yeah, yeah," Mercy said. "I'm sure she's going to make a wonderful hostess someday. And I'm sure a guy as awesome and powerful and good-looking as you will be at the top of her wish list."

I grinned despite everything. My blush felt as bright as Adem's. "You think I'm good-looking?"

"Did I say that?" Before I could react, she leaned forward

and kissed me. Her lips were softer than I expected, and they coaxed mine to part before withdrawing just as fast. "Oops. You and Barbie aren't an item, are you?"

"Who's Barbie?"

She shook her head and laughed. "You really are adorable, you know that?"

I laughed with her. "And you really are nuts."

Her eyes flashed before lowering in what I could have sworn was embarrassment. "So they tell me," she said. "But then, it runs in the family."

I guess I was doomed never to sleep in the land of the blessed.

Mercy crawled into a cranny at the altar's base and, with her soldier's training, dropped off in an instant. I lay with my hands clasped on my chest, heart beating madly, thoughts zooming forward and backward like a protograph gone haywire. I imagined the power building in me, flowing outward like a shower of glowing tears.

For the first time, it seemed to me, I saw what it meant to be the leader of a survival colony. To be a man like Laman, a woman like Aleka. Even a man like Udain. To try to hold it all together when everything around you was trying to tear it apart. To know, deep down, that no matter how hard you tried, things would get broken, hopes would fall short, lives would slip through your fingers. There were so many people I would have saved if I could have. Soon. Wali. Laman. Korah. And every one of them I'd lost.

I glanced across at Mercy's sleeping form. In a few hours, I might lose her, too. I might lose me. The thought of my own death felt more real than it ever had. Facing the Skaldi at the nest, in the cage, I hadn't had time to think about death. I'd been too busy fighting for my life.

I sat up, hands between my knees. I remembered something Laman had said to me before he died: *There is no luck left in this world.* That was just like him, gloomy and bitter to the end. But he'd also said, the very last words to leave his mouth: *You can't choose the life you're given. But you can choose the kind of man you want to be.* There might be no luck, no way out, no chance. But there was still choice.

Not Asunder's version of choice. Not Udain's. A *real* choice. A choice that came from me.

I rose and went to Mercy, stroked a dark curl that had fallen across her forehead. Her fingers laced through mine, whether in sleep or not I couldn't tell. Her arm contracted, pulling me down beside her. I couldn't hold her with my hands bound, but I moved as close to her as possible, felt her wriggle until the curve of her body shaped itself to my chest. We lay like that for hours, me listening to the sounds of her quiet breathing and my own thudding heartbeat, however many hundreds of breaths and hundreds of beats it takes to fill up a night. I wondered if, reversing the breaths and the beats, that's what her night was filled with too. Her soft inhalations and exhalations had the ease of sleep, but the pulse in her arm had quickened to a desperate, silent whine.

That's how Archangel found us when the moon rose and the fires sprang to life at the altar's crest.

"The Scavenger awaits," he said, his voice surprisingly soft in the perfect stillness of night. "Come with me now, and all will be revealed."

Nessa had hidden her knife beneath her chest covering.

When her arm lay flat against her side, you could barely see it. She kept her arm by her side almost all the time.

Still, I couldn't convince myself Mercy was right. The blankness in Nessa's green eyes, the eerie floating movements of her tanned limbs made it seem she'd surrendered. Try as I might to catch a hint of anything familiar, she ignored me entirely, gliding behind Asunder up the silvery stairs as if he was a heavenly body guiding her orbit.

At least she was spared the manhandling me and my companion suffered. "Come with me" apparently meant something unique to the colossus Mercy called her brother: he'd no sooner spoken than he yanked us to our feet by the cords around our wrists and wrenched us around to face their children and ours, who jeered at the sight, their faces pale in the light of the moon. Then he shoved us up the stairs, paying no regard to the fact that they yawed dangerously, gaps showing where stone had crumbled away. The children followed us to the altar's summit, muttering a low, wordless chant in tune with the cadence of their feet. Mercy cried out to our giant captor as his rough hands threw us ahead of him.

"Ardan!" she said. "It's me. It's Mercy. You don't have to do this!"

He looked away, her words only doubling the force he applied to our backs.

"Ardan." She tried once more. "This isn't you. I know this isn't you. Don't listen to him!"

But he didn't respond, and though I wanted to believe his averted eyes meant he was ashamed, I'd have had an easier time believing a rock could feel shame. When I glanced across his broad chest at Mercy, I saw she'd given up her efforts to reach him, a calm resolve settling on her face that I tried to match. It dawned on me that I might have to choose between her and my colony, the family I'd found seven months ago and the friend I'd sworn to help. I might even have to choose between her and Nessa. The choice had seemed a lot easier when it wasn't right in front of me.

Another few steps, and we exited the staircase at the altar's peak.

We stood on a bare, circular sheet of stone, as much as fifty feet across and hundreds of feet above the plain. The twin horns of the altar loomed above us, seeming to sway in the red glare of the torches. Twenty or more members of

Asunder's colony crowded the platform, the children deserting us to join them. It was then that I saw Nekane, her hands behind her back and a rope around her neck, standing with bruised limbs and frightened eyes in front of the horns. There was still no sign of the old woman. I had no time to communicate anything with Mercy before Asunder stepped forward, Nessa moving to his side. He threw his cloak behind him and raised his arms to the torch-lit sky, the staff of bone pointing upward like a claw protruding from his closed fist.

"Now you come to your trial at last, Querry Genn," he said. "You have imagined you might elude the one who waits. You have trusted to the ways of the despoilers, thinking their power the only one that holds sway over these lands. But as ever, you underestimate the might of the Scavenger of Souls, and you hope in vain."

Flourishing the staff, he pointed at the altar's horns.

"Behold!" he cried. "His vengeance comes!"

His voice echoed and died. Nekane was flung aside as if the sound had physically struck her. I struggled to free myself from Archangel's grasp, but I couldn't do it without risking a burst of power. Then I saw that something hung between the horns of the altar.

It took me a second to recognize the shape as a human body.

Its skin flared as red as the flame-soaked rock, so that its naked arms and legs seemed to form an X of flesh and stone. At first I thought it was covered with blood, until I realized the red was the color of its own flesh, a solid red without the tiniest hint of whatever hue its skin might originally have been. Its head had fallen to its breast, masking its features. But it wasn't dead. Its chest gasped for air, and its blood-red hands, bound tightly to the surrounding rock, flexed feebly. Something on its chest caught the light of the torches and flashed with a light not their own.

Archangel's hands fell away. Asunder smiled and let me approach. The apparition raised its head, and though its face was puffy and scarlet I knew who it was.

Wali.

I tried to say his name. The word grated in my mouth like shards of stone.

He swayed, unseeing, unhearing. The ring on his chest swung with his body's motion. His mouth opened in a groan, his teeth and tongue the same deep, shocking red as the rest of his body.

And then he spoke. I couldn't tell if he was talking to me, or himself, or someone else. His words came out as cracked and dry as the scorching air.

"Forgive," he said. "Forgive me."

His eyes opened. Solid red, they stared at me in blind agony.

"Let me go," he rasped. "Please, I beg you. Let me go."

I hesitated, reached a hand toward him, saw the torch-light glint off the memory ring. Then Asunder lowered his staff, touching Wali on the forehead, the same place he'd marked him before. A violent shuddering gripped my chest as I watched it happen.

The spot where the staff had touched him throbbed as if something alive moved underneath the skin. Wali tensed, throwing his head back, gritting his teeth so hard I heard them grind against each other. My mouth and nose filled with the tinny taste of blood, and I couldn't tell if it was real or imagined, if I was the one being attacked or the one doing the attacking. Wali's arms and legs stretched irresistibly taut, until at last the joints of his hips and shoulders began to tear. A scream filled my ears. The spot on his forehead ripped open, and I saw the thing beneath bulge outward.

For a final second Wali's mutilated body hung in the altar's grasp, his sightless eyes turned to me. "Querry," he said. Then the scar split from his forehead down the length of his chest, and the creature emerged from the host it had consumed.

The newborn Skaldi fell to the stone. The ring Wali had worn spun for a moment and lay still.

The power in my chest erupted, and the Skaldi ignited with a ghostly moan. It tumbled from the precipice, flaming through the night sky like a falling star.

Asunder watched it all happen with a triumphant smile. Without a word, he gestured with his staff, and the children of Survival Colony 9 separated themselves from the crowd. Ignoring the hands I reached out toward them, they marched to Asunder's side, spreading out to form a ring around him.

They faced me, an army far stronger than the warriors Mercy and I had slain.

"The Scavenger of Souls reigns for all time," Asunder said. "You may kill one or many, but always he will call more to come to him, always he will claim the flesh of those who oppose him. You have seen what becomes of those who challenge our ways. Now you must choose whether others of your people will follow the condemned one into darkness."

I turned to face Mercy, saw her struggling in her brother's arms, her curses bouncing off him as ineffectually as her blows. I calculated what would happen if I attacked Asunder, but I already knew: the children would die with him. I tried to meet his eyes, but as always they evaded me, slipping away like a lost memory.

"What do you want from me?" I said.

He laughed, a hollow, mocking sound. An image clawed into my mind, an image of myself caught between the altar's horns, my body being torn to pieces, a vast gulf of blackness opening to swallow the world. My knees buckled at the imagined pain, far worse than anything I'd felt in real life.

"And then what?" I spat out.

"And then it ends," Asunder's voice sounded in the burning air. "All doubt, all sorrow, all suffering. The Scavenger of Souls will gather all into his embrace, and the world will be renewed."

"And my people?" I said. "What happens to them if I agree?"

He smiled the smile of the Skaldi, a scar and a skull.

"It is not given to you to know the future," he said. "Choose, and the all-powerful one will prepare your judgment."

I looked at the children, imagined them squirming in the altar's grip, helpless as toys shaken by a giant's hand. My eyes fixed on Nessa's, and I saw in their green depths an intensity none of Asunder's slaves could have possessed. Her lips shaped the word *no*, but I had already made my decision.

I stepped before Asunder, holding my hands out.

"Take me," I said.

His smile yawned impossibly wide. Two of his warriors stepped forward, holding bonds to tie me to the altar. As they positioned me between the horns, Nessa moved to Asunder's side, her long blond hair screening her face. For a second, I saw the shape of her stolen knife through the wrapping she wore.

Then the knife was in her hand, the blade glinting red as it plunged into Asunder's chest.

His eyes flew open as if in pain. But a moment later his body shuddered and split from chin to stomach, wrapping Nessa in the Skaldi's bloodless embrace. She screamed, and I could have sworn I saw the glowing currents of her life being sucked into the depths of its body.

"Nessa!"

Her name burst from me at the same time as the flash of light. The pulse swept over the Skaldi and its victim, flinging the creature back, leaving Nessa gasping on the stone. I reached for her, but before I could touch her I felt an irresistible pull latch onto my arms. The warriors with their bonds were down, their flesh red and smoking, but something else drew me toward the altar's horns, a force as strong as a magnet. I couldn't resist as my hands gripped the stone of the horns, couldn't pull myself loose as a power stronger than any I'd ever felt reached down into my gut and began to feed.

It was the altar, I realized as pain tore through me. The altar itself was draining the power from my body. I tried to make it stop, but something deep inside the stone drew it from me like blood from an open wound.

Mercy's face flashed before me, her eyes and mouth open wide, but I couldn't hear a word she was saying. A second later Archangel appeared behind her, and she disappeared in his arms, still shouting wordlessly. The Skaldi had risen from the stone, a grotesque combination of man and monster, Asunder's shape cloaking a hollow core. Its skeletal arms clutched the staff, and when it touched my forehead, I saw Asunder's older daughter frozen in the rock, her mother cocooned around her, the child's frail arms held up in a plea or a prayer before they turned to ash and sloughed off to reveal the pallid bone.

That was the last thing I saw before golden fire exploded around me like a supernova.

Warriors fell before the onslaught, some landing on the

platform with bodies charred beyond recognition, others flying from the altar's peak. A pulse shook the stone, a vibration like the buzz of Udain's beam, only as strong as a tremor and growing stronger with each passing second. I turned my head to see my shoulders straining against the horns, my arms consumed by the fiery glow. My eyes dropped to my chest, and I saw only the vaguest outline of my own body swathed in pulsing, streaming light. It was as if I *had* no body, as if I'd been turned to pure energy. Dimly, through pain and terror, I realized what was happening.

The altar was the rift, the portal to the Skaldi's home world. My own power flowed through it, and I couldn't stop it from feeding on me.

The pain rose to a scream in my ears. I felt the threads of my life begin to tear. I bit my lip in an effort to shut the power down, to hold myself together. But I was growing weaker by the second, and my flesh seemed to dissolve into nothingness.

I was no longer I.

I was a flicker, a thought, a final memory.

I was an explosion of fire.

The sky filled with a deadly yellow light. It spread until it erased everything, blotting out the torches, the altar's horns, even, while the light lasted, the moon and stars. I floundered in an absolute void, unable to see my own body, fearing that when it ended I would find myself not only blind but erased like the rest of the world.

A howling gale blew over me, and the light vanished.

The altar shuddered. Sensation returned to me just as the horns let go, pitching me forward onto punishing rock.

Pain shot through my frame. I hardly dared look at my arms, but when I did, I saw that they remained attached to my shoulders. The burning field of energy had disappeared, leaving only my weak, aching flesh. When I tried to call the energy back, a few feeble sparks played at the tips of my fingers before dying out completely.

I struggled to stand, failed, rolled onto my stomach. The altar was empty except for a few skeletal remains I couldn't identify. The Skaldi that had taken Asunder's body had been reduced to a pile of black cinders, the bone staff lying streaked with fire on the glassy stone. I choked on my own bile and the taste of ash. Then I saw, through a haze of tears, someone clinging to the altar's summit, just above the stairs. Every inch an agony, I crawled to the figure's side.

It was Archangel, his cloak burned to nothing, his mighty shoulders charred like a tree half-consumed by fire. But he was alive, and when I neared him he pushed himself upward and stood, wobbling on legs that had been burned as badly as his back. That's when I saw others on the stairs beneath him, people his body had shielded from the explosion: Mercy, the unconscious Nessa, and the six missing children of Survival Colony 9. Nessa's long hair seemed to have been singed at the ends. Farther down the stairs, Nekane clung to the rock, shaking but alive. The kids' faces were frozen with fear, but they looked at me with the first sign of recognition I'd seen all day.

Archangel took a wobbly step then fell, thudding to his knees on the platform. Mercy flew to him and tried to hold his body upright, but he was too heavy. He collapsed, eyes closed, breathing roughly. She reached down and touched his cheek, and for a second his lips moved in a hint of a smile. Then she turned to me, and through a mask of grime and tears, I saw the look of anguish in her eyes.

At first I thought it was because of what had happened to her brother. But when I peered over the altar's edge, I saw the real reason.

From horizon to horizon, the black land erupted with flashes of fire. The plain crested like a wave, and when it fell the stone cracked open, peeling back like the scar of a gigantic Skaldi. More fissures appeared, smaller, glowing with pale yellow light, stitching the ground with an infinity of scars. Shadows split the fire, and from each of the holes a figure wriggled: pale, stunted, catching itself with skeletal arms before dragging its wormlike body to the surface. As the Skaldi fought free into the burning air, the wounds on their chests opened hungrily, and even from my elevation, I nearly suffocated on their death stench. The moment one creature made its way to the surface, another materialized behind it, and another, and another. There was no counting them. They covered the plain like maggots on the carcass of a leviathan.

I knew instantly what had happened.

The portal had opened again. *I* had opened it. My own power had been drained by the altar, and the creatures had flooded back through the hole in space and time.

I remembered Udain's words: *The consequences are beyond anything you can imagine.* He'd been right. I'd thought only of saving my colony, and this was the consequence he had foreseen.

The army of Skaldi squirmed on the broken ground at the base of the altar, their claws scratching against the glassy stone. I felt weak as a baby, with no power left to face them. I watched as the first one set its clawed fingers on the altar steps.

Mercy's hand gripped my arm. "There's still a way," she whispered.

"How?"

Her eyes grazed the creatures below. "Stay here with Ardan and the little ones. I'll see if I can draw them away. Then you go."

I glanced once more over the edge, saw the thousands of creatures swarming the impact zone. "There's way too many. You'll die."

A trace of her old smile touched her lips, and she rolled up the arm of her uniform, showing me the tracker. The pulse had grown so strong her skin undulated like a desert flower opening to the light.

"I've still got a few tricks up my sleeve," she laughed.

I opened my mouth to say something, but she leaned

forward and closed it with a kiss, a real kiss, letting me feel the softness of her lips and taste the salt of her tears. I had no memory and no idea how to kiss her back, but her touch taught me the way. When she pulled back at last, I felt a tiny flicker of strength filling my body, and I knew what I had to do.

"You're staying here," I said. "I'm the one who did this. And I'm the one who's going down."

For once, she stared at me, speechless.

"I've got the best chance against them anyway," I said. "And Ardan will need your help. He's your brother, Mercy. You owe it to him."

Her dark eyes filled with tears. Then her arms went around me, and she squeezed so hard it hurt. I felt the tracker against my back, fluttering like hope.

"So go, get out of here," she said, releasing me. "Kick some Skaldi butt. I'll take care of the others."

She gave me one more kiss, just a light peck on the cheek. Then she playfully shoved me toward the stairs. I rose on legs that quivered with more than weakness and was about to take my first step down when a sparkle on the stone caught my attention. I stooped, touched Korah's ring. Cold and lifeless at first, it warmed when I gathered it up, as if responding to the beat of my heart.

I held it in my palm, weighing. I looked back at Mercy, who smiled and whispered a farewell.

Leaning heavily against the rock, I descended the spiral staircase. By the time I reached the bottom every part of me was trembling. I took the last turn and scanned the plateau.

The Skaldi had gone still and silent. Moonlight rimmed their backs, an ocean of them in the dry, dead land. I closed my eyes, took a deep and halting breath. I knew I couldn't fight them all. But I also knew I had to try.

Gripping the ring like a promise, I summoned all the strength I had left and took one final step down.

PART THREE

MYTH

A moon rose over the desert, a single bright stitch in the dark sky.

Dust and bare rock and dunes rippled out beneath it, stunted trees clinging to life between the arid land and chalky heavens. It was a place I could never say I loved—what was there to love?—but it was the only place I'd known. I breathed it in, felt the dust coating my face and hands. Clouds scudded across the moon, breaking its light like rapid blinks of an eye.

"There's a storm coming," someone said, stepping up behind me. I turned and saw my mother. Aleka. The commander of Survival Colony 27.

She was with my brother, Yov. Both wore their typical camouflage uniforms. He wore his typical sneer.

Through blowing veils of dust, I saw the tent they'd come from, the tent my older brother and I shared. A memory jumped into my head: a memory of Aleka visiting me after Yov was asleep to help me sound out the words of my one book, a threadbare book with faded pictures and half-gone cutouts of huge armor-plated reptiles that had once walked the land until a hunk of fiery rock from outer space put an end to their reign. But she hadn't read to me in years, not since we lost the book in an evacuation, not since Yov's height and hatred grew to their full size. The tent stood in the center of camp, with other tents around it, a portable generator or two, thirty or forty additional people—men, women, and teens—milling around like shadows made of dust. I started to ask Aleka a question, when all at once the dust blew away and everything changed.

We were standing in the second of three concentric rings formed by human bodies. Six children, the youngest ones in camp, occupied the central circle. I held one of their hands. It was a defensive posture, the kind we never adopted unless we weren't sure where our enemy might be coming from, who our enemy might be.

Skaldi, I thought.

I watched it happen.

It started with a tall man whose name, I remembered, was Avel. One second he stood there gripping a flame-thrower, the next his body collapsed, the weapon clattering to the ground beside what was left of him. Another colonist reached for it, a teenage girl named Hezka, but she jerked back unnaturally, stumbling out of formation. A third colonist sent a stream of fire at her, only to watch her skin curl up like a scrap of paper. The outer ring collapsed, colonists running to escape a creature whose position was impossible to tell. Aleka shouted for order and the middle ring stood firm, but her words flew past the others like handfuls of dust scattered by the wind of the creature's rampage.

One by one, the fleeing colonists fell. Yelling words I couldn't hear over the chaos of pounding feet, Aleka grabbed the abandoned flamethrower and pursued the creature.

She tracked it through camp, following the trail of bodies. It consumed them all.

She wheeled when the final body sank to the ground, turned to me and Yov and the others who stood in an ineffectual barrier around the little kids. Her voice issued a warning that was more like a scream, and I watched the man closest to me shrivel like a piece of plastic thrown in the fire. The next instant, I felt my gut twist inside out, and I knew the Skaldi had taken hold. My hand flew free from the kid I'd been protecting, and if I didn't know better I'd have expected to watch my own body crumple and fold like an emptied shell.

But what happened next I didn't expect at all.

A blinding light exploded from my body. Yov and Aleka were tossed in the air, landing with soft thuds and rolling over, stunned but alive. The little kids took the force of the white-hot blast, their bodies disintegrating as if they'd been consumed by Skaldi. The kid whose hand I'd been holding splattered my face with ash. For an instant I thought I saw the

Skaldi leap clear, an arc of light that shot like an arrow straight for Yov, who was cursing and struggling to stand. Then I staggered and fell, just as Aleka dragged herself toward me with the flamethrower trained on my face.

Then I was rushing along a black tunnel toward daylight, knowing nothing about my past—not my name, not my family, not anything. There was only one thing I knew for sure.

The power in me had killed those children. My body's reaction to the Skaldi had wiped them away as surely as if the creature itself had attacked them.

I didn't want that power. And I didn't want to remember what I'd done.

I only wanted to forget.

My body hit the ground hard, and my eyes opened to a blinding white light. For a moment I thought I was still there, out in the desert with Survival Colony 27, the light exploding from my body. Then I realized it had all been a dream—or not a dream, a memory. A memory of the night I lost my memory. Everything I'd seen was true: the attack, the colonists falling before the creature's onslaught, the children falling before my own.

I knew now why Aleka hadn't been in any hurry to tell me about that night.

I attempted to sit, but the instant I moved, a sharp pain squeezed the breath from my lungs. I ached everywhere, not just my back and arms and legs, but everywhere. My forehead. My fingers. My teeth. I didn't know where I was, had only a dim memory of something closing in on me, overwhelming me, smothering me . . .

I closed my eyes, tried to concentrate. When I opened them again both the present and the past swam into focus.

I was lying in bed, not on broken stone. My uniform was intact, except for my bare feet. The light came from an identifiable source, a long tube that hung over my head. The pain and weakness came from the attack at the altar, and from whatever had happened when I faced the Skaldi in the impact zone. I had crash-landed back in my body, and it was taking me a long time to claw out of the wreckage.

Too long.

Concentrating all my attention on my legs, I inched them over the side of the bed, felt them drop like stones to the floor. Using their weight to lever my torso up, I pulled myself into a sitting position, more aware of the muscles straining in my abdomen than I'd ever been. With my palms flat on the bed and my feet pressed against the floor, I took a couple breaths as deep as I could manage and shoved myself upright.

I wobbled but didn't fall. I'd come to a temporary agreement with gravity, which told me it wouldn't drop me if I upheld my end of the bargain.

A pair of boots sat by the bed. I tugged them on with clumsy fingers. Lurching as if these were my first steps, I made my way to the door. I knew now where I was. The sheets, the fluorescent tube, the whitewashed walls, the uniform that had been just as spotless until my flight with Mercy across the impact zone: Udain's base. The small protograph screen on the wall gave me a specific location: Mercy's room. Somehow, I'd come back. I couldn't have walked here, not after the attack at the altar. So someone must still be alive. Someone who cared enough to transport me, put me in bed, and wait to see if I'd wake up. Someone like Mercy.

But how long had they been waiting?

I needed to find out what had happened. To Mercy, and Nessa, and the kids. Even if that meant discovering their deaths were on my hands too. I hadn't done any of it on purpose—the children of Survival Colony 27, the opening of the rift at the altar, the loss of Soon and Wali—but that didn't change how I felt. Guilt staggered me as much as the burden of my own body. Guilt *was* a body, or more than one, all the deaths I was responsible for a weight I knew I'd carry for the rest of my life.

My hands fumbled with the door, but there was no knob, nothing but a keypad. The code could be anything, and I didn't have time to punch random keys. So I punched the door instead. Pain ignited in my knuckles as I hammered at it, but it wouldn't give. I took a step back and threw myself against the thick metal, which did nothing except bruise my shoulder. I fell back, breathing hard, gravity threatening to break our brittle accord. I drew a breath and yelled.

"In here!" I shouted. My voice sounded husky and raw. "I'm alive! In here!"

No one came.

I looked around the room. No windows, no other doors. No way out.

One way out?

I squeezed my eyes shut, called up as vivid a memory as I could of the Skaldi attacking me. I felt the sick twisting of my gut as clawed hands clutched at my soul. I inhaled their death stench, heard their moans echoing deep inside. I didn't know if memory could do what an actual attack did. But I was desperate to get out of the room, and that must have been what tilted the odds in my favor.

The pulse rippled from me like a wave. When I opened my eyes, all that was left of the door was a ragged hole, molten around the edges. Its heat pricked my skin as I squeezed through.

There was one more door between me and the outside. It suffered the same fate as the first.

I stumbled from Mercy's quarters into the compound's cement courtyard. Bright daylight assaulted me. Quickly I oriented myself, spotting the guard tower that stood by the front gate, the building that served as Udain's headquarters, the smaller building that housed the infirmary. From the direction of the gate, I heard the buzzing sound of the perimeter fence. Someone was shouting, words I couldn't make out from this distance. If I listened closely, I thought I heard not only human voices but something else, a single long howl like the sound the Skaldi had made the night Survival

Colony 9 fought them at their nest. We'd believed, or at least prayed, that we had defeated them that night. Feeling dizzy and sick at heart, I summoned all the energy I could and raced for the gate.

When I drew level with the cage, I saw that the compound's power had been restored: the pale glow, washed out by daylight, infused the bars and the twenty-foot palisade of the perimeter fence. The cage itself was empty, the remains of the Skaldi cleared away, but up ahead I saw human figures lining the interior of the fence to either side of the front gate. Twenty, maybe thirty of them. All wore the uniform of Udain's camp, and from what I could tell they were a mixed group of men and women, grown-ups and kids. My eyes caught a couple more in the guard tower, aiming energy rifles at the fence. When I closed within a hundred feet, I saw what they were shooting at.

And I also saw that they had no chance of taking down their target.

The dusty plain outside the compound seethed with Skaldi. I only had to look at their numbers to know this was the army I'd summoned at the altar: they emerged from the gleaming black expanse of the impact zone in columns at least a hundred across and double that deep. They crawled toward the perimeter fence, each row shearing off in sparks of yellow flame as they made contact with the beam, which must have been set to burn, not just to stun. The stench of their flaming bodies—a smell somewhere between rubber and cooked flesh—mingled with the rot they produced on their own. Many bodies lay smoking and motionless on the plain, but the creatures behind them merely climbed over the carcasses and crawled inexorably toward the compound. Thirty people—thirty battalions—couldn't hold them off forever. Eventually, the bodies would pile so high the creatures would simply spill over the top of the fence, and then the compound would be overrun.

I took a step toward the survivors, knowing that against an army this size there was little I could do except die along with them. But then I froze when one of the figures in the tower turned to face me.

She was tall, and so thin her uniform hung on her like a tent draped over a wooden frame. Her cheekbones pressed against her wasted flesh, the hollows of her eyes seemed as cavernous as a skull's. She held her rifle in her left hand, and I realized with a sick lurch that her right sleeve hung empty, flapping uselessly at her side. But her eyes were the same gray they'd always been, and they blazed in her pale face with the determination I'd always known.

She was my mother. She had survived. And she was leading the battle against the creatures I had summoned to our home.

"Aleka!" I called out, and my voice carried across the courtyard, over the din of battle.

She must have heard me, because she responded with a quick nod before turning back to the creatures at the fence.

I ran to join her, and as I drew closer, I realized I knew the others as well. Mercy, small and agile, danced along the fence with her rifle, zapping any creature that didn't fall victim to the beam. Nessa, her hair cut short like my mother's, her uniform jacket stripped off to show tanned arms covered in muscle and blood, stood at the head of a ragtag army: Keely and Bea and the other children of Survival Colony 9, still tiny but hardly children anymore as they wielded guns in defense of the compound. Zataias had stripped down to the waist, and the energy rifle he held looked enormous against his puny arms and ribbed torso. The guards from Udain's compound—pimple-faced Geller, the one Mercy had called Ramos, and others—stood among the child warriors. A few of my comrades I didn't see—Tyris, and Adem, and Nekane—and there was no sign of Udain. But the rest were there, looking weary and wounded but as resolute as their leader, who waved them on with her one remaining arm and shouted from the top of the tower.

I'd nearly reached the fence when one of the Skaldi forced itself through the sparks and landed at Mercy's feet. Preoccupied with another creature, she didn't react as it reached a shaky hand toward her. I yelled a warning, but my words were drowned out by a roar that came from the tower.

I looked up and saw a man the size of two men leap to the ground, his long brown hair flying as he landed with a ground-shaking thud in front of the prostrate creature.

Muscles bulged on his bare chest and arms, stretched his too-small camouflage pants. The Skaldi, dazed from its contact with the energy beam, didn't resist when he swept it into his embrace and squeezed, its fleshless body bursting under the pressure. Mercy laid a quick hand on his forearm as he dropped what remained of the creature, then she went back to her work at the gate, firing at emboldened Skaldi that tried to work their claws through the gaps in the fence.

It was her brother, Ardan. His giant body was covered with a patchwork of scars from the fire that had scored him at the altar, but his broad face revealed no trace of pain or fear. He was back, fighting by his sister's side—and fighting, I could easily see, with every ounce of strength he'd possessed as his father's lieutenant.

But fighting, I could also see, a losing battle.

The Skaldi kept coming without end. They dragged themselves toward the fence, and no matter how many fell before the energy beam, there were ten more to take their place. Now that Ardan's victim had taught them they could pass through the fence without fatal damage, more of them began probing the gaps between fence posts, sticking their arms and heads through while others shoved from behind. The smoke and stench of their smoldering bodies filled the courtyard. Some of the creatures avoided the front gate altogether, fanning out around the compound to entry points the few members of Aleka's forces couldn't defend. With the creatures' numbers, they'd soon be able to form a ring around the entire base, and there was no way thirty soldiers could prevent them from finding a way in.

Aleka must have realized it too. Strapping her rifle to her back, she climbed down the ladder of the guard tower, moving far more quickly than her emaciated frame and single arm would have led me to believe. When she reached the ground, the others retreated from the fence to join her. Mercy lingered to shoot a few stray Skaldi over her shoulder. I pulled up beside the group just as she did.

I looked at the defenders, sweaty and dirt-streaked, wide-eyed with exhaustion. Mercy shot me a grin, and I felt a fever start in my blood that had nothing to do with the energy beam.

"Querry," Aleka said. Her face had lost flesh, but not its ability to hide whatever she was feeling. "Welcome back."

I responded with the first thing that came to mind. "How long was I out?"

"Three days," she said. "Udain's forces returned with you and the others yesterday."

"The others?" I said. "Where are they?"

"Adem and Nekane are helping Tyris and Doctor Siva with the wounded. The old woman has not returned from Athan's colony." Her eyes tightened with a moment's pain, then they became chips of granite once more. "Otherwise, all are present and accounted for."

"And Udain?"

She frowned. "We've had some trouble with him, I'm

afraid. Udain is no longer the man you knew, Querry."

Before I had a chance to ask what she meant, a loud crackling caught my attention, and I turned to see a pyramid of Skaldi tumbling over the gate. None moved beyond a feeble twitching when they hit the ground, but others had begun to climb the wall of bodies behind.

"I suggest we continue this conversation elsewhere," Aleka said with the ghost of a smile. On her gaunt, whittled face, it reminded me of Yov's lopsided grin. "To the bunker!" she called, and everyone followed her as she moved off at a brisk jog to the rear of the compound.

As we ran, I saw sparks raining from the fence at every point we passed, smelled the odor of burning bodies on the breeze. The Skaldi were forcing their way in all around us.

"Where are we going?" I asked.

"The generator," she answered tersely, her eyes trained ahead.

"But—"

"There's an underground bunker and escape tunnel accessible via the generator room," she explained. "Built in the days this compound was a military installation. In case the brass needed to flee their own failed work."

"This was where the Kenos trials started?"

"The very place," she said. "Udain restored the compound after the wars, but the trials had begun long before."

"Oh." I glanced at Mercy and Nessa, who seemed to be doing a good job of ignoring each other. Then I said softly to Aleka, "I sort of knocked off the door the last time I was here."

"Yes, I noticed," she said, the wisp of a smile softening her features. "Not to worry, Querry. Where we're going has been well defended against incursion."

We ran on, retracing the path Mercy and I had followed the night we left the compound. When we reached the generator, Mercy let out a low whistle at the sight of the dangling door. "Love what you've done with the place," she said. "But wouldn't it have been easier just to spray-paint 'Querry was here'?"

Nessa tossed her hair, apparently forgetting it had been cropped too short to toss. I guess she remembered a moment later, because her cheeks flamed beneath her green eyes.

Seeing them all here, restored and alive, I felt a shiver travel through me that I must not have had time for at the scene of battle. I'd brought an army of Skaldi to the world, risked all of their lives. Yet here Mercy was, still looking at me with her flashing eyes, still teasing me with her jokes. And here I was, still feeling my heart stutter when I remembered her lips meeting mine. The kids clustered near me the way they used to: their hands twining with mine, their faces showing no awareness that I had killed others just like them. Ardan glowered at me, but not in a hostile way—just in the way I figured a big brother looks at the guy his sister is pressing up against. Did no one realize what I'd done? Did no one care?

"Guard our rear, Mercy," Aleka said. "If anything comes remotely close, blast it."

"With pleasure," Mercy said.

"Querry first," Aleka said, and I was about to squeeze through the cockeyed door when Ardan yanked the whole thing off its final hinge and flung it in the general direction of the Skaldi. He cut me another challenging glare before I started down the steps.

The others followed. Mercy's gun let off a few short bursts, the Skaldi moaning in response. Then there was nothing but our footsteps pinging in the empty room. I wondered at how silent it was, and then I realized the glow that should have lit the room and the vibration that should have stirred the walls were missing. The box that had housed the final drone had been opened, revealing nothing but the bands that had held the prisoner in place.

"The drone," I said.

"Udain has removed it," Aleka said. "I've no doubt he's secreted it somewhere, but we can't convince him to tell us where."

She nodded into the gloom. I saw what I hadn't noticed in my previous visit: a door to the side, on the only wall that didn't hold the drone boxes. Aleka leaned over, punching a code into Udain's wrist cuff, which circled her calf, way too loose even there. The door slid upward without making a sound. Beyond lay a cement tunnel, lit by fluorescent bulbs. I had only a moment to wonder how she'd gotten the cuff when a huge shadow moved and a voice spoke from within the tunnel.

"The drone is safe," Udain said in a tone so numb I knew I was hearing the only words he had left to say. "I'm responsible for it. I'm responsible."

The former commander of the Kenos Project stepped out from the tunnel, ducking his whitened head beneath the low doorframe.

But even Aleka's warning couldn't have prepared me for how much he'd changed.

Where he'd once stood erect and indomitable, he now shuffled forward, his shoulders stooped as if they could no longer bear the weight of his giant frame. His uniform, once so pristine, was befouled with dirt and speckled with ragged holes as if it had been burned. His braids had come loose, his long white hair hanging in grimy strands over his cheeks and forehead. And the lines of his face had deepened so much they looked like cracks carved into solid rock by eons of water and wind.

His eyes were the worst, though. Still dark, still intense, but without the spark of angry pride I'd seen only days before. They darted from face to face with no hint that he knew or cared who we were.

"Grandpa!" Mercy called out, bounding forward to give him a hug. She barely came up to his chest, and as she clung to him, I thought I was seeing her as she'd been years ago when he'd taken her into his care.

Now, though, he looked down at her in confusion and doubt. His hand stroked her hair, but his words were the same mechanical refrain as before. "The drone is safe," he said softly, as if he was telling her a bedtime story. "I'm responsible for it. I'm responsible."

"What's wrong with him?" I whispered to Aleka.

"He's been this way since his return from the impact zone," she whispered back. "He ceded control of the compound to me, then retreated into his own private world. Tyris thinks it's trauma or shock, but we can't rule out the possibility that he's suffered a stroke. In either case, we've been unable to discover what he's done with the drone."

Mercy peered into her grandfather's face, her eyes sparkling with tears. Ardan approached them, and I realized he was even taller than Udain, though maybe that was only because of the stoop in his grandfather's shoulders. Ardan laid a hand on Udain's arm, and the old man's eyes wandered from Mercy's face to his.

"Grandfather," Ardan said. "We must leave this place. Will you come with me?"

Udain looked at him helplessly, his lips beneath his

yellowed mustache mumbling the empty words.

"It's Ardan, Grandfather," the young colossus continued. "Give me your arm and I'll take you from here."

Mercy squeezed the old man's side before moving to make room for her brother. Gently, but with a strength I knew couldn't be resisted, Ardan laid his hand on the old man's elbow and steered him back into the tunnel.

At first Udain let himself be led, the bewildered look remaining on his face. But a few paces into the tunnel, he stiffened and began to fight against the pressure of Ardan's grip. I caught sight of Mercy's face as she jumped forward to help, saw the alarm in her eyes. Udain pulled free and began swinging an arm dangerously, forcing her to duck out of the way.

"No!" he bellowed. "The drone must be protected. I'm responsible for it. I'm responsible. Let me be!"

A moaning sound from outside made us all turn. At the top of the stairs, a jumble of shadows showed that some of the creatures had revived and were almost on our heels.

"Take him, Ardan!" Aleka shouted. "Mercy, guard our retreat. The rest of you, inside. Now!"

Without a moment's hesitation, Ardan tightened his grip around his grandfather's arms and lifted him from the ground as easily as he had lifted people half the old man's size. Udain moaned, the sound eerily like the Skaldi's senseless voices. But he couldn't fight his grandson's full strength, and his moans were his only form of protest as Ardan held him and sprinted down the tunnel.

Mercy's gun pulsed behind me. Skaldi screamed, the smell of their burning bodies wafting down into the room's stale air. With Aleka waving us ahead, we crowded after Ardan.

"Now, Mercy!" Aleka ordered.

Mercy threw herself into the tunnel. A second later the Skaldi came pouring down the stairs. A second after that, Aleka activated the button on the cuff, and the door slammed closed. Bodies reverberated against it, but it held.

I turned to look down the tunnel. I could hear Ardan's echoing footsteps, but the corridor branched into three a few paces ahead of us, and I couldn't tell which route he'd taken.

"Where to now?" I asked Aleka.

"Follow me," she said.

She took the rightmost of the three branches, and I fell in step beside her. The tunnel carried ahead for long minutes, angling steadily downward and cutting left and right, broken every hundred yards or so by a door. Aleka used the cuff to open each one, closing them on the other side. Though I wasn't 100 percent confident Skaldi in large numbers couldn't force their way through, I felt somewhat reassured when I realized the route wasn't a straight line but a maze, with multiple options leading the wrong way. Our course only looked direct because Aleka walked it so confidently. I tried to match strides with her, and was surprised to discover it wasn't as hard to do as it had once seemed.

To keep my nerves from bubbling over, I asked her a

question I thought she might answer. "How's the power still running?" I said. "With the drone gone?"

"The compound was designed to run on stored energy for several days," she answered. "In case the drones were captured or destroyed."

"Do you think Udain destroyed it?"

She looked at me sharply. "If he had, we'd know it. The drone is extremely dangerous, Querry. We need to locate it before the Skaldi do."

There was no accusation in her voice, but I couldn't help thinking of what Udain had said before Mercy and I left the compound. *You're dabbling in forces you don't understand.* He'd been right. And now he himself was another victim of my ignorance.

"I'm sorry," I told her.

Her eyebrows lifted. "For what?"

"Everything." I couldn't begin to think where to start. "You told me to—to take charge. And I tried. But all I did was make things worse. And now . . ."

She didn't slow her stride, but she cast one of her long, appraising looks on me. Her eyes seemed enormous in her gutted face. I felt exposed, as if she could see everything about me, everything I couldn't. But I didn't expect what she said next.

"This doesn't begin with you, Querry," she said. "Now why don't you go talk to Mercy?"

I turned and saw Mercy walking at the back of the crowd,

her rifle slung over her shoulder and her head lowered so all I could see were her dark curls. I had to squeeze past everyone else to reach her, but Nessa moved out of the way, giving me a look that was almost a smile as I passed. Then she tossed her missing hair again and took my place beside Aleka, the two of them exchanging words too quiet for me to hear.

Mercy didn't look up when I joined her, but she slipped a hand through my arm. "You okay?" I said.

She shrugged.

"Tyris is really good with people. She might . . ."

Mercy looked at me, smiling through tears. "Grandpa's one tough hombre," she said. "But I think he's fought his last war."

I put my hand on hers, tried to communicate sympathy through my skin. For years, she'd dreamed of escaping her father and grandfather. But now that her dream had come true, it had to hurt.

"What happened?" I asked her. "Out there?"

Her eyes grew distant. "The Skaldi swarmed you. Bucketloads of them. But somehow you fought them off. I don't even think you were conscious, but your body kept doing its thing, and they kept falling back. Still, it looked to me like you were going to go under. And I said to myself, it figures. I seem to have a talent for losing the people I love."

My heart double-stepped at her final word. "I thought you were going to die too," I confessed.

"I'm not sure I know what death means anymore," she

said. "When Grandpa finally showed up, we were in bad shape. The Skaldi had pretty much given up on you and started to climb the stairs. But you'd stunned or burned enough that he could clear a path to us. And then Geller . . ."

"Geller?"

"That's right," she said with a small smile. "He helped me bring Ardan and Baldilocks down. The little ones too. They didn't want to leave at first, but we wrestled them away and came back to base. With Geller chugging along in the moon buggy, of all things." She laughed. "Glory hound that he is."

Up ahead, the back of Geller's pimpled neck reddened, so I knew he was listening in.

"And here's the crazy thing," Mercy continued. "Once we got the kids patched up, it was like they were back to normal. Blondie and Aleka, too, when she finally woke up from surgery." She gestured toward my mother's missing arm. "You said the staff is like an electric shock. But I guess the shock wears off. That must be why he had to keep touching people with it. Otherwise they'd have come back, remembered who they are."

"Sometimes," I said, "remembering who you are is the worst part."

She squeezed my arm, and we walked on in silence. Our steps echoed along the corridor, covering up the small hitch of sorrow I thought I heard in her breath.

The tunnel continued for a half mile or more, zigzagging as it went. Finally we came to a door that was much larger—

and, with its rivets and steel plating, better reinforced—than the others. The muzzles of what seemed to be energy rifles jutted from its corners, positioned so that anything that came down the tunnel would be unable to avoid the blast. For the first time in what felt like years, I relaxed, realizing that Aleka's words were true: the bunker had been designed—and, thanks to the genius of Athan Genn, enhanced—to stop Skaldi from getting in. It was just a pity the people who'd engineered this fortress hadn't put as much thought into not waking up the monsters in the first place.

The door groaned open when Aleka placed the index finger of her left hand on a plate so well disguised I couldn't tell it from the rest of the door. Behind that door stood another, just as impregnable, and then one more. She moved so efficiently through the bunker's various safeguards, it was easy to forget she'd fled this place more than fifteen years ago.

"Welcome to the war room," she said as the final door creaked open.

I stepped into a space that seemed as large as the cavern of *Grava Bracha*, lit by a flat white light from fluorescents high overhead. The light revealed a sterile expanse of cement walls and polished metal furniture, including a long, gleaming rectangle surrounded by chairs in the room's center. One of the chairs, at the midpoint of the table, rose slightly higher than the rest, and it occurred to me that the bunker *was* the model for Asunder's canyon kingdom: the labyrinthine tunnels, the cavern, the throne. Suspended above the table and running its entire length was a five-foot-high, flat white screen I recognized as a protograph, though much longer than the one in Udain's headquarters. A few people milled around the table, including Ardan with his hand on his tottering grandfather's arm. But only a single figure sat there: Doctor Siva in his spotless white uniform, his hands flowing across the tabletop as they operated some kind of controls embedded in its surface. As he manipulated the controls, the protograph flickered with choppy, black-and-white images, and I realized that unlike the one I'd watched aboveground, this one was double-sided, providing a view to anyone seated on either side of the table. The images flashed by too fast for me to see what he was viewing, but I noticed that Udain watched the screen intently, as if he could find in the flow of frozen memories an answer to the confusion that had settled over his mind.

He didn't watch long, though. Doctor Siva switched off the screen and rose from the table, and with Ardan keeping careful guard, the old man was led to the back of the war room, where Tyris and Adem and Nekane tended to teen soldiers lying on a row of cots.

"They'll see to Udain," Aleka said. "There's not much we can do for him, but a sedative should calm him down. Perhaps, in that condition, he'll be more receptive to questioning." Mercy was about to pull me away when Aleka continued. "Mercy, can you and Nessa check on the condition of the weapons? I want to show Querry something."

Mercy looked less than thrilled, but she did as Aleka asked. I couldn't tell if she was more annoyed to have our private conference interrupted or to be paired with Nessa.

Aleka placed her only hand behind my back and guided me to the table. We sat side by side next to the commander's chair, staring up at the empty protograph. Aleka touched one of the buttons in the table and the screen hummed to life.

"Did you know that people who've lost limbs can feel their presence years afterward?" she said. "Or at least, so I've heard. I'm too recent an amputee to attest to that."

I'd tried to avoid thinking about her missing arm, but now I asked, "Does it hurt?"

"It's not so much pain," she said. "When I woke from the touch of Athan's staff to find the arm gone, it was like waking from a dream. Though my mind told me my body was changed, my body refused to believe. It clung to a vision of itself that was no longer true. To some extent, I imagine it always will."

She touched the buttons deftly with her single hand, and I heard the sound of the protograph searching. Then she paused the recording, and though the screen was still blank, I could tell she'd reached the spot she was looking for.

"I know you want the answers to what lies in your past," she said. "But I need to ask you, Querry: Are you absolutely sure? What I'm about to show you will change you. And once you've seen it, you'll never be able to go back to the way you were."

I stared at the empty screen hanging over my head. What

could be hidden there that would change me so much? "I need to know, Mom. I feel like I've been walking around without a part of me for—well, all my life. I need to get it back."

She smiled and raised her hand from the table to touch my cheek. "I can give you that," she said. "Are you ready?"

That seemed too big a question to answer, so I simply nodded.

"I'll leave you here, then," she said. "I think it should be just the two of you."

"The two of who?"

But she didn't say another word. She touched the play button with a slim finger, then stood to join the others at the back of the room.

I turned my attention to the screen.

The blank white rectangle filled with light, and an image sprang to life from its depths. What appeared there was the face of a boy, years younger than me, with long dark curls and dark eyes ringed by thick eyelashes. He sat alone in a canvas chair, with nothing behind him but darkness. I was about to turn to get Aleka's attention when I noticed the boy's hands tinkering with something offscreen, and I realized what I was seeing: the protograph recording the finishing touches of its own creator.

Athan Genn.

The boy spoke, his voice soft but focused. "Is it working?" He looked over his shoulder and yelled, "Hey, Dad! I think it's working!"

A deep voice from beyond the screen rumbled in response.

"Wow," the boy said, returning his attention to the screen. "Um, okay, this is really awesome. I can't believe it's working!" His face broke into a huge grin, showing a couple gaps where teeth were missing. "This is Athan Genn, and what you're watching is my first . . . What?" He looked back over his shoulder, then addressed the protograph again. "My dad says I should time-stamp it. So okay, this is, um, September twenty-third, the year two thousand sixty-two, and the time is . . ." His eyes left the screen, then returned. "Five o'clock in the morning. Oh. Duh. Military time. Oh-five-hundred hours. This is so cool!"

A blur moved behind him, and a massive hand, much larger in proportion to the boy than you'd expect even from an adult, appeared on Athan's shoulder. The child looked up at his father's face, hidden beyond range of the protograph screen. "Should I keep going?"

Udain rumbled an indistinct response, and his huge body moved off.

"Okay," Athan said, turning back to the screen. "Like I said, my name is Athan Genn, and this is my first recording on the machine I built to keep records for the colony. So we won't ever forget. The recordings are backed up on an off-site server, and they can be remote-accessed from here. . . ." His hand fumbled for something, then held it up in front of the screen: a metal cuff, identical to the one Aleka now wore except much smaller. "I'm going to work on some other cool stuff, like fast-forward and freeze-frame, but this is only a bare-bones prototype. So you'll just have to sit and watch me talk!"

He laughed giddily.

"Anyway," he said. "Status update. Our scouts report that the Skaldi population seems to have stabilized, though of course it's hard to tell. The human population is at a historic low. We count fourteen survival colonies containing a total of just over nine hundred people within a seventy mile radius of our location, which is . . ." Again the offscreen voice sounded, and Athan turned to listen, swiveling back when it was done. "Okay, my dad says not to disclose our location. I think he's been listening to Laman too much. Because this is top-secret stuff!" He made a face and went on. "But the point is, Skaldi numbers aren't growing, but human numbers keep on declining. Which supports our theory that the Skaldi can't survive autonomously. The surge of energy they get from their victims doesn't last. It's like they're sending it somewhere else. Back to their home world, probably, by some means of electrical conduction. Shooting it back through the wormhole. What Dad calls the interdimensional anomaly."

He grinned again, as if delighted to be using such big words.

"Dad says a parasite that consumes its host without the possibility of reproduction is an evolutionary dead end. So the Skaldi don't make sense as an invading army acting on their own behalf. He figures they must be someone else's tools, biological manufactures sent to absorb energy for a dying planet." Again the gap-toothed grin. "I like to call the ones who sent them here the Creators. And their home world Skaldi City."

His hands tinkered with the offscreen recording device for a moment, and the image of his face centered and narrowed. Then he returned his eyes to the screen and continued.

"Drone trials have reached a critical phase, and it's becoming clear we need a permanent settlement to continue the work without interruption," he said. "We've discovered why human ribosomal DNA rejects the Kenos master sequence, but we're not sure exactly how to fix that. And Melan says we still haven't cracked the code to the mitochondrial DNA. We lost a ton of research in the wars, according to Dad. Which is why I'm feeding all our data into the remote server. Using encryption, of course." He smiled, and I could see his pleasure at being someone his dad trusted with such important work. "I'm thinking we should take another stab at embryonic stem cells, and Melan agrees. We just have to convince Dad it's worth the effort after what happened to the last batch."

The way he said that, as if he and Melan were stirring a pot of soup instead of culturing human cells, sent a cold wave across my scalp.

"But I think we can make it work," Athan went on. "We have some info on the basic drones Dad and his team created in the early years of the war. The ones that enabled the

Skaldi to flood the interdimensional anomaly." He smiled as the words rolled off his tongue, and I realized he was using that expression as much as possible, showing off in front of his new toy. "But I'm thinking if we can find a safe place to continue our research, we should be able to get into the mitochondrial DNA, which will give us a shot at boosting the energy level to where it'd shut the Skaldi down for good. I know I can convince Dad to stop listening to Laman and being such a chicken if I can just show him the results of our last—" He stopped, eyes widening guiltily, a kid remembering that his every word was being recorded in a format his father could watch anywhere and anytime he pleased.

"But like I said," he continued, his voice lowered as if that could keep his recording from being overheard, "I think we're just about ready for the next phase. And I'm positive Dad will be really pleased with the results." He smiled, and then he stared intently at the screen and slowly pronounced words I never thought I'd hear from his child's mouth: *"Aya tivah bis, shashi tivah bracha."*

The screen flickered, erasing his face for a moment. When it returned, the background had changed, bright sunlight revealing a desert backdrop. The recording was grainier too, the image jittery. When Athan smiled, his face seemed to be moving in slow motion, and his lip movements didn't quite match his words.

"Testing," he said. "Testing." He squinted, then smiled broadly. "Dad would kill me if he knew what I was up to.

Which is why I had to create this separate folder. I'm the only one who knows it's here, and it takes voice recognition to get in. How do you like my secret language, Athan?"

He cracked up, a boy talking to himself while he plotted behind his father's back.

"I've got something much bigger than the drones planned," he confided to his phantom self. "And I'm going to be storing all the information here. I'm sick of working on those things, spending every free moment with a bunch of brain-dead freaks. And I'm sick of Dad's protocol that says we can't use our own DNA. He's the one who started the wars, so who is he to tell me what to do? Plus I'm their creator, so why shouldn't I be their father for real?"

For a moment the child's eyes grew dreamy.

"Drone trials will continue, of course. Got to keep the public face going or Dad will get suspicious. But if I can find the remains of the Kenos laboratory, I'll have everything I need to get started on my *own* research. The kind of stuff no one ever dreamed of, back when all they could think about was building soldiers and bombs. I'll need girls, too, but—well, I can get girls."

The grainy image seemed to blush at the thought, but he kept going.

"Dad will see. He'll have no choice when he sees what I can do!" His dark eyes danced, throwing off sparks of light reflected from the desert sun. "*Aya tivah bis, shashi tivah bracha.* Over and out."

The screen went dark. I leaned back in the cold metal chair, a sick feeling crawling down my spine. It wasn't only the strangeness of watching someone whose life and death I'd already witnessed talking so confidently about his future. It was the realization of why Aleka wanted me to see this particular recording out of all the ones she could have chosen. I didn't know how she'd broken into Athan Genn's private files, but I knew why.

Athan had succeeded. As a boy, he'd dreamed of using his own genetic material to father generations of half-human, half-alien children, and as a man he'd done it.

"I'm one of them," I said to myself, though I felt the presence of my dead father and creator hovering near me as I said it. "Athan made me. With Aleka. I'm part-Skaldi."

I had enough composure to check on the wounded mem-
bers of our combined colonies as I knew Aleka would expect
me to, then I took myself to an empty room and stared at the
wall in stunned silence.

It wasn't really a room. More like a closet, though without shelves or supplies or anything else. I chose it because it
was the only place I didn't need to know a code to enter. The
only place with an old-fashioned doorknob.

I had to dodge Mercy to get there. Not knowing what
I'd seen, she kept pursuing me, saying she wanted to intro-
duce me to Ardan. There was no way to tell her I wasn't in
the mood for a Genn family reunion. Watching the light that
shone from her eyes, and the crestfallen look when I shook
free from her, was almost as hard as learning the truth.

The truth. The truth that my father was a madman. And
that I was his monster.

Blind, useless fury bled from me. I couldn't believe how stupid I'd been. Everything added up, and yet I'd persisted in believing I was just an ordinary human being with a strange little habit of draining energy and shooting it back when the opportunity arose. I remembered hunting inside myself after I'd learned about the Skaldi attack that stole my memory, wondering if any part of the creature was still there, never knowing it had been there all along. And I remembered something Korah had asked me, the one time we really talked. *Do Skaldi know they're Skaldi?* She'd meant when they take control of someone, the way they took control of her just days after that conversation. She couldn't have known when she asked me the question that she was asking someone who proved the answer was *no*.

Beyond the anger at myself, there was anger at Athan: stale, thick anger like a scab that starts bleeding when you pick it off. There was anger at Udain and his accomplice Melan, the ones who'd treated the boy genius like some kind of king, feeding his ego to the point where he must have figured he could have anything he wanted. Gadgets. Girls. His own race of hybrid children, including me.

And there was anger at Aleka. My mother. Intelligence might not have been one of the traits Athan bred in his creations, but it didn't take a genius to figure out she'd been a lot more than his lab assistant. The fact that she'd lied to me all this time became understandable now that I knew how much the lie covered.

255

There was no end to it. No chance with Mercy. No point in being here at all. I wished the Skaldi had killed me any one of the multiple times they'd had the chance. Except I guess they couldn't kill their own brother.

I stayed a long time in the small, empty room, feeling as much a prisoner of its four walls as I'd felt in Asunder's canyon. I was about to leave when I sensed someone hovering outside the door and a voice I knew said softly, "Knock, knock." Embarrassment at my hiding spot flooded me as I opened the door to face Aleka.

She looked a hundred years old. I'd always told myself her hair was blond, but the truth was it had all gone gray, a flat sandy gray like the canvas of an old tent. The lines across her face reminded me of how the land looked after a rainstorm gouged it into streams that instantly ran dry. And though I knew her gaunt body was still wrapped with strength, the terrible imbalance of her missing limb screamed at me that she'd already set her feet on the road to death, that all the things that could kill you in this world—violence, disease, Skaldi—had taken their first chunk out of her and would never let go until they were done. They'd taken my father, my half brother, my friends. They would take everyone I knew.

Except *they* weren't they. They were me. I was death, and I'd only learned it now.

"Querry," Aleka said, and I tried not to watch the cords of her neck tighten as she swallowed. "I think I owe you an explanation."

"I think you owe me a lot more than that."

A strange expression crossed her face as she cocked her head to examine me. "So judgmental. So hard. You weren't always this way."

"Yeah, well," I said, "being a monster will do that."

"You're not a monster," she said. "You're my son."

She sat on one of the chrome metal chairs that littered the huge, hollow chasm of the war room. I couldn't very well stand in the doorway of a storage closet with her sitting there staring at me, so I joined her. Or didn't exactly join her. I sat in another chair is what I meant.

She watched me sit. Alert, keen-eyed as always. I don't think I'd ever hated her more.

"Did you sleep with him?" I said. It seemed like a stupid question considering what I'd just learned, but I wanted to set the record straight at the start.

"Yes," she said, meeting me with a level gaze.

"So then me and Mercy . . ."

"No," she said. "Athan suffered from infertility, a condition not uncommon after the wars. All of his children are products of experimental procedures. Some, like the young of his colony, are clones. But you and Mercy have quite separate genetic histories."

I felt a surge of guilty relief at hearing this. It didn't change what Athan and Aleka had done, but at least it meant I didn't share blood with Mercy. How that would make a difference once she discovered what I *did* share blood with,

I had no idea. "Mercy's no clone," I said. "Neither is Ardan."

Aleka sat back in the chair and sighed. "It's complicated, Querry," she said. "And I'm not sure where to start."

She was quiet for a long time. I studied the creases beside her nose, the cracks lining her lips. I was about to say something when, as usual, she beat me to it.

"How old do you think I am?" she said. It startled me, made me feel like she'd been eavesdropping on my thoughts. I mumbled something I knew she wouldn't be able to hear.

"I'm forty years old," she said, which startled me again. My guess had been more than a decade older than that. "I was twenty-five when you were born. Twenty-two when I had Yov. Athan was much older. That first recording was produced two years before I was born. But Yov's father was only twenty-one when I became pregnant with his child. Twenty-one when he died."

She leaned back, running her hand through the coarse stubs of her hair. "You know he died in a Skaldi attack," she said. "The one that led me here. We were members of Survival Colony Fifteen then. Years later, when I joined Survival Colony Nine—just after the attack that took your memory—I feared Laman might still have communication with his family. So I lied to him, told him my husband had survived the earlier attack. If word got around camp that I was your mother, I was hoping Laman—and you—wouldn't trace your birth back to Udain's compound."

"Did it really matter that much?"

"It did to me," she said. "I had loved Yov's father for as long as I could remember. And when I lost him, I lost the will to live."

She reached out, bony fingers gripping a palm-size screen. It flickered to life, and I realized it was a portable protograph, the miniscule image speckled and gray. It showed a woman with long pale hair sitting in a metal chair, the same kind we were sitting in now. She was obviously pregnant, her belly huge. But her arms and neck and face had gone beyond gaunt and passed into skeletal. And her eyes, eyes I knew so well, stared emptily at the recording device. I noticed printed characters, too small to read—maybe a name or number— stitched across the front of the plain white gown she wore. While she sat there, two technicians in white coats fiddled with her right arm, probably prepping her for the tracking device everyone in Udain's colony carried under their biceps. Their backs were turned to me, but I thought one of them might have been a younger Doctor Siva. My living mother let me look at her past self for a minute, then she snapped the device off and stowed it in her breast pocket.

"I have no memory of the day I was admitted," she said. "Yov was born days later, but I didn't—I couldn't care for him. I wouldn't touch him. I couldn't"—she swallowed painfully—"I couldn't feed him. Fortunately Mercy's mother was still nursing, and she gave Yov what I couldn't. All I had to give the world was pain. I lay in bed, ate nothing, spoke no words. When they brought my baby to me, I turned my head away. He was nothing to me, only a reminder of what I'd lost. A reminder of my pain."

I stared at her trembling chin, the tears creeping down her cheeks. "It was you, wasn't it? You had to kill your own husband."

"I set his body on fire," she said in a whisper. "Before the Skaldi could complete the transformation. Because I knew if I let it finish, if I let it look at me for even a moment from behind his eyes, I wouldn't have had the strength to destroy it. I would have fallen at its feet and let it take me and my unborn child with him."

A tear slid past her lips, poised at the end of her sharp chin, reflecting the light of the room. The next thing I knew she was sobbing, her head buried in her hand, her empty shoulder jerking ineffectually as it tried to bring the missing limb over her face. For a second I let her cry, then I rose so fast my chair clattered to the floor. I put my arms around her, feeling the thinness of her body, even thinner than I imagined, like the woman in the protograph, a handful of bones. I held my own mother like she was a child, and she cried so long and hard I thought she had stored these tears for the past twenty years of her life.

When her breathing finally eased and her eyes lifted, I let go. She smiled at me, her face a teary mess. I righted my chair and sat, and she nodded as if she understood.

"Athan came to me in the infirmary," she said. "Where Siva had tied me down so I couldn't cut myself, started force-feeding to keep me alive. I don't know if that was standard protocol on suicide watches or if Athan had ordered it especially for me. He visited me every day, and at first he said nothing about his—his work. He just talked. That voice of his—you've heard that voice. It was the same then. It was like the first ray of sunshine after a darkness a thousand years long. It lifted my head from the pillow, tore my eyes from the shackles on my wrists. It told me I was beautiful, and strong, and—and desirable. I'm sorry, Querry. I know this isn't what you want to hear."

"It's okay."

"I don't know if it was love," she said. "I'll never know if he truly meant all the things he said, or if he'd seen something in me—in my eyes, my blood, the shape of my face— that led him to believe I'd suit his purposes. All I knew was that when he said those things to me, I was finally able to rise from my bed, to hold my baby in my arms, to smile at his smile. I had been dead for months, and when he said those things to me, I came to life again."

I clasped her hand in both of mine, felt the fragility of her bones, but also her strength. She brought my hands to her mouth and gave them a dry kiss before letting go.

"For the two years I stayed in Udain's camp," she continued, "I was Athan's assistant. His assistant, and his—I don't know how to say this."

"'Lover' works," I said.

"Okay." She nodded, sniffled. "I knew about Hadiyah, of

course. His wife. Her milk had saved my baby's life, but even that didn't stop me. Mercy takes after her. Did you know that?"

I shook my head.

"Of course not." She smiled in an embarrassed kind of way, making her look much younger for a fleeting moment. "For years, Hadiyah had been Athan's principal collaborator in the secret experiments that paralleled the drone trials. As you've seen, he'd quickly grown dissatisfied with those stunted aberrations, creatures without mind or will. He wanted to create a legacy for himself: children who were human in body and mind, but Skaldi in their power to dominate. And to destroy."

"So Mercy is part-Skaldi too?" For some reason, that upset me more than knowing what I was myself.

"Mercy is free of Skaldi genes," she said. "The first trials were not successful, Querry. All resulted in miscarriages or . . . defects. Ardan represented a major breakthrough, but not a successful fusion of human and Skaldi. In his case, Athan speculated that the recessive gene for gigantism prevented the assimilation of the Kenos genome. Beryl, though physically capable of absorbing energy, was born with a profound intellectual disability. Mercy was too young to realize it, but her older sister was more a child than she."

"The staff," I said. "It's her, isn't it? It's what's left of Beryl."

"It must be," she said. "Infused with the energy her body absorbed from the drone years ago."

Her gaze retreated from mine, and she stared emptily at her own hand, her mouth turning down in bitterness or anger.

"Then Mercy . . ." I prompted.

She looked back up at me. "Athan suspended the trials for almost five years after Beryl's birth. Mercy is the product of in vitro fertilization, using her parents' genetic material exclusively. Meanwhile Athan spent those years searching for a new approach, and a new . . . subject."

"You."

She nodded. "A willing subject, honored to be chosen. In my case, he tried something unprecedented in the Kenos trials: inserting Skaldi DNA directly into my ova. He'd come to the conclusion that the male gamete created an imbalance, a weakening of the Kenos properties." She smiled again. "I suspect he knew this from the time Beryl was born. But as you've learned, it can take years for the male members of the Genn family to admit they might be the source of a problem."

"Or never," I said.

"True enough," she said with a short laugh. Then her face grew serious again. "I need you to understand something, Querry. I was not a dewy-eyed innocent, much less a victim. I understood what the experiments were intended to do, and I recognized the risks. I also knew they didn't require us to—that Athan and I didn't need to—"

"It's okay," I said. "I get it."

"Thank you," she whispered. "But whatever misgivings I

had were overcome by the power of his . . . persuasion. He convinced me we were building something beautiful, both in the laboratory and in the—the other places we went. Building it in my own body. I needed to feel that way, Querry. Not just the physical beauty, but that I had something to give to life. That I could strike back against the darkness. That instead of it overwhelming me, I could become the vehicle of ending its reign."

"I know the feeling," I said.

"Power is a tempting thing," she agreed. "Especially when it comes in the guise of love. He gave me a ring, in secret. One of two rings he'd salvaged from the time before. Of course I couldn't wear it publicly, but I kept it with me, close to my heart. I—"

I fished in my pocket for the ring I'd nearly forgotten was there. My fingers closed on it, pulled it free. She stared in disbelief.

"Where did you get that?" she stammered.

"It's a long story," I said. "I thought it was Korah's."

She reached out to touch the ring, but when I tried to drop it in her palm, she gently pushed my hand away. "It is Korah's," she said. "I gave it to her when we joined Survival Colony Nine. She was ecstatic, because it nearly matched a ring Wali had found in the desert. She would never have asked me for it, but when I saw her face . . ." She shrugged awkwardly. "I decided I had carried it long enough, and it was time to let it go."

I watched her eyes as they drank in the ring, and though she was lined and gray, I thought I saw in those eyes the person she'd been, the young woman who'd given everything for love. I slipped the ring back in my pocket, and a look of pain crossed her face. But it gave way to the look I knew best, the stern intensity of her older, sadder, truer self.

"For a long time," she said, "I convinced myself Athan would leave Hadiyah and come to me. I told myself their relationship was only that of scientist and subject, while ours was so much more. As we got closer to the trial of the drone he'd prepared at his father's bidding, I became certain he'd declare his love for me openly. Once the Skaldi threat had been eliminated, what reason could there be to keep it a secret?"

She shook her head and sat brooding, staring at the floor a long time before she went on.

"Of course, when I saw what happened in the desert that day, the accident that killed Beryl and Hadiyah and all the others, I woke from my illusions and realized what I had done. And afterward, when Athan returned to the compound so dangerous and unstable, ranting that the Scavenger of Souls would come to chastise me for my sins of the flesh, I knew I had to get away from him. I cut the tracker from my arm—I'd show you, but it's the arm that's gone"—she flapped her missing limb, the shoulder moving despite the absence beneath it—"and fled with Yov. I was carrying you at the time, as I'm sure you've already figured out. . . ."

"Math," I said.

". . . and yet I had no idea *what* I was carrying. For those last six months, I lived in fear of what might emerge from my body. I even considered terminating. . . ." She bit down on her lip and went on. "My fears were allayed by your birth. You developed normally, showed no signs of the Skaldi material you'd inherited. But then, when you were three . . ."

I tensed. "What happened?"

"You were attacked," she said simply. "One of them infiltrated the colony that had adopted us and went straight for you. It happened in the impact zone, outside the canyon. The result was the rockslide where we were taken by Asunder."

I could barely ask the next question. "Did I kill anyone?"

"No," she said. "But there were severe injuries, as well as the damage you saw to the land. The reaction was so extreme I began to feel you must have acquired a heightened ability to absorb energy from the accident that occurred before your birth. I tried to convince our commander your power could be useful, but he wouldn't listen. He feared the Skaldi were tracking you, and that others would soon follow. I was given a choice: end your life, or leave with you and Yov, never to return." She lifted her chin defiantly. "It was never a question which option I'd choose."

I stared at her, not sure whether to be thankful or appalled. She'd saved my life—but at the expense of other lives, people who'd never known they were letting a ticking time bomb into their camp. After her commander's ultimatum, she must have decided never to reveal my past to anyone else. The children of Survival Colony 27 had been destroyed by that secret. So many members of Survival Colony 9 had died for it too. And now . . . Tears burned my cheeks as I thought about the impossible choice she'd made, the impossible life she'd spared. I knew that I'd be haunted forever by her choice. She'd kept me alive only to bear the burden of what I was.

"You should have chosen the first option," I said.

She reached out with her single hand to touch my face. Her eyes held me, wouldn't let go.

"Listen to me, Querry," she said. "And listen well. Vengeance is not a program for living, any more than despair is. It's no accident Athan produced a child outside the Kenos trials and named her Mercy. After all he'd lived through, all he'd done, he was seeking forgiveness—for his father, his people, and most of all for himself. But he never found it. He allowed himself to be consumed by guilt and grief and rage, and in the end all he found was death. You may be Athan Genn's creation, but you're also your own man. You don't need to let the Skaldi win."

"*Am* I a man, though?" I said.

"You're the child of my body," she said. "I've watched you grow for fifteen years. But only you can answer that question."

I tried. I thought about all the people I'd known, all the people I'd loved. Skaldi weren't able to love, were they? I thought about my mother's faith in me, the jobs she'd given me to do, the trust in her eyes when she'd told me to take over from her. Mercy, too. She might have thought of me as a mutant killing machine at first, but now she thought of me as much more, didn't she? But then I remembered all the people I'd let down, all the people I'd hurt. All the people who'd died because of me, directly or not. Could I ever forgive myself for that? Were Skaldi capable of forgiving, and of being forgiven?

I didn't know. All I knew was, I'd asked for the truth, and I'd gotten it at last.

Aleka eyed me knowingly. It struck me that she'd been only a few years older than me when she lost her husband and gave birth to her first child. While that thought lasted in my mind, it seemed to close the distance between us. What had she known back then about life and love, choices that cling to you for a lifetime? What did she know now?

"You okay?" she said.

I took a deep breath. "I've been better."

"What are you going to tell Mercy?"

I looked at her, at the smile on her lips. Everything was a secret with her, and nothing was. "I'm not sure, Mom," I said. "I'm working on it."

"You should talk to her," she said. "Sometimes people will surprise you."

I said nothing. I was dealing with enough surprises at the moment.

My mother's gray eyes flicked over my face. Whatever she saw, she didn't push. But she nodded once, and then she was back to business.

"We should check on the others," she said. "Secure as this bunker is, it's a temporary respite, not a long-term solution. And the matter of the missing drone still needs to be addressed. One way or another, we'll have to come up with a plan."

"I'm with you," I said, and gripped her hand as I stood.

That was when the lights went out.

In the total darkness Aleka's chair scraped against the concrete, then her hand squeezed mine with a strength like iron.

"Querry."

"Mom."

"Listen to me," she said in a whisper so low I could barely hear it over my thudding heart. "Keep your back to mine. When I move, you move. When I stop, you stop. Don't let me lose you."

I pressed against the sharp bones of her back. She sidestepped, and I followed.

"I'm going to try to get to the power," she said. "It's just across the room."

"But that's where it'll be."

"Unless it's gone hunting."

"Who is it?"

"Everything in the bunker responds to biometric signature. Mine. And Siva's."

"But how . . . ?"

"Someone must have been infected up above. And then it jumped to him. I was distracted, should have thought. . . . At this point it could be anyone."

"No one screamed."

"No one can see it coming."

Mercy had been closest to them at the gate. And she'd been the one who stayed behind to hold them off in the generator room. I prayed silently it wasn't her, knowing my prayers didn't matter, knowing that even if it hadn't gotten her out there it might still come for her in here.

We inched sideways, stepping so lightly we were like twin ghosts. I strained into the darkness. The room was deadly quiet.

"Do we have flamethrowers?"

"Not readily available."

"What about your rifle?"

"It's jammed. The creature knew what it was doing."

"We need light."

"Stay with me, Querry. We'll get there."

Something rushed past us, close enough I felt the air shiver. Still I couldn't hear anything except our constricted breathing and the slight rustle of our uniforms touching. My body itched to strike out at the thing, wherever it was. But I knew if I let the power loose with us standing back-to-back, I'd set her body on fire.

"Almost there," Aleka breathed.

For a second I thought I saw a flash of light in the distance, so sudden I couldn't be sure. It illuminated nothing, not the thing that had made it, not the darkness surrounding the thing. At first I thought it was the power trying to come back on, but it was too weak for that. It was almost as if some moving object had flared briefly then extinguished itself—or moved too fast to a new position for my eyes to follow.

It was as if the flash itself had moved.

"Aleka," I said. "Mom. Look for a light. A quick pulse. If it gets close, warn me."

"What is it?"

"It's the Skaldi," I said. "It's giving off some of the energy it swallowed. It's—there!"

Another flash darted across my visual field, instantly folding into darkness.

"I can't see it," she said.

"I just did."

"Where is it? Is it getting closer?"

"It's— I think it's closing in."

Her hand reached for mine, gripped so hard it hurt. "It can't touch you."

"I'm not going to let it get you, either."

"Querry." Her whisper had no breath in it. "You have to fight it off. Otherwise it'll take everyone in the room."

"I can't." Visions of children's bodies coming apart filled

my mind. She'd seen it happen. She knew what she was asking. "Mom, I can't."

"You have to."

"You're all I have left."

"This is about more than me and you."

"Mom . . ."

"Do as I say!" she snapped, louder and more angrily than I expected. She shoved with her one hand, and in the dark separation between us I sensed the thing moving in for the kill.

"Mom!"

A spark.

A moving flare.

The fire caught.

A pulse, bright as the sun, filled the room.

In its glare I saw the Skaldi attached to her, its scar split wide, preparing to suck her in. Then its body caught fire and sloughed to the floor. The light died almost the instant it appeared, only to be replaced by the dance of flames across my mother's body. I saw her mouth widen in a scream.

"Mom!"

I leaped at her and threw her to the floor, dousing the flame with my body. Darkness fell again, and I felt her chest heave, heard her ragged breathing. Footsteps and shouts sounded from across the room. My hands burned, and the air I drew into my lungs stank with the odor of charred flesh.

"Querry." Her fingers touched my face. I could feel the

rough skin where she'd been burned. "Find Mercy. She knows how to reset the signature."

"Mom, no. No. Please, no."

"Find her." Her hand traced my cheek before falling to the floor.

I stepped clear of her and searched the darkness until I heard a sharp scratch and caught sight of a red flare. The footsteps resumed, and in seconds Mercy, Nessa, and Ardan appeared in the ruddy glow. I tried not to falter at the sight of my mother's body stretched on the floor, angry burns covering her, the black remains of the creature enclosing her in a ring of ash. The wrist cuff lay open near what was left of her leg, its cold curve like a cruel smile.

Mercy dropped to a knee beside her. Aleka touched her face, whispered things I couldn't hear. Mercy scooped up the wrist cuff and stood, gesturing for Ardan to pick my mother up, then headed toward the control panel. Nessa held the flare, lighting the way. When we arrived at the panel, Aleka reached up with trembling fingers and swiped the touch pad, and the room filled with light. I blinked, willed my eyes to adjust. The burns I'd thought were bad in the flare's wavering glow revealed themselves fully: the shriveled creature Ardan held in his arms, its hair and clothes nearly gone and its flesh the red of a body turned inside out, bore no resemblance to the woman who'd been my mother.

With Aleka's bright eyes following her every movement, Mercy entered the code to reprogram the control panel. I thought she'd substitute her own signature, but she nodded at me, and I reached out numbly to press my index finger against the touch pad. When the panel whirred and an image of my own print appeared briefly on its surface before being pulled into the metal's depths, I knew I was now in control of the compound.

Ardan carried my mother to the bunker's medical wing, where Tyris and Adem watched the giant lay her on one of the beds. Neither of them made a move to tend to her, though. Even if Doctor Siva had still been alive, everyone could see she was beyond their help.

I stood beside her, leaned over to kiss her cheek, burned and reddened as it was. I thought about the woman I'd known, pale-skinned, gray-eyed, severe and serene. The woman who'd led two colonies, fought monsters and insurrections and her own lasting grief. I thought about the long road she'd traveled from the young woman she'd been, the expectant mother I'd glimpsed in the protograph the first time I'd visited Udain's compound. The years that followed had whittled her body down to nearly nothing, but somehow her spirit had remained strong. Now she stood at the road's end, and I could do nothing but hold her hand as she took the final step into the darkness.

Her eyes shone, her lips moved. "Mercy," she said, and Ardan's sister moved to the bed beside me.

But Aleka wasn't talking to her. "Mercy," she said again, her eyes fixed on me.

I nodded. Her face relaxed. I hoped that, when she made it to the other side, she'd arrive like that. At peace. Whole.

Healed.

"I saw him," I said. "In a dream. I saw Yov."

Her eyes brightened, gray as the moon.

"Maybe you'll . . ." My voice trailed off. *Maybe you'll see your husband*, I was about to say.

Her ruined face tried to smile.

"I love you, Mom," I said. "I won't let them win."

Her eyelids closed, the skin as red and blistered as the rest of her face. I touched her cheek one last time as she died. Grief would have overwhelmed me if anger hadn't burned it away. Not anger at her. *This doesn't begin with you*, she'd told me. And it didn't begin with her, either. None of this would have happened if not for Athan and Udain Genn. And none of the choices they'd made would have been necessary if not for the monsters that roamed the land above us, the creatures from beyond the stars. Forgiveness could come later—forgiveness for my creator, my people, myself.

For now, vengeance was all I had.

"Get the others," I said to Mercy. "Tell them this is the night the Skaldi die."

My first official act as commander of Survival Colony None was to order the destruction of the base I commanded.

The *None* was Mercy's idea. Something about how that was almost *Nine*, but with an *O* for "unknown." Like most of her jokes, it didn't make much sense, and it didn't seem like the right time. But my next official act was to ignore that.

We wrapped Aleka's body in a sheet and eased her onto a storage shelf in the infirmary, where a sedated Udain slept beside his wounded soldiers, his feet spilling off the edge of a normal-size cot. From the location where my mother had fallen I collected the two things not so badly burned as to be useless: a pistol that had fallen from its holster—silver like the one she'd lost to Asunder's colony—and the battered but still functional miniature protograph. A search of the war room turned up the remains of Doctor Siva, heaped on the floor beside the table, identifiable only by his white jacket. Everyone else was accounted for, which meant that the creature had infected him before he'd gone underground. To be certain there wasn't another one, Mercy subjected everyone to the military version of the Skaldi trials: a flat black wand that hummed with the same energy as the guns. I wished Aleka had thought to use it on Siva before she locked the war room door, but I guess she'd had too much faith in the man who'd twice saved her life to suspect him. And she'd been too eager to show me the protograph recording to perform the act that might have saved her own life.

I sat with Mercy at the war room table while she showed me the basics of the compound's integrated network. She'd been clingy ever since Aleka's death, snuggling up to me with her arms draped over my shoulders and her cheek pressed against mine. Not like she was trying to start something, just attempting to console me—or to scare off Nessa, who she practically hissed at every time the girl came near. Still, the touch of her hands seemed wrong, especially since I was the only one who knew why it seemed wrong. I wiggled uncomfortably, and she got the idea—or at least, the idea that I wasn't ready for anyone to get close to me yet. Like so much else, the full story of who I was and why it would never work out between us would have to wait for later.

"So the entire compound's visible from here?" I said.

She guided my hands to the proper buttons, and a glowing map appeared on the screen. Thousands of pinpricks of red light swarmed the surface compound's outline like a disease.

"That's them," she said.

"Yeah," I said. "I kind of figured that out."

We zoomed and scanned the image, focusing on the tunnel to the bunker. A handful of red dots sprinkled the passageway up to the first door, but after that there was nothing. Those few were probably holding the corridor while others searched for a different way in. At least for now, they hadn't found it.

"Is there another entrance?" I asked.

"There's a rear escape"—she moved my hands over the controls until a long, straight tunnel appeared—"right there. It extends for miles to the east, out into the desert. But our friends don't seem to know about it."

"What about the drone?" I said. "Shouldn't it show up on the map?"

"Apparently not," she said. "But I can work on finding it if you want."

"Hm." Something about the way she said that told me she was just being something she never was: polite. "So we slip out the back way . . ."

"And blow them to kingdom come before they know we're gone," she said with a smug smile. "Check this out."

She called up a map of the compound's final fail-safe: charges set in a ring around headquarters that could be detonated by the commander, turning the area above-ground into an inferno. This could all be accomplished, she announced confidently, through the remote function on the wrist cuff I'd locked onto my right calf. But her glee turned to bewilderment, and then to fury, when she discovered the remote wasn't working. She monkeyed with it far longer than I thought was prudent before spitting out that it had probably been damaged in the fire. Other hardware—the guns, the protograph—had responded to my signature and come back online, but the charges would have to be set by hand.

My hand.

"You'll need a guide," Mercy said when I told her the plan.

"No way, Mercy."

"Oh, come on!" she said. "It'll be just like old times!"

Nothing will ever be like old times, I thought. "I'm your commander, you know."

"Ha!" Her expression was about what I expected, but the motion she made with her finger was new to me. "Command *this*."

I didn't have the time or energy to fight her, so I gave in. I'd have to ask about the finger thing later.

I assembled the others. All of the kids volunteered to join us, including Zataias, who raised his hand so high it was like he thought I was picking an "it" for a game of freeze tag. I ruled him and the rest of the kids out immediately, plus the injured colonists and medical personnel. Geller must have been high on Mercy's praise from earlier in the day, because he volunteered too, but I told him I needed him to stay with Udain. Tyris tried to make a case that we might need her if the plan went wrong, but my answer was that if the plan went wrong, there'd be too many little pieces of us for her to do a thing about it.

In the end I decided on just me, Mercy, and Ardan. Any more I was afraid would attract too much attention. Any less I was sure would produce my first mutiny. Nessa hadn't said anything while I described the plan—probably because Mercy was staring daggers at her the whole time—but now she insisted on both her and Adem coming along. Though Adem looked like he was strangling when she volunteered his name, he didn't refuse. I considered telling them no, which would have pleased Mercy, but I found myself saying yes. Maybe it was because I knew how solid Nessa was. Or because, with her hair cut short, she looked a lot like my mother.

We took the bare minimum in terms of supplies. Energy guns, the miniature protograph to chart our course and keep track of Skaldi, the wrist cuff in case some of its functions still worked, a flashlight, a set of walkie-talkies. I left Aleka's pistol on the war room table, asking Tyris to bury it with her if we didn't return. Her team would exit the compound via the rear passageway, with Geller and most of the other guards transporting their former commander. If my team didn't make it, the others would try to pry the drone's location from Udain. If and when we regrouped, we would hold funerals for Siva and my mother.

We arranged a meeting place and an "if we're not back by" time. I was about to make one last check of everything when Mercy touched my arm. "Querry."

I stopped.

"I'm sorry about your mom. I don't remember her from when I was a kid, but she seemed like a great lady."

"Yeah," I said. "She was a lot like you."

She laid a hand on my cheek, looked at me with her dark eyes. When I looked back, it was like I was seeing the girl I'd begun to think about being with through the ghostly image of the girl I knew I never could. Then the first of those girls grinned.

"With the possible exception," she said, "of the lady part."

We finalized plans with the others, then turned the protograph on and headed back into the tunnels.

No sooner did we set off than Mercy dropped behind with me and tried to sneak a kiss. Which I thought was kind of inappropriate, considering what had just happened. But like she said, she was no lady.

I shook her off, edged away. That was hard to do in the narrow tunnel. "Not now, Mercy."

"Come on, live a little," she said. "This is the first free moment we've had since you woke up." She batted her eyelashes. "And for all we know, it might be the last."

"Later," I mumbled. Ardan had turned his head and was looking suspiciously at us, so that gave me the excuse I needed.

Mercy, though, didn't seem fazed. "To be continued," she said, giving me a quick kiss before skipping ahead to join her brother. "And just as a reminder," she shot over her shoulder, "I am not exactly renowned for my patience."

Ardan offered me one last scowl before nodding to his sister and turning to concentrate on the road ahead.

I walked right behind them, with Nessa and Adem in the rear. We marched for a half hour without a word, the brother-sister team consulting the protograph and communicating as quietly as our footsteps, with nods and glances and hand gestures. We'd just approached a door that looked identical to all the doors we'd passed when Mercy paused, letting out a breath. It sounded like a gale-force wind after all the silence.

"What's the problem?" I asked in a whisper.

"Take a look at this," she said.

She held out the protograph, and we all clustered around it. She'd switched the view to the surface level, and what it showed was a mass of Skaldi surrounding what appeared to be Udain's headquarters. "Uh-oh," I said.

"Yeah," she said. "The little buggers are standing right on top of the charges. They've shifted position since the last time I checked. Almost like they know we're coming."

That was the last thing I wanted to hear. And the last

thing I wanted to tell her was *why* the Skaldi always seemed to know when I was around.

Nessa leaned in closer. "Is there another way?"

Mercy gave her a look. "Another way to do what?"

"To set the charges," Nessa said. "Like, from underground."

I could see Mercy warring with a response. "There are tunnels all over the place," she said through her teeth. "But the charges are at surface level. We have to be outside to get at them."

No one spoke for a long time. Then Nessa said, "So we need to create a diversion. We need to split into two teams, one to draw them away and one to set the charges."

"*Them* happens to be about two thousand Skaldi," Mercy said. "In case you hadn't noticed."

"I noticed."

"And are you volunteering for this suicide mission?"

I stepped between them before my first official action as commander ended in a fistfight. "Enough, you two," I said. "Nessa's right. Mercy, what's the closest tunnel to the generator room?"

Mercy muttered to herself while she scanned the protograph, making very little effort to prevent the rest of us from hearing what she was muttering. Ardan filled the space beside her, double her size but not half as vocal. She quieted down only when she found what I'd asked for. "There," she said. "If we come up on the outskirts of the square, we'll be within spitting distance of the generator. What's your plan?"

"Fire on the generator," I said. "That should attract at least some of their attention. Meanwhile the second team sneaks over to headquarters and sets the charges."

"And which team is which, may I ask?" Mercy said.

Before I could answer, Nessa spoke up. "Adem and I will create the diversion. The team that sets the charges will need Ardan's strength and Mercy's knowledge. How much time do you need?"

Mercy glanced at her brother. She seemed to be having a hard time keeping her breath under control, though I had no idea why. It was obvious she didn't like Nessa, but we were all in this together.

Finally she answered. "We'll need to set at least two to take out the Skaldi on the inside as well as the perimeter. Depending on our luck and how many flesh-eating alien monsters decide to get in our way, that could take us any- where from ten minutes to forever."

"We can give you ten minutes," Nessa said. Adem, I thought, looked pretty green, though the light in the tunnels was gray white. But he swallowed a lump the size of his fist and nodded.

"Great," I said. "Mercy, let's go."

She held her hand out to Nessa in exaggerated polite- ness. "Right this way, princess."

Mercy and Ardan led us onward. After a few minutes Mercy signaled for another conference, the two of them por- ing over the protograph. Mercy's brow knotted in concentration before she pointed the way. We wove through a new set of hallways that looked like the old set of hallways, and I could feel an angry silence radiating from Mercy that I couldn't explain. Her mood was really starting to fray my nerves when she said, "Stop."

I peered ahead. The corridor was indistinguishable from any we'd walked in the past hour.

"We're close," Mercy said. "Through that door and up the stairs."

Everyone held their breath and listened. The tunnel was absolutely silent. Mercy spoke my mind before I could.

"No pulse," she muttered.

"You think the beam's down?"

"Possibly. The Skaldi might have taken it offline in the war room."

"My signature wouldn't have brought it back?"

"Depends on what the thing did to it."

"If it is down," I said, "will that make a difference with the charges?"

"It'll sure as hell make a difference in terms of our ability to *get* to the charges."

Nessa spoke up again. "Not if we can anticipate their movements—"

"Oh, for God's sake!" Mercy snapped, forgetting to keep her voice down. "There's an army of Skaldi ten feet above our heads. You think you can *anticipate* them? What are you going to use? Tarot cards? Divining rods?"

Nessa shook her head but said nothing. I reached out toward Mercy. "I think she just means—"

"Bug off!" Mercy snapped, shaking me away and storming a short distance down the tunnel.

I caught up to her. She didn't make any effort to elude me. "Mercy, what is wrong—"

"I'll tell you what's wrong!" she exploded. "Every time Skinhead opens her smart-ass little mouth, you're all, *Wow, what a great idea!* Since when did she become so high on your list?"

"You're . . ." I couldn't believe I was about to say this. "You're jealous?"

Apparently that was the wrong thing to say. "You are such a flipping idiot," she said. "It would be lovely if everything was about you, wouldn't it? But it's not. Did it ever occur to you this might be a trap?"

Now she'd totally lost me. "A trap?"

"Yes, a trap," she said. "Designed to march us straight into their waiting arms. Or mouths, as the case may be."

She held out the protograph. At first I couldn't make sense of it: where a moment ago there'd been a mass of red lights so dense it was like a puddle of blood, now there was only a single dot, pulsing weakly in the center of the screen. Then I realized what I was seeing: our own position. Underground. And with the red light of a Skaldi right in front of my eyes.

"I'm kicking myself for not catching it before," Mercy

said, her voice finally under control. "But I was focused on where we were going, not where we are."

"Who is it?" I whispered, wondering if it might be me.

She shrugged. "My money's on Little Miss Diversion. That minx has been raising my hackles from the get-go."

I decided not to risk asking what a minx was. "But she passed the test."

"There's only one test I'm convinced by," she said, fingering her rifle. "The question is, do you want me to fry her cupcakes now, or are you in a gambling mood?"

I glanced up the corridor at the three shadowy figures. Ardan's posture appeared as stolid as ever, Adem's as indecisive. But I sensed that Nessa knew what we were talking about. If, that is, it was really Nessa.

"Contact Tyris," I said in a low voice. "Don't tell her what's going on. I just want to know their position in case anything happens to us."

Mercy switched on her walkie-talkie, but only static filled the line. I took a deep breath and steered my gaze back to the end of the tunnel. Mercy waited, the light too dim to tell if it was expectation or annoyance I saw in her face.

"This is what leaders are for," she said, handing the protograph over. "To make the tough calls."

I deliberated a moment longer, then tucked the protograph in my pocket and nodded toward the door. "Tyris and the others will have to fend for themselves. Keep an eye on

Nessa. But don't shoot unless I say so. We're sticking to the plan."

Mercy spoke no word of objection, but I felt her silence behind me like a blade in my back.

We rejoined the others, and together we inched toward the door. It opened at the touch of my finger on the keypad. The stairwell beyond was unlit, and so dark I couldn't tell if anything waited in the shadows. I thought of lighting our way with our flashlight, but I didn't want to alert them. With me in the lead and Mercy gripping her rifle in the rear, we crept up the stairs. When we got there, I touched the button beside the door.

It opened onto a courtyard swarming with Skaldi.

Darkness blanketed the square, the perimeter fence visible only as black uprights against the dead gleam of the impact zone. But I could make out the humped shapes that filled the area in front of us, wriggling like an enormous hive. A rot worse than thousands of corpses emanated from bodies that had never been alive to begin with. They hadn't detected us yet, but without the beam to immobilize them, it was only a matter of time before they did.

The generator stood fifty yards away. Nessa and Adem would have to sprint through the Skaldi to get there.

"Satisfied?" Mercy said to no one in particular.

Nessa turned to her, hefting her rifle, and for a moment I thought she was going to use it. Mercy must have thought so too, because her own rifle rose to Nessa's chest. But then

Nessa clutched Adem's hand and pulled him from the door-way. He stumbled forward and stood shakily beside her.

"We can do this," she whispered fiercely. "For Aleka. And Wali."

For a moment Adem looked stricken. Then I watched his back straighten and his face take on a determined expression I'd never seen. Nessa gripped his hand and squeezed before turning to me.

"Go," she said. "Be careful. Work fast."

Then she and Adem were leaping through the Skaldi, firing bursts that lit the night. The creatures responded sluggishly at first, moaning and tumbling over each other in their confusion and panic to get away. Soon, though, they seemed to realize they were thousands against two and began streaming in the attackers' direction. In seconds so many bodies blocked the way I could no longer see any-thing of Nessa and Adem except the pale sparks from their rifles.

"Stay close," I said to Mercy and Ardan. "But not too close."

"You planning to drop a Querry bomb?" Mercy said.

"You never know."

We crept toward Udain's headquarters, keeping low. Or, in Ardan's case, as low as a nearly eight-foot-tall human being could. Though many of the Skaldi had followed Nessa and Adem, hundreds still covered the yard, so many that some lay squirming on each other three or four deep. When we reached the edge of the square I signaled to Mercy and Ardan, and they stooped—or loomed—by my side.

"They should be there soon," I said.

We waited for a long minute, listening for the sound of Nessa's and Adem's rifles. But all we could hear were the Skaldi's moans.

"This is taking way too long," Mercy muttered.

"I'll go in," I said. "You two follow. Try to keep them from closing behind us. Let me know when we reach the charges."

Mercy grabbed my arm. "You're forgetting one thing," she said. "You're the only one who can set the charges. If you go under like you did at the altar, we're all screwed."

She was right. I froze, seconds ticking by like hours. Still I heard nothing that would indicate whether Nessa and Adem had reached their target. In the dim light, Mercy's eyes flashed a grim and mirthless *I told you so.*

Then, all at once, the compound to our right was illuminated by a blaze of yellow light, the ground shaking beneath our feet. Sparks twisted into the sky, drawn upward by the column of smoke they lit. The Skaldi in the courtyard, attracted by the explosion, began to migrate toward the generator building. I suspected they would find nothing left of it. I hoped they wouldn't find any sign of the two who had demolished it.

But I couldn't think about them. We had our own job to do.

"Now!" I shouted at my companions.

Mercy sprinted through the gap in the Skaldi's ranks, with Ardan a step behind. I followed. Over my shoulder, I heard Nessa's and Adem's rifles coming alive again, the howls of the creatures they hit.

The mass of Skaldi had recovered from their initial surprise, and some came streaming toward us, clumsy but determined, moaning in fury or pain. Mercy hit the ones in our path with her energy rifle, their scars peeling back before they exploded into flying fragments. Some tried to circle behind, but Ardan was sharp, and he nailed them before they had a chance to form an effective group. The wild thought flashed through my mind that we could destroy them all this way, without worrying about the explosives. But I saw the countless shadows moving in the darkness, I remembered the few survivors of our combined colonies marching slowly through the tunnel with the body of my mother, and I knew we had to stick to the plan.

Mercy stopped without warning and fell to a knee. At first I thought she was hurt, but then she signaled and Ardan came to her side, understanding immediately what she needed him to do. She entered a code into a touchpad embedded in the cement, and a square metal plate popped free, exposing corners a normal human being could probably pry up with a crowbar. Ardan used his hands. He gripped the edges of the plate and pulled, and in a single motion the plate came free and flew into the night, colliding with a Skaldi and slicing its body in two.

Mercy put a hand on his forearm. "That's my big brother."

His face shifted in the slightest of smiles.

While the injured thing wriggled helplessly and its fellows streamed over it to reach us, Mercy grabbed my hand and pulled me down by her side.

"There," she said. "Work your magic."

I reached into the hole and, guided by Mercy, manually set the charge. The Skaldi fell back before Ardan's energy beam. In seconds we were done.

"Let's set the other and get the hell out of here," Mercy said. "I can try for the one that'll do the most damage."

"Your call," I said, and we were up and running with Mercy in the lead.

She stopped in front of the cage. Even with the power out it was empty, as if the creatures had some dim memory of what it was meant for. In its center, just visible in the light of the burning bodies that had sprung up around the compound, I made out the black scorch mark from the creature I'd destroyed almost a week before. The three of us entered the cage, and Mercy knelt at this spot and punched the code into a keypad I'd been too busy fighting that first night to notice.

"Will two be enough?" I said. "To take out most of them?"

"The best laid plans," she said with a smile.

Ardan wrenched the scorch-streaked plate from the ground, and once again I used the signature my mom had given me to set the charge. When I was done, I stood, wiped my forehead with the back of my hand, and looked at my two companions.

I realized the compound had gone quiet. No moans from the creatures, no crackle from the distant fires or from Nessa's and Adem's rifles. I looked around us and saw that the Skaldi had advanced as silently as shadows, thousands of them, forming a solid circle just beyond the cage. A soft exhalation like a rustle of fabric passed through them as the scars on their bodies yawned open, their stink enveloping us as if we'd already been pulled inside. I glanced at the door to the cage. It was closed, and something told me it wouldn't open at my command.

The Skaldi waited. They had no reason to hurry.

"Which one of you is it?" I said to my companions. "Or were you working together all along?"

They dropped their eyes. I took out my mother's protograph and flicked it on, scanned and zoomed until I located the four white lines that indicated our cage.

A single red dot glowed at its center.

"I could kill you both," I said.

"It's not me," Mercy said. Ardan stood impassively, saying nothing.

I walked to the bars of the cage. The Skaldi outside waited hungrily.

"There's one way to find out," I said.

I grabbed the bars and poured everything I had into them.

A pulse passed through me, almost as strong as the one I'd felt at the altar but nowhere near as painful. With an explosion of sparks, the compound's power sprang back to life.

The perimeter fence hummed with energy, pale gold against the night sky. Stark white spotlights swept the courtyard, showing the huddled bodies of the Skaldi, their faces turned upward in what might have been shock if they'd had features to show it. Then they fell back, moaning in agony as the energy surrounded them. The cage buzzed with so much power I felt momentarily dizzy. When I stepped to the door and touched the bars, a crackle of fire leaped from my fingers and the door flew open with a clang.

I turned to face the two who shared the cage with me. Ardan stared back with an uncharacteristic expression of amazement. Mercy shook her head sadly, then withdrew a gun from its holster.

Not the kind that fired the energy beam. Aleka's pistol. She held it outstretched, and I jumped back. I couldn't read the thoughts in her eyes, but I could see something foreign there, something that passed like a shadow behind a lighted window.

"Oh, Mercy," I said.

She stood unmoved, staring back with haunted eyes. I remembered the night I'd watched Korah die at the hands of the Skaldi. I felt the power build, and I tried to steel myself to kill the second girl I'd ever loved.

"I told you," she said. "It's not me. And I can prove it."

The gun swung to the side, settling on the hulking form of Ardan.

"I love you, big brother," Mercy said.

And then she fired.

The bullet tore through Ardan's massive chest.

But there was no blood.

"I'll take him," I said.

The Skaldi in Ardan's form tried to flee the cage, but the energy beam weakened it, and it fell to its knees with a crash that shook the cement pad. I took a step toward it, ready to end his suffering, when the giant frame shuddered and the Skaldi tried to escape.

It leaped from his throat, his face, his chest. It burst him like a torn cloak. It was almost free of him when, amazingly, the hands of the tattered giant grasped the creature, clutched its torso, and squeezed. It raked him with its claws, fighting to free itself from the body it had counterfeited, but he held on, arms that somehow obeyed the human he'd been holding on to the Skaldi he'd become. Those powerful arms constricted, and the Skaldi responded with an otherworldly moan of confusion and pain. Its host body was dead, had to be, but it clung to the monster that had hollowed it out and wouldn't let go.

With a final, enormous effort, Ardan's arms ripped the thing free of his body and flung it to the ground, where it lay motionless except for a convulsive quivering.

The remains of the man staggered to his feet. One side of his face had slid into a gaping cavity, the other side appearing like melted wax with a single dark eye peering furiously from the chaos of flesh. Mercy's gaze never left that face as it warped and flowed. He tottered as he approached her, and at last his legs gave out and he sprawled on the floor of the cage, stretched out full length, his arm reaching for Mercy. There he lay, heaving like a mountain erupting, holding himself together through a force of will I couldn't conceive.

Mercy fell to her knees beside the thing that had been her brother, her hand brushing hair from his tortured forehead.

"Mercy," he groaned, and the voice was still Ardan's, except it sounded hollow, as if it issued from the pit of his chest. "Forgive me."

With one shaky hand, he reached up and awkwardly touched Mercy's hair, the motion delicate and uncertain, as if he feared he might break her. Gradually, though, as his fingers flowed over the crown of her head, they recovered the tender pace I was sure they'd once known. Mercy leaned down and stroked her brother's ruined face, coaxing a last smile from his lips.

"I went willingly with our father into the desert," he spoke, his words slurred and broken. "I served him not from compulsion but of my own free choice, pledging myself to the power he commanded. I stole the innocent from their homes, bore them to the canyon to serve his ends. I built him an army, won him brides. It was only when I saw his plans for you that I knew what I had done." His smile held a second longer before slipping from his face. "Do not mourn for me, Mercy. I am at peace. I have paid."

His body began to crumble. Mercy tried to hold him, but the effort was finally too much, and his frame fell apart, sliding through her fingers in a shower of golden sand. Mercy threw herself on the ground, and for a second I thought I saw wisps of light curling around her like soothing hands. I watched them twist into the air, where they vanished in the glow of the compound. Nothing remained to mark the place he'd been, unless it was his sister's anguished cries.

I waited until the worst of her tears had ended, then knelt beside her. She took my hands and let me pull her to her feet. For the briefest of moments her head sank to my shoulder as she clung to me.

"I'm sorry," I said.

Then we were running through the open door of the cage and past the stunned bodies of the Skaldi. Mercy aimed her rifle and pulled the trigger, but the only sound that came from the spent weapon was a low whine. She threw it at her feet. I glanced in the direction of the perimeter fence, but it seemed impossibly far away with the hordes that lay between us and escape.

"How long until the charges blow?" I asked Mercy.

"Thirty minutes." Her voice had recovered its calm, but tears tattooed her face in the light of the beam. "Of which we've already wasted ten. What's the plan?"

I turned to see Skaldi creeping toward us, weakened by the beam but drawn by the living energy in their human prey.

"Nessa and Adem," I said. "They might still be alive."

We ran for the generator shed, dodging burned and dazed Skaldi. We reached the place only to find a smoldering pile of rubble. There was no sign of the two, but their rifles lay beside the ruins. Mercy picked one up, testing it. Like her own, it had expended its charge.

"They're gone," I said, hardly believing the words as they left my mouth. "We need to get back underground. It's our only chance."

With Mercy in the lead, we returned to the stairwell that had brought us to the surface. The Skaldi tried to crawl after us, but we closed the door to hold them off. At the bottom of the stairs I flicked on the protograph, scanning and scrolling through the labyrinth of tunnels. Everywhere I looked I saw trails of red dots, like blood cells flowing through an intricate system of veins. All the paths that I could find that led away from the blast radius ran straight into them.

The Skaldi had breached the tunnels. There was no place to go. Ardan was dead, and Nessa and Adem too. And in minutes, we would join them.

Mercy leaned over me. In the depths of her eyes I saw the ghostly outlines of tunnels, the map of the world below. Finally she said, "There!"

I stopped the image on a cluster of tunnels so densely woven it looked like a spiderweb. No Skaldi had penetrated it so far as I could tell. "You know where that is?"

She took the protograph from me and scrutinized the screen. "Aleka briefed me on the tunnels. But she never said anything about this."

I wondered if my mother would ever stop keeping secrets from me, even after she was dead. "Can they withstand the blast?"

Mercy shrugged. "Ask me fifteen minutes from now."

"That's the best you've got?"

"The best I've got," she said softly, "was beaten out of me by this crummy world a long time ago."

"I'm sorry," I said again, realizing with new force how inadequate it was to say. The worst thing about this world, I thought, was that it gave no one a decent chance to grieve. "Lead the way."

With Mercy holding the protograph and me shining the flashlight ahead of us, we set off at a run in the direction she judged the tunnels lay. The fact that the charges might blow at any second bothered me less than the mood of my companion, who kept a tight silence I knew her too well to try to break.

After running for what seemed like hours but couldn't have been more than minutes, we entered a part of the tunnel system totally different from the rest: unlit, suffocatingly narrow, and filled with a rank smell of mold or decay. The protograph indicated that we were traveling west, the exact opposite direction the rest of our colony was moving. And it also indicated, via a timer function Mercy had discovered, that we had only a couple minutes before the charges went off.

Which made it especially problematic when the tunnel came to a dead end.

"Perfect," Mercy said, giving off a short laugh.

I grabbed the protograph from her, desperately looking for another way out, finding none. "What do we do now?"

She might have been about to answer when the tunnel quivered, dust and chips of cement raining down from overhead. A split second later, a powerful explosion shuddered through the reinforced concrete, then another, this one even stronger than the first. The walls groaned, and in the beam of the flashlight I saw them begin to buckle. Then the floor trembled and the ceiling cracked with an ear-splitting screech. I leaped for Mercy, who shouted something I couldn't make out just as the ceiling collapsed.

That wasn't the worst part, though.

The worst part was when the floor did too.

\||||/

Mercy coughed, her mouth dangerously close to mine.

"Damn, you sure know how to show a girl a good time," she said. "But seriously, what were you planning to do for an encore?"

I couldn't see anything, but I felt her body on top of mine. I tried to move, only to discover I couldn't. My lungs burned with the effort and my tongue felt thick and heavy in my mouth, but I squeezed out a couple words. "What happened?"

"The charges went off and we dropped to some kind of sublevel. Where I think you cushioned my fall. *Cushioned* being a relative term, of course." She sighed, the sound coming out more like a wheeze. "My hero."

I felt her wiggling, heard her scratching against stone. A dim light opened in the darkness, and her shape squeezed through. But when I tried to roll over and follow, I found that I couldn't budge.

"Mercy?"

Her face, plastered with white dust, appeared in the window she'd opened. "You okay?"

"I'm—" I didn't want to answer that too quickly. "I'm kind of . . . stuck. Can you give me a hand?"

She reached through the hole. Her fingers were as white as her face, except where blood tipped the nails. "Upsy-daisy."

She gripped my hands and tugged. I felt the strain in her arms, but still nothing moved. Her face grew serious as she squinted into the rubble behind me.

"Your foot's trapped," she said. "Something on your ankle, I think."

"I can't feel it."

"Your foot? Or the something?"

"Nothing." Sweat trickled into my eyes. "I can't feel anything down there."

"Okay," she said. "Don't panic. Let me just . . ." She wiggled into the hole headfirst. "There's some debris," she announced. "This is going to take a minute."

I waited, dust choking my throat and sweat burning my eyes, while Mercy cleared the wreckage. I lost all sense of time as she worked. Finally she removed whatever was pinning me, and with her help I crawled through the hole. I lay on the floor beside the mound of broken concrete, staring at a sputtering light in the ceiling. The cool air opened my throat after the stifling weight of my almost grave.

Mercy crouched beside me. "It's your ankle," she said. "I wouldn't look if I were you."

I looked, and then wished I'd listened to her. Something, maybe steel rebar from the concrete, had pierced the Achilles tendon of my right foot, the open wound oozing chalky blood. Seeing the torn flesh just beneath the metal control cuff chased away the numbness, replacing it with bone-deep pain. "How are we for supplies?" I said, trying to change the subject.

"No water, and the pistol's a pancake, if that's what you're asking. I assume the protograph is defunct too?"

She searched through the pile, laughing humorlessly as she pulled the device free. The miniature screen had snapped in two, the pieces held together by a couple wires. She let it drop to the floor.

"How are we going to find our way out?" I asked.

"That remains to be seen," she said. "You wait here. Don't run off."

She stood and paced down the tunnel. I tried not to think about the pain, which had begun to crawl up my calf and was working its way into my knee. Within minutes she was back, looking strangely excited.

"I know this place," she said. "Or at least, I've heard of it. The tunnel widens just ahead, and there's a monorail leading west. This must be one of the old bomb silos they built back in the day. To shuttle warheads from place to place. Come on, I'll show you."

She wrapped a strip of cloth as best she could around my ankle, then hooked my arm over her shoulder and pulled me to my feet. I swayed, tried to balance on one leg. I wouldn't have succeeded without her arm around me. With me leaning my entire weight on her, we limped down the tunnel until it curved and widened. Unlike the tunnels we'd been in so far, this one was circular, and much taller, maybe fifteen feet at its apex. Most of the lights were out, but the few that were left provided enough illumination for me to see that a rail ran down the center of the floor, along a broad red stripe painted on the concrete. A rhythmic throbbing as if from buried machinery sounded just at the threshold of hearing. The tunnel, Mercy announced, headed due west, straight under the impact zone.

"Should we go that way?" I said.

"We're sure as hell not going back the way we came." She smiled and raised her eyebrows. "So let's explore."

She left me for a moment while she searched the tunnel. She wanted me to sit down and rest, but I leaned against the wall instead. The effort of walking had made the pain climb all the way up my leg, and getting off my feet might have been a relief. But if I returned to the floor I wasn't sure I'd be able to stand again.

Sheer exhaustion threatened to break my vow when Mercy returned, dragging some kind of cart down the rail. It was small, but the two of us could just squeeze in, with her helping me every inch of the way and then practically climbing onto my lap.

"I think this is what used to move the missiles," she said. "Now we just have to hope the power's still on."

I doubted it would be, but miraculously, it was. She pressed random buttons on a control panel, and the cart inched forward on its own, picking up speed as it went. It glided forward at a comfortable rate, faster than we could walk but not as fast as the trucks we'd once had in Survival Colony 9. As we moved deeper into the tunnel, the throbbing sound became louder, seeming to come from all around us, or from inside my head. Our path wasn't entirely straight:

it curved gradually this way and that, though Mercy insisted our direction was still basically west. If she was right, the solid black weight of the impact zone rested above our heads, with the base and our companions falling farther behind with each passing moment. I searched the tunnel for exit routes, but it was all smooth gray concrete.

"Sit back," Mercy said. "This is as close as we're going to come to a roller coaster, so enjoy the ride."

I tried. But the thought of what lay above, and the lancing pain that now consumed one whole side of my body, made it hard for me to relax. It didn't help that Mercy had wrapped her arms around me and laid her head on my shoulder, and in the cart there was no room for me to move away.

The rocking motion of the cart made me drowsy, and I felt Mercy's soft breath on my neck, her fingers mechanically stroking my hair. I had no idea how much time had passed or whether I'd stayed awake through all of it when her voice startled me. "What the—?"

She untangled herself and slammed a button on the control panel. Our personal means of transportation eased to a stop.

Mercy climbed from the cart and stood in the tunnel, hands on hips. She wasn't looking ahead. She was looking above, where the tunnel walls curved to the ceiling. We'd reached a place where almost all the lights were out, and the pulsing sensation was strong enough to make the floor shake. In the opaque light of a lone, flickering bulb, I followed her gaze.

"Are you seeing this?" she murmured.

I was.

The tunnel had changed over the distance we'd traveled, not only in color but in composition. The concrete had been replaced, or maybe covered over, by something that glistened in the faint light. At first I thought it might be water leaking down the walls, but it was thicker than that, a coating like gel. Rather than the concrete's solid, nondescript gray, this stuff had a pearly hue, with faint threads of pink woven through it. When I took a deep breath, I realized the cool, dry air of the underground silo had thickened, becoming slightly humid. My nose twitched with the hint of an odor I knew all too well: rotten, decaying. The smell, like the throbbing sound, threatened to grow stronger the deeper we went.

And that wasn't all. The light was so bad I couldn't be sure, but the walls of the tunnel seemed to be moving—pulsing rhythmically, as if they were the gullet of some enormous creature. Slowly, the painful stiffness in my limbs making me think I must have slept part of the ride, I climbed from the cart and hobbled over to stand beside Mercy, who instinctively put her arms around me and saved me from a fall. From close up, there was no doubting it: the walls shifted, slithered, surged. The tunnel swam with shapes that seemed to be trapped beneath a membrane stretching up the curved walls from floor to ceiling.

The shapes of Skaldi.

Their bodies hung suspended all around us. They moved, held by the living tunnel, rolling and squirming as if they were drowning. The skin of the tunnel bulged and rippled where their limbs pressed against it. One creature thrust its blunt, empty face against the membrane, which strained outward, finally bursting to let the head free. I saw then that its head was smaller than usual, a knob barely larger than my fist, and that the scar that should have snaked down its face was closed, only a faint line visible where it normally would be. Before the rest of the thing's body could emerge, the membrane sealed again, sucking the creature back into place with the others.

The creatures in the walls bulged and retreated like the beating of some misshapen heart. Something told me why they couldn't get loose.

They weren't ready yet.

Not ready to be born.

"Oh my God," Mercy said, as if she'd picked up on my thought. "Querry, look at the cart!"

I turned. Dimly visible in the half-light, I read the single word in raised red letters on the cart's side.

SCAVENGER.

"This silo is for Scavenger missiles," Mercy said. "Grandpa used to talk about them. They're called that because they deliver their payload to multiple targets at once. He always made it sound like they were nukes, but . . ."

"They weren't," I said. "They were delivering drones."

"And the altar," she said. "It must have formed over the silo when Athan's—when my dad's device failed. Do you think we're underneath it now?"

"We couldn't have come that far," I said, not at all sure of our coordinates. "But I'm guessing the tunnel goes all the way there. That's where they emerge. When they're ready. When they're called out by a strong enough burst of energy."

Holding me upright, Mercy edged closer to the tunnel wall. The Skaldi swarmed toward us, locking onto our life-force, restrained only by the membrane. Her face turned toward mine in horror.

"He must have known, then," she said. "Grandpa must have known about this place all along."

I smiled, though that was the last thing I felt like doing. "Maybe he wanted to forget."

We stared at the things hanging above us, the monsters that had devastated our world. Mercy's arm tightened around me, and this time I didn't try to move away when she rested her head on my shoulder. I wasn't sure anymore if she was holding me up or if I was holding her. I remembered discovering the Skaldi nest in the desert, the network of tunnels that enabled them to move through the land undetected. I'd thought the nest was their home, until Udain told me they'd come from another world, spinning around another sun. Skaldi City, a place beyond time and memory.

But he was wrong. Wrong, or lying, whether to me or to himself.

"There's no rift, Mercy," I said. "This is the Kenos laboratory. This is where it all began."

Leaving the cart braked behind us, Mercy and I scouted back the way we'd come until we found a door in the tunnel wall.

It swung open at a touch. Lights blinked fitfully on, revealing a room not much larger than Udain's office. But it was filled with so much equipment there was barely space to move beyond the couple feet at the entrance. Machines like giant metal cabinets stood against the walls, lights flashing on their surface. Metal gurneys blocked the center, while other machines hovered nearby: some with knobs and dials and clear plastic tubing, others with sharp gleaming instruments that looked like saws or knives. There was a metal chair by the door, and a large metal desk crammed between the towers at the far end of the room, with a chaos of vials and tubes and syringes strewn across its surface. A lamp curled over the instruments, its bulb unlit, looking as if whoever had sat there had left the room for the night and would be back the next day.

And distributed against the corners of the room, suspended in vertical glass cylinders that contained a pale ocher fluid, were four bodies.

Lifeless bodies.

One of them was Skaldi. Fully Skaldi. Featureless face, skeletal arms, body cavity, paddle tail. It hung in its tube in a posture of frozen menace, as if it had been sealed in the act of making its jump to a human victim.

The other specimens weren't quite Skaldi. But they weren't quite human, either. One had the Skaldi's empty body but humanoid arms. Another had a face, though it wasn't the kind of face you'd want to see on anyone you knew. The fourth had the beginnings of legs, as if its tail had split and feet were emerging from the severed ends. Taken together, the four looked like a series of pictures showing the evolution from Skaldi to human, or a slow-motion sequence of the Skaldi taking over a human body.

And there was one more, strapped to a gurney with its arms and legs splayed. It looked like a cross between a human being and a Kenos drone: oversize head, empty eye sockets, spidery limbs. Its chest collapsed inward like a sinkhole. The expression on its withered face was one of outrage, as if the instruments that lay on the gurney beside it were still probing its lifeless body.

I knew this place. Knew it like a nightmare deeper than memory, from a time before *I* was I.

This was the place I'd been born.

Or maybe not born.

Made.

Athan had found the remains of the Kenos laboratory, as he'd dreamed of doing. What he'd found there was the project that had started the wars, then been stalled by the wars: the breeding of monsters to use as weapons and warriors. He'd taken as much of the previous generations' research as he could to advance his own. And when the device he'd built at his father's bidding had destroyed him and he'd fled into the desert, he'd left the lab, the immature Skaldi, everything. Not living, not dead. Not finished.

Waiting. Thousands of them, in a place that could breed millions more. Waiting for the day the Scavenger of Souls would return and release this final plague on our world.

"Mercy," I said. "We should get out of here."

"Is it your leg?" She looked at me with concern, but I could tell her thoughts were elsewhere.

"No," I said, though the truth was I could barely stand. "It's just . . ."

"Give me a second," she said. "I promise this won't take long."

I lowered myself into the chair while she squeezed through gurneys. "Hard to find good help, isn't it?" she said to herself as she surveyed the cluttered desktop. Then she squinted, frowning. "Well, look what we have here."

She raised her hand, holding another portable protograph.

This one was in perfect condition, without a scratch or dent to mar its shiny surface. But it was even smaller than Aleka's—suited for a child's fingers, not a man's.

"Is that . . . ?"

"Athan's? No doubt." She fiddled with the screen, trying to get it to come on. "Maybe it'll show us the way out of here."

"I think . . ."

Her eyes rose to mine.

"I think there's only one way out," I said.

She shook the protograph as if that might make it respond, then swore silently and dropped it in her pocket. "The altar?"

"I'm guessing."

A noise made us both jump. Mercy spun to take in the room. "What was that?"

"I'm not sure." My eyes flicked around the crowded space. "But I'm pretty sure it wasn't a pony."

She looked blank for a second, then smiled. "Why, Querry," she said. "Did you just make a funny?"

She helped me from the chair, her arm bolstering me, our attention shifting to the room's hidden corners. We had reached the exit when I caught movement out of the corner of my eye. I stared hard at the experimental subjects in their cylinders, but all were still.

Yet in one of the tubes, bubbles climbed slowly through the yellow fluid.

"Mercy," I said. "The Skaldi—the specimens. They're alive."

"I sure hope the crazies aren't catching," she said. "Those babies are stone-cold dead."

"No, they're not," I said. "They're in suspended animation. Look"—and I pointed at the wires running from each cylinder. "They were being kept sedated by the energy beam. But someone must have cut the power."

"Who?" she said. "The evil janitor?"

"Whoever," I said. "We've got to get back to the cart."

We backed out the door. The lights died as we exited. A faint luminescence exuded by the tubes showed the creatures flexing as they came out of their comas: clawed fingers opening weakly, blunt heads swiveling toward us. The pitiful monster strapped to the gurney pulled feebly against its bands, its sunken face stretching in the motion of a silent scream.

Mercy lingered in the hallway outside the door. I knew what she was thinking. There were so many secrets here, and once we left, we'd never discover them all. "Let's go, Mercy."

She looked longingly at the room, but didn't resist as I pulled her away.

"This was a trap," I said.

"No shit, Sherlock. Any chance you've got turbo boosters on those spindle shanks of yours?"

"That's next year's model." I clenched her hand, and she pulled me back toward the cart, my useless leg dragging behind me. I swore I heard footsteps that weren't ours trailing us, but with the noise of my boot scraping the floor, I couldn't be sure.

We reached the spot where we'd left the cart. The embryonic monsters struggled with renewed vigor above our heads.

But the cart was gone.

Mercy turned to me with something like a smile. "I'm beginning to think ours is not an entirely healthy relationship."

She left me sitting on the tunnel floor while she searched a short distance ahead for the cart, but we both knew she wouldn't find it. When she returned, her face and eyes were calm, with a look of inevitability I didn't like to see.

"You go," I said. "With luck you can outrun them."

"Still trying to get rid of me, huh?" she said. "Maybe I like unhealthy relationships."

She sat, wrapping her arms around me. When I turned to her, I found her lips on mine. They moved invitingly, drawing me in, while her hand on the back of my head pulled me closer. It was all I could do to break away and whisper a single word. "Mercy—"

Then the footsteps I thought I'd heard resolved themselves into a steady drumbeat, and Mercy jumped to her feet as a figure stepped from the shadows.

"What the hell," she breathed when she saw him. I couldn't blame her.

It was Geller.

His pimpled face spread in a smile. He held two objects: an energy rifle, and the bone-white staff. Behind him, clustering out of the darkness at the edges of the tunnel, came ten or more of Asunder's warriors, armed with spears and stone knives.

"Kind of a private moment here," Mercy said.

Geller's smile didn't change. But when he spoke, his voice was rapid and jittery, and his eyes shone with fearful enthusiasm.

"It is as our lord Asunder foretold," he said. "The children of the despoilers have fallen into a snare of their own devising. The day of the Scavenger of Souls is upon us at last."

They tied us with the brown ropes and hauled us far up the tunnel, where the cart was waiting. Mercy told me to blast them, but even if I'd been able to summon the energy, I couldn't do it with Geller's rifle trained on her. "Thought you true believers weren't into techno toys," she gibed, but he merely smiled. The smile turned to a manic laugh when he discovered my mother's mangled pistol, and he handed it mockingly back to Mercy, shoving it in her holster while she recoiled at the touch of his hands. My biggest fear was that he'd touch her with the staff, and I tensed every time he approached. But he did nothing but hold it up for the others to admire, waving it wildly over their heads as if he was their new king.

And I guess he was.

They loaded us into the cart, and Geller operated the controls to get it going. He must have understood the system better than Mercy, because whatever he did had us sailing down the tunnel at top speed, whipping around curves under a canopy of unborn Skaldi. Against the screech of the wheels and the howl of the wind, I shouted a few words into Mercy's ear.

"Geller's parents," I said. "What happened to them?"

"His mom died in the accident," she yelled back. "His dad was taken by Asunder. He lost a sister, too. Why?"

"Just wondering," I said, though I'd expected an answer pretty much like that.

An hour or more passed with the rumble of the cart and the roar of the wind the only sounds in my ears. The air grew increasingly hot and sticky as we traveled west, and the mass of Skaldi above our heads thickened to the point that we could practically have reached up to touch them if our hands hadn't been tied. Any thought we might have had of jumping from the cart was flung away by its speed, plus when I looked back I saw another cart racing after us, probably occupied by Geller. All I could do was hold on to Mercy as we careened toward the end of the rail line.

Finally the cart slowed, then came to a rolling stop against thick rubber bumpers. We'd arrived at a huge circular cement pad that lay at the bottom of a cement cylinder, as wide as the pad and shooting up into darkness far above our heads. A few stray Skaldi clung to the sides of the cylinder, but the heavy mass from the tunnel had finally thinned out and then vanished. Looking straight up, I could easily imagine that the altar of the Scavenger of Souls reared into the sky above us. Warriors dressed in their caveman outfits appeared from the shadows. They dragged us from the cart while its partner came to rest against ours and Geller stepped out, rifle and staff in hand.

"Come, children of the light," he said to them. As before, his voice sounded unnaturally fast, like someone nervously trying to get through a speech. "*Nidach asa minach*. The Scavenger awaits."

They scaled the walls with us slung over their shoulders, their bronzed hands gripping rungs affixed to the inside of the cylinder. Mercy and I were too tightly bound to do anything except stare as the cement pad dwindled to a dot the higher we climbed. It got to the point where I had to close my eyes to prevent dizziness from making me fall despite the warriors' grasp on me. I didn't see where we exited, but when I felt the outside air on my face, I opened my eyes to find that they held us at the base of the altar, dawn light breaking from the east. So many warriors ringed the stone mountain, along with the cave-children who now belonged to Geller, it was obvious he'd emptied the canyon to witness the consummation of their dead leader's prophecy.

Geller waved the staff, and Asunder's people bowed low to the ground. He took the time to touch every one of them, the staff descending to their shoulders the way Asunder had done in *Grava Bracha*. I couldn't help noticing, though, that his hands shook, and once or twice he had to repeat the performance when he missed his target. When he'd finished, he signaled with a nod, and the warriors who'd brought us topside grabbed our arms.

Mercy struggled ineffectually as they pulled us toward the stairs. "You little prick!" she shouted at Geller. "I should have wasted you when I had the chance!"

Geller ducked his eyes for a moment, a flush darkening his scabbed face. But then his smile returned, the feral smile he'd learned or copied from his dead master.

Mercy turned to me. "Kill them!" she screamed. "Hit them with everything you've got!"

"I can't," I said. "I'll kill you too."

"Then kill me," she said. "I'd rather die that way than *his* way."

I reached inside, tried to summon the power, but got no response. I looked at Mercy, and her eyes told me she knew. Her furious cries cut my ears as the warriors' feet pounded toward the summit.

At the peak of the altar, the scene was laid the way it had been for Wali's sacrifice: warriors holding spears and torches, packed so densely I could just make out a small figure between the horns. The rising sun bathed the summit in blood-red light, and Geller, coming to stand where Asunder had stood, flourished the staff awkwardly, like someone doing a bad imitation of the prophet's elaborate gestures. It would have been funny if not for what he planned to do. But when the warriors stepped aside and I saw what was bound between the horns, my heart caught in my throat.

It was the drone.

Small as a child, bleeding pale yellow light against the red of the dawn, it hung there with its oversize head lowered to its chest and its emaciated arms dangling like threads from the altar's horns. My hair rose at the touch of its crackling energy. The new ruler of the Shattered Lands stepped toward it, his lips moving silently as if reciting something he'd memorized, and the drone's head jerked upward, blind eyes staring into the sunlight. I knew that the moment Geller contacted the creature with the staff it would explode, drawing the Skaldi that swarmed below into the upper world.

And this time, there would be no one left to stop them.

Geller reached out with the staff. His eyes shone, and his hand shook. Watching him, seeing his fumbling attempts at fulfilling the ritual, it struck me that he was just a kid, only a few years older than me. Maybe Mercy's age, even younger. Too young to inherit Asunder's mantle. Too young to have lost his family in the tragedy that had claimed his master, too young to play the part of his surrogate father. His pimpled face was as scarred as Asunder's, but his scars were the scars of a boy, not a man.

We were both Athan Genn's creatures. The only difference between us was that I'd known my mother, too.

And I remembered her final lesson.

"Wait," I said, and Geller paused, his eyes shifting to mine. The girl named after that lesson looked at me sharply, but I ignored her. I had no idea if this was going to work, but I figured we were going to die anyway, so it was worth a shot.

"The drones and I are brothers," I said. "Made by the hand of your master. To serve the same purpose."

Geller's eyes narrowed. I talked fast.

"I should join my brother," I said. "If this is to be the end, I should share it with him. With what's left of my family."

"All will share the same end," he said, but I thought I heard a note of uncertainty in his voice.

"The more power you command, the more surely the Scavenger of Souls will come," I said. "With me at my brother's side, the end will be certain."

"The end is certain," he said.

"Not always," I said. "It can leave things undone. Let me join him, Geller. Let us finish this together, so all suffering can come to an end, and you can be with—with the ones you lost." I caught his eyes, held them. "I promise."

Geller lowered the staff, his look at once hesitant and keen. He licked his lips as if deciding.

Then he gestured for his warriors to bring me forward. They gripped my arms and dragged me toward the horns.

"Are you insane?" Mercy whispered.

"Must be," I said, giving her a quick smile before they tore me away from her.

With the drone already bound to the altar, the warriors

had to circle behind the horns to place me there. I balanced shakily on a single foot, hovering over the stunted creature like Archangel over a normal-size human being. I could feel the power radiating from its body, could hear the rasp of its tortured breathing and the crackle of its energy agitating the air. Where its feet touched the surface of the altar, black rock melted to liquid glass. I braced myself as Geller took the final step toward us, the staff raised, an eager light in his eyes.

"The Scavenger of Souls is merciful," he said. "May he come for us all at last."

When he touched the staff to the drone's forehead, it erupted with power.

The pulse of energy flashed in my eyes, giving me a quick glimpse of Geller's smile—a softer smile, like the winning, gap-toothed grin of the young Athan on the protograph screen. Then the pulse consumed him, tearing the smile from his damaged face, sweeping the fragments of his body into the void. All that was left of him was the staff, which clattered to the ground at the drone's feet. The warriors who'd tied me to the altar were next to shatter into dust, their wide-eyed expressions reminding me for an instant of the children of Survival Colony 27. But before the crackling energy field could extend any farther, I tore myself free of my singed bonds and wrapped myself around the creature, hugging it to my chest. It screamed in senseless agony as power poured from it, but unlike the other times I'd been assaulted by the Skaldi, I didn't try to strike back. Instead, I opened myself to the energy streaming from it, welcomed that energy into my own body. Athan Genn had designed me to drain energy from other living beings, to store it in my cells forever. He'd made me stronger than the Skaldi, resistant to the beam that crippled them. If Aleka was right, the accident that had destroyed him had made me even stronger than he anticipated. What my limits were I didn't know.

But I was about to find out.

The drone glowed with power, a furnace of light. Warmth at first, then unbearable heat spread through me as its life-energy flooded my system. It was like holding on to the sun. I knew the only way to gain relief was to let go, to allow some of the energy to bleed back out. But I also knew that without me to contain it, the drone's full power would be released, and the Skaldi colony beneath us would be freed. So I bore down, clutching the creature to my chest, pulling its power into my blood and bones. Bright lights exploded in front of my eyes, shaping themselves into images in my mind. I remembered carrying Keely the night we found the Skaldi nest. I remembered clasping my mother's body just before she died. And I remembered holding Mercy, and knew I never would again.

Because as I gripped the burning drone to me, I felt my own body begin to burn.

A look of dim awareness dawned on the creature's inhuman face. It struggled in my arms, mindless panic emanating from it, limbs flailing as helplessly as an infant's. I gripped its hands gently and held on, melting with it, letting its energy fuse us into one. My senses were failing me, but still I didn't stop. I had passed into a realm beyond pain, beyond feeling, and all I knew was that I was going to die. A memory darted through my thoughts, something Laman used to say to us in Survival Colony 9. *Never leave anything behind.* But he knew, didn't he, that in the end you have to leave everything, and there's no going back to retrieve it?

A rumble shook the stone beneath us, and with a deafening screech, the summit of the altar split between the horns. A minute passed before a clawed hand emerged from the yawning depths, then the entire creature clambered onto the platform. Its scar shivered, opening at the scent of fresh prey—Mercy—on the altar's peak. But before it had a chance to attack, its body collapsed, shaking as if with palsy. It made a final attempt to rise, but its arms trembled with the effort, and finally it disintegrated, cracking along the seam of its scar and sliding to the black stone. Within seconds, all that remained of it was a pile of dust, picked over by the wind.

Another creature ventured above, and another. Like the first, these new arrivals emerged into the sunlight only to collapse helplessly onto the rock, unable to get their quivering arms under them to push their bodies upward. When they tried, their arms folded, then shattered into dust as if a gale had struck them. It wasn't long before I was surrounded by their dusty remains, wasn't much longer before the wind blew all that was left of them over the glassy stone and out into the distance. No more emerged, and the only movement was that of the drone twitching beneath me.

Even that stopped soon. It lay there with its mouth and eyes fixed open, its body limp in my embrace. It sparked a final time, then its light blinked out like a fistful of candles and its spent form joined the dust at the altar's peak. The crackling noise died from the air, and all that was left was a slight scent of ozone. The split summit settled back into place, sealing the scar as if it had never been. I lay beneath the horns, unable to feel the sun on my face, the jagged stone at my back. On the final verge of thought I reached out to the Skaldi slumbering deep beneath me, to see if any more had responded to the drone's call. But everything was quiet. The Scavenger of Souls had come and gone. It was over.

A dark shape moved at the corner of my vision, and I saw Mercy hanging over me, her hands reaching to cup my face.

"Mercy," I said.

She put a finger to my lips. "The feeling is mutual. Let's not spoil it with a bunch of words."

"I'm sorry," I said.

"For what?"

"For . . ." *Leaving you*, I thought.

"Hey." She smiled. "It's been a hell of a ride. No complaints from this girl."

She leaned forward, and through the blur of my own tears I saw the silvery trails on her cheeks. Then she moved so close her face was all I could see.

I couldn't feel her lips on mine, but I knew she was beside me as I closed my eyes and sailed into darkness.

I stood in a city.

It wasn't any city I knew. Certainly not one of the cities Laman used to talk about, with their massive white towers flickering with lights and long, sleek trains speeding past on elevated tracks. Nothing like the twin compounds I'd passed through either, the shelled community where Laman had settled and then lost Survival Colony 9, the military base where my creator and his father had done their deadly work. This was a different kind of city, with tall rounded towers the color of red sand and curved lanes that glittered in the sun as if they were spattered with crushed diamonds. A city that rose out of the desert like a living thing, stretching languorously in the midday sun.

Mercy was with me. She had her arm wrapped around my back, and when we walked, I leaned on her, moving with a stiff and clumsy gait. When I glanced down I saw why: my right foot was nothing but a curled stump, the shape you'd get when one of the little kids molded a human figure from river clay. I felt no pain, though. There wasn't enough of the foot left to feel anything.

We walked toward the center of the city. Shaded archways beckoned to us, while leafy plants trailed from circular windows and lined the paths with ribbons of green. When we looked up, we saw long garlands strung between the towers, twisting and curling in a way that made me think they were fluttering in the breeze. It wasn't cool, exactly—the desert sun was always there, a reminder we couldn't escape—but it was tolerable, heat you could grow used to if you let yourself forget about the waste beyond.

And there was something else about this place, something I couldn't put a finger on. Something familiar. As if I'd seen it before, or heard someone talk about it a long time ago. Someone who'd spoken of a place just like this, a place whose curved lanes and secret alcoves promised discoveries but not terrors, a chance to find something new instead of only more chances to lose.

Mercy looked around as we walked. "Nice," she said. "Don't you think?"

"Really nice."

"Not the kind of thing a survival colony would have built," she continued. "Something left over from the time before?"

"Could be."

"No sign of Skaldi, either," she said. "Come to think of it, no sign of anyone. Where in the world do you think they are?"

"I don't know." But even as I said it, I felt that I *did* know, that we were on our way to meet the ones who lived here, and that I was the only one who knew the way to find them.

We kept walking. I realized others had joined us, people from our combined colonies. Tyris, Nekane, Adem. Zataias and the rest of the little ones, including the children of Asunder. Ramos at the head of a force of Udain's soldiers and Asunder's warriors. Nessa too, her hair still short and her eyes still green, though her face seemed harder and sadder than it had before. Others, though—my mother, and Wali, and Soon, and Udain, and all the people we'd lost from the survival colonies I'd known—were gone for good. I knew I wouldn't find them here.

We rounded the last of the towers and came upon a huge concrete structure rearing out of the heart of the city, a curved shape as if a giant ball had been half buried then sliced open to reveal its hollow inside. A circular platform jutted from the base of the raised semicircle, easily a hundred feet across and fifty deep, while cement canals snaked from the stage into the surrounding city. No water flowed through them, though. Cautiously, we advanced onto the stage, our steps echoing against the soaring roof, amplified so much it reminded me of the tramp our colony had made when it was whole. Looking out over the city from this spot, I realized it lay within the canyon, but not a part of it I'd traveled, the walls vague and misty with distance.

Mercy stood beside me, her eyes sweeping the city. "No electricity. No running water. Nobody home. This place is dead."

"I'm not so sure." The same inkling tugged at me as before, the sense that there was something here yet to be discovered. "It feels . . . dormant. Waiting."

"For what?"

I shrugged. "For the right time, I think."

Mercy laughed. The sound pealed high and clear against the vaulted ceiling, carried across the city. I felt like I hadn't heard that laugh in years. "Well, I think it's time it stopped waiting," she said playfully. "Time for it to wake up."

I turned to her. "What did you say?"

"I said it's time," she repeated. "To wake up."

I tried to grasp her words, but for some reason they eluded me. She took my hands, peered at me with her intense black eyes.

"It's time, Querry," she said, the laugh gone from her voice. "It's time to wake up."

Her face hovered over me. A bleariness around her eyes made me think she'd been crying. But then I focused—or she did—and the look was gone, replaced by a tender expression I had thought I'd never see again.

"Hey," she said softly.

"Hey."

"You're getting to be quite a project," she said, her lips curving into a smile. "Not a lot of girls would've stuck around this long."

I tried to smile back, but a wince sliced through the smile. My body was a wilderness of pain. "Mercy?"

She laughed, just as she had in my dream. Its details had grown slippery, but the laugh I remembered. "That's the name."

"Where are we?"

"I'm thinking you're not in shape for a bunch of coordinates. So I'll just say we're by the river. And a good long way from where we were."

I tried to sit. Mercy looked doubtful, but she helped me up. That's when I saw that my hands, my arms, my legs were coated in bandages. The wrapping around my right foot was lumpy, misshapen, not like the contours of my foot at all. I reached down to undo the covering, but Mercy gripped my hand.

"Let it heal," she said.

"What happened?"

Her face hesitated, but she answered. "Whatever you did back at the altar burned you pretty bad. So bad the control cuff melted and fused with bone. Tyris had to take most of the foot off."

"Tyris is here?"

"They're all here," she said. "Come on, let's get you up."

Balancing against her, I stood and took a look around. I recognized the place instantly. It was the site where we'd laid Laman Genn to rest, back when I was a member of Survival Colony 9 and Aleka its new commander. His tombstone protruded from the soil, maybe tilted a little from what it had been. The inscription remained unchanged. We'd left this place in search of the mountains . . . how long ago? Days, weeks, months flowed into each other like dunes in the dusty ground.

"How did we get here?" I asked.

"Slowly. But surely."

"But—" I knew this was a stupid thing to say, but my mind was too tangled to say it any other way. "Did I die?"

"That's a matter of opinion," she said. "Your heart stopped for a brief time, so I guess that counts."

"But now I'm . . ."

"Alive." She smiled. "Thanks to the staff, which seems to have given you the jump start you needed. And no one could be happier than me."

I looked away from her smile, so brilliant it almost hurt. I remembered something she'd said to me in the tunnels. *I'm not sure I know what death means anymore.* But I was pretty sure I did know. Aleka was dead, and Laman, and Korah, and Wali, and the little kids from Survival Colony 27, and so many people in my life. They were all gone. They were never coming back.

"Mercy," I said, my voice breaking.

"Shh," she said, and she held me while I cried.

When it was done, the others drifted over. Bruised and ragged, with eyes that stared in exhaustion from gaunt faces. But alive. Tyris. Nekane. Adem. The kids. Ramos and the other guards. As in my dream, some of the children and warriors were those who'd once been Asunder's, though their numbers weren't as great as they'd been that final day at the altar. Nessa was there too, her uniform in tatters, her face and hands so blackened with grime it seemed to have sunk into her skin. Adem looked pretty much the same. Mercy whispered that the two of them had survived the blast at the compound by hiding in another tunnel, then clawing their way to the surface. They'd been met by Tyris's team, which had set out across the impact zone in pursuit of Geller. Mercy told me that Geller had ambushed the others in the escape tunnel, using the staff to draw from Udain's broken mind the final drone's location. It didn't surprise me when she revealed that Udain had hidden the drone in the part of the tunnels she and I had been trying to reach when the walls caved in. But when I asked her what had happened to her grandfather, her eyes grew teary again.

"The staff was too much for him," she said. "And there was no way to transport his body. It's okay, Querry. It was his time."

They'd buried him where his headquarters had once stood. They'd buried my mother right here, beside an empty grave to mark Wali's memory and a final grave containing the bone that was all that remained of Mercy's older sister. Tyris had emptied Aleka's body to preserve it for as long as possible—something Doctor Siva taught her, not the same as what the Skaldi did—but in the end they'd been unable to wait. I'd been unconscious, according to Mercy, for almost three weeks. I supposed it was better this way. I wasn't sure I wanted to see the wreck of my mother's body in the pitiless desert light. Nekane led me to the grave, which she'd prettied up with a garland of pale pink flowers. The smoothed ground looked peaceful, vacant and still. I'd always thought of my mother's face as a mask, and now the desert dust had taken its place. A mask over an emptiness, with no more secrets to hide.

I stayed by the grave a long time. Mercy hovered nearby but let me be. Before I left, I took the ring I'd carried all this time from my pocket. It had melted in the drone's fire, its shape twisting so it would no longer fit on a finger. I'd thought about burying it with Korah's remains, but it seemed right to return it to its original owner. Or if not that—I had no idea who its actual owner was, someone who'd lived and loved and died in the time long before—at least to close the circle of life and death as much as I could. I dug a small hole in the ground beside my mother's grave and buried the ring there. I thought I might cry, but I guess all my tears had already been shed.

"Bye, Mom," I said, and turned from the grave.

Mercy came to help me. As we hobbled off, Nessa

approached, her strides sharp and jerky. She walked right past us and fell to her knees beside Wali's grave, and I'd have gone back to her if Mercy had let me.

I never got a chance. Adem stepped over to where Nessa knelt, hesitantly reached out a hand, tapped her on the shoulder. She looked up at him, and I saw that she was crying, the tears cutting streaks through her grimed face. His long arms went around her, and she let herself be drawn in while she cried.

"You don't know the things I saw," I heard her say. "In Asunder's camp. The things Wali died to try to save me from. Sometimes—sometimes I can still hear Asunder calling my name."

She lowered her head to his shoulder and cried, while Adem's calm voice spoke words in her ear I couldn't hear.

When night fell, the others wandered off, leaving Mercy and me alone. For once the sky was relatively clear, giving us a view of actual stars. We spread a blanket on the barren ground and lay back, side by side. She turned to me, her breath tickling my chin. I wouldn't say it smelled sweet—no one's breath did—but it was warm, and I felt comfortable lying there beside her, no pressure and no expectations.

But then, with every breath, every heartbeat, she started inching closer, and I kept inching away. I sat up before it got to the point where there was nowhere left to inch.

"You're not scared?" I said.

"Of you? Please." She draped an arm across my chest to

pull me back down. "I could kick your ass on a good day. And you're obviously not having a very good day."

"But I'm—" I didn't know what to say. "You saw what happened at the altar. You know what I can do. That doesn't scare you?"

Her eyes searched mine, black as the night around us. "I just told you," she said. "I'm not scared of anything anymore."

I thought about that. I wondered if I could ever say it about myself.

"Make the beam," Mercy said.

"What?"

"You heard me. Snap your fingers or whatever, and show me some of that old-time Kenos religion."

"You're serious?"

"Am I ever not serious?"

I rolled onto an elbow, reached inside. I imagined circuits closing, cells communicating, energy bubbling up from somewhere deep in my blood or bones.

But I knew right away I was wasting my time. There was an emptiness in me where there'd been something before. That part of me, at least, was dead. And I realized how glad I was to let it go.

"I can't," I said.

"I suspected not. Whatever you did at the altar baked your biscuits for good. So no worries, right? I can get as close as I want."

"But—"

"With you it's always *but,*" she chided. "*But* I'm a human firecracker. *But* I'll crisp your unmentionables. *But* I'm half-Skaldi."

"I—" I looked at her, stunned. "You knew?"

"Of course I knew," she said. "How do you think Aleka got into Athan's private files in the first place? Turns out his ability to program voice-recognition software was a bit, shall we say, primitive in those days. All it took was a vocal resemblance—a family resemblance—and, open sesame!" She smiled. "Plus, you may have forgotten, but you kind of let your big ugly secret drop at the altar. With that whole 'I am his brother' speech. Very stirring."

"Okay," I said. "So then you know why you and I—why we can't . . ."

"I know nothing of the sort," she said. "The only thing I know for sure is this."

She sat up, wrapped her arms around her knees, took a deep breath. I tried to take a breath of my own but couldn't. My heart was pounding as if it had never stopped, and all the air seemed to have disappeared. Either that or it had rushed in to crush us in its grip.

"My father and grandfather," she said, "spent their whole lives fighting monsters from beyond the stars. All their lives, searching for the Scavenger of Souls, trying to predict the moment of his coming. But do you know where that got them? You know where they ended up?"

I shook my head.

"Back where they started," she said. "Fighting monsters they built beneath their own feet, monsters they built inside their own hearts. The monsters were never beyond their reach. The only thing beyond their reach was the people they could have known, the people they could have loved. The people they could have *been*, if they'd only let themselves."

She pointed upward, and my eyes found the brightest star in the sky. A planet, maybe, or a vanished sun, its light reaching us long after it was dead and gone. And there it was, blinking in the dark emptiness of space, calling out to those who could read its message.

"I know I'm here," Mercy said. "I know this is where I want to be. And I know you're who I want to be here with me. What else is there to know?"

She put her hand on mine. She drew close to me, and her lips parted, and then she was kissing me, and I was kissing her back. The voice in my head that told me this was impossible was drowned out by the feel of her hands caressing my face, the warmth of her breath, the touch of her tongue tapping mine. Lightly, like a question. I pulled her down beside me and held her, kissing her, forgetting everything, remembering everything. She drew away for a moment to trace a single tear from my cheek, and I had no idea why I was crying. For us, maybe, or for them. For all the things I couldn't remember, all the things I could but couldn't change. For the end of the world, or the beginning.

"This is our home, Querry," she whispered. "This is where we belong. Let the monsters go back to Skaldi City. Stay with me here on Earth."

EARTH EPILOGUE

When the past comes to haunt me, I remind myself we had to travel there to find our way here.

We left our camp by the riverside with reluctance. The graves felt like our extended family, and I think we knew that if we moved on we'd never visit them again. But I had to make a decision, and the dream that had led me home tugged at me, wouldn't let go. I felt sure the city I'd seen in my dream existed, and I was determined to find it. Of all the places we'd been, all the encampments we'd found or made, I was convinced this was the one where we could finally stop our running. The one we'd been searching for all along, but could never find so long as the creatures of our nightmares remained.

For the first few weeks after we broke camp, we saw them from time to time, enough to make me believe they were the remnants of the army that had invaded Udain's compound, or stray members of the underground colony that had found their way to the surface. But they were weak and listless, dragging themselves aimlessly across the desert with heads bowed and scars caved in to cover the emptiness inside, too feeble even to make their signature moan. They didn't respond when we approached, didn't look up, didn't change course or prepare for the attack. Some we found motionless, on their backs, staring with empty faces at the bright blank vault of the sky. Others grew pale and flaked into dust as we watched. After a while we didn't see them anymore. I sensed the relief that flowed through everyone in camp, and I shared it, though mine wasn't quite the same. After all, these final survivors were my brothers too. I was glad to see them go, but just as glad to see them finally at peace. I suspected they were as weary of the fight as the rest of us.

It was months before we found what I was looking for. Months for me to master the crutch Nekane carved, until I got so adept I could keep pace with everyone except Mercy. Months for Zataias to start an unexpected growth spurt and Keely to make that subtle shift where you knew he wasn't looking at the world through a pure child's eyes anymore. Months for Nessa and Adem to grow close—and for him to grow eloquent in her presence—until one morning I saw them walking behind everyone else, hand in hand, his face a shade of red even Asunder's cloak couldn't match. It was months for our supply of food, all of it filched from the ruins of the compound, to dwindle and fail, the pinch in our bellies to start again. No Skaldi, we learned, didn't mean no hunger. For me and Mercy, it was months to discover each other, months to fall in love, which meant months to discover we already had. The vow she'd made my first night back she never broke: she wasn't afraid of me, or of anything, anymore. No matter how many days passed, I still couldn't say the same for myself. But when I was with her, I could believe a time might come when my fears would finally be laid to rest.

We paced the river beyond the impact zone, past the rock city and into the canyon. There we found green vegetation clinging to the walls and carpeting the floor, cooler-than-usual air, a wholesome smell breathing from the clear-flowing river, which widened and deepened as it unfurled toward the north. We came upon a green pool, so bright it glowed like a second sky shaming the brown sky above, with ranks of tall tufted grass blooming in the muddy shallows. Tyris dabbed her tongue in the water, tasted it on her lips, and pronounced it safe for bathing—which we did, splashing and shrieking like the little kids, emerging as clean as any of us had been in our entire lives. To our great surprise, when we exited the pond we were met by the women of Asunder's colony, free from his power now that he and his staff were gone. Our surprise was even greater when they led us to *Grava Bracha* and we found the old woman there, seated in ragged splendor on the stalagmite that had once been Asunder's throne. The women had nursed her back to health with the aid of Melan, who vanished shortly after we arrived, hiking to the east to fulfill whatever destiny was his. Now she presided over the women as a sort of grandmother, if not a guru. At night, we'd sit with her under the deep purple canopy of the sky, our campfire etching shadows into her puckered face, crowning her pure white hair with gold. Her tales of the time before held us all spellbound.

"It's a beautiful night," she always began.

"A storytelling night," Nekane would respond, and then the old woman would smile and tell another of her tales.

Her name, she told us, was Chelle.

We lived with her community for a month, learning what they had to teach us, before moving on again—all of us except Nekane and Asunder's children, who chose to stay. Deeper into the canyon the vegetation grew wilder, bushes and river reeds springing up in chaotic profusion. The buzz of insects and the sweet scent of decay led us to groves of trees—not the stunted, leafless trees that grew in the desert, but trees twenty feet tall, their branches forming a shady canopy, their foliage sprinkled with brighter green orbs. These Tyris proclaimed safe to eat, and we stuffed ourselves, biting through soft pockmarked rinds to savor the fleshy fruit beneath. We did find evidence of Asunder's raids—in particular, an enormous ditch gouged into the canyon floor, as broad as the green pool was long and filled to overflowing with heaps of blackened metal. When we stood at its lip, we saw dented fuel drums, tires, wire-mesh screens, vehicle grates and fenders, aluminum doors and window frames, flashlights, lanterns, propane tanks, camp stoves, tent frames, pots and pans, truck batteries, rearview mirrors. It was hard to tell with so much junk littering the top, but I thought I saw the roofs of convoy trucks lining the bed beneath. And there were weapons, enough to supply an army, plus the other army it was fighting. Near the surface lay the tanks of flamethrowers, the spray-painted 9 identifying them as ours. The galling smell of oil and baked plastic hung heavily in the air.

The sheer waste of it tightened my throat with anger. I considered climbing into the pit to search the tarred trash for Aleka's stolen pistol and my red-handled pocketknife, but Mercy talked me out of it.

"Let it go, Beam Boy," she said. "Let it go."

We stayed just long enough to say a prayer for the dead, then left. I walked away with Mercy's hand in mine, but not without taking a long look back.

And then, one morning, we came to a part of the canyon where the walls fell away to reveal miles of open land and the city sparkling in the sunlight beside the unspoiled riverbank. Strange sounds filled the air: high-pitched, quivering, full of clicks and beeps and crackles. They seemed to come from somewhere far up on the canyon walls, and not from one place but from lots of places all at once. At first we tensed nervously, but then Tyris told us not to worry.

"Birds," she said. "Those are birds."

We entered the city to the sound of the birds' morning carols. Everything was there: the towers, the avenues, the giant dome. Seeing it at last, I knew why it had felt so familiar in my dream.

I'd been here before.

I'd been born here.

Aleka had fled Udain's compound when she was pregnant with me. There was no way, it struck me now, she could have escaped without someone's help, no way she could have made it across the stone desert with a two-year-old at her side and an unborn child months from delivery. She must have relied on someone else: a sympathetic guard, someone angry at Athan for what he'd done, someone she continued to trust until the day both of them died—Siva. It was Siva, I was sure of it, who'd helped her cut the tracker from her arm so she could get away, Siva who'd offered to go with her— but when she refused, it was Siva who helped her steal one of the compound's vehicles so she could drive into the canyon on her own. The city she found must have been built before the wars, protected by the canyon walls from the worst of the damage, hidden from the ravages of the Skaldi. And then Aleka arrived, giving birth to a child everyone assumed was human, a child who would fulfill that belief until age three, when they ventured beyond the safety of the canyon and the Skaldi tracked him down.

I understood now what a risk my mother had taken in leading us to the canyon. Though she'd had no way of knowing that Asunder had claimed its southern entrance in the years after the attack on me, she must have believed the city was still prohibited to her, the sentence of exile still in force. Living out in the desert with Survival Colony 27 and then Survival Colony 9, she couldn't have known that the city was no longer alive—that the attack had signaled the Skaldi, who'd overwhelmed her lost home and the people who had driven her from it.

We strolled the empty lanes beneath the rounded towers. In places I saw where the bodies of Skaldi had crumbled, pale shapes like shadows in rooms protected from wind and rain. We reached the stage I'd seen in my dream, found a plaque on the rear wall that told the city's history: that it had been built as an experimental community, an artists' colony and an exercise in sustainable living in the years before the wars. Cisterns—now cracked—had collected rainwater, a wetlands had flushed the sewage clean, sagging wind towers had provided energy. The area behind the dome was crisscrossed with garden plots, all gone to weeds. So much had fallen into disrepair in the years since the city had been deserted, it was hard to imagine the thriving community it had once been, even harder to imagine it becoming such a place again.

"Well," Mercy said, squeezing my hand, "you called it. Not that I doubted you, of course."

"Of course."

"Kind of a fixer-upper, though." She shucked her jacket,

muscles playing beneath her glossy skin. "What say we get to work?"

We did. We found storerooms full of tools to supplement our own meager supply, construction materials to fortify the turbines and seal the cisterns and canals. Mercy had been tinkering with her father's protograph during our trek north, and she'd finally unlocked its most precious secrets: information on building and growing things, breeding plants to resist toxins, culturing bacteria to replenish the soil. With that knowledge and an eager team of workers in the members of our combined colonies, Adem supervised the work necessary to revive the wetlands. I discovered that, even when he talked—and he talked nonstop with Nessa at his side—I couldn't understand a word he was saying. I'd barely known him before, hadn't been able to tell if he was smart or stupid, scared or just plain shy. Now I realized that the entire time the rest of us had been busy running and hiding from the Skaldi, he'd been devoting all his brainpower to the problem of what to do if the Skaldi ever disappeared. He'd already rebuilt human civilization in his mind. All he'd been starving for were the know-how and materials to work with.

Mercy relinquished the protograph to him, and he dug deeper. New canals, roads, and other improvements sprouted under his hand. For a while we relied on the groves and berry bushes in the mid-canyon to keep us fed, while we waited for the seeds Chelle's colony had given us to bloom in the gardens we cultivated. One of the plants was topped with oblong brown tufts that felt at once fibrous and elastic, almost like skin. These, the women had told us, weren't for eating but for braiding or weaving into an infinite variety of forms, just as Asunder's colony had done to create their clothing, their torches, their ropes. As the days passed and the work progressed, other survivors trickled into our community, loners and parentless children who'd been on their own in the desert or holed up in the ruins of cities until something they couldn't name—a feeling, a hint—told them to come out, guided their feet all the long miles to us. Five years into the rebuilding, we had a community of almost two hundred, far smaller than the city could hold but far larger than any survival colony had been. The new people brought skills and stories and strong backs we needed to keep us going, and our leader was happy to welcome them into the fold.

That leader wasn't me, though. For the first few weeks everyone looked to me for the go-ahead, but it soon became obvious that our real leaders were Nessa and Adem—him to supervise the individual projects, her to oversee the grand design. There was no vote, no coup, but by the end of our first year they'd assumed the roles they were meant to have. Mercy, meanwhile, turned her attention to security, which covered everything from registering weapons to repairing outer defenses to mediating disputes. Ramos served as her deputy—which, so far as I could tell, meant her uncomplaining gofer and whipping boy. She carried Aleka's battered and inoperable pistol as the sole insignia of her office, and she told me time after time that much as she'd gotten a charge out of being a soldier in war, it was much, much better to be a soldier in peace.

Me, I was more comfortable with the kids, the way I'd always been—and since Nessa believed, once we got settled, that there was a need to teach our young ones and the others who appeared from time to time, that became my job. We converted one of the buildings behind the dome to a schoolroom, and there I spent my days. Sometimes I'd lead my students into the canyon, walking as always with my crutch, remembering the chains I used to form with the youngest members of Survival Colony 9. There'd been so few then. Now the chain felt endless, with me at the head and all the others joining hands behind me. How a chain so fragile could hold was a mystery I couldn't begin to answer.

Once a year, on the anniversary of the day we discovered our new home, we held a ceremony. Very simple, with stories and songs and thanks. Zataias volunteered to lead, and though he was no older than twelve when it started, he was the perfect one for the job. He'd memorized all of Chelle's stories, as well as adding some of his own, and he recited them in a deep, rich voice, something you'd never have guessed when he was a wide-eyed kid watching the world with silent wonder. At the end of the day, using paper from the fibers of another plant Adem had cultivated, I worked with Zataias on jotting down all the stories we could remember, trying to preserve a permanent record of the times we'd been through. It grew to hundreds of pages before I decided it was done.

Other, private ceremonies we performed on our own. Wedding vows we shared only with each other.

Mercy wakes me, as always. She retains her soldier's training, her preference for early rising. I keep my penchant for sleeping late. Being lazy, she says. Thinking, I say. Dreaming. Hoping.

But today's different. When she calls, I open my eyes at once, the mist of sleep scattering before the sunlight.

She stands at the window of our tower apartment, framed by the day. When she turns to make sure I'm up, I see her rounded belly, straining against the uniform top she still likes to wear. At our last visit, Tyris said it could be any day now. Eighteen-year-old Bea, training to take over as healer when the time comes, smiled, saying how nice it would be for a new baby to join Nessa and Adem's. Their son, born two months ago, they named Wali. His hair has started to come in in curls, so he may live up to the original.

Mercy's already decided on names. If it's a boy, Ardan. A girl, Korah. I ask her if she wants to burden our child with the weight of the past. She tells me the past is a burden only if we let it be.

She may be right. But for me, it's not that easy. Often, I'll wake from dreams I remember all too well and lie in bed, feeling Mercy breathe beside me, staring into darkness until it goes away. But the daytime isn't safe either. Too many things I do, teaching a kid to read, eating a meal with Mercy, climbing a hill with her to watch the sun set—all can bring the past gliding back like a phantom, and then I'm stranded there again, in the compound, the tunnels, at the nest, the river, the circle of children, the altar, feeling as if I never left, as if no time at all stands between then and now. It's not always bad: there are times when memory feels like a cool stream carrying me back for glimpses of what I left on its shores. The poolside, the place where Korah and I stole an almost kiss. My mother, gray-eyed and wise. Laman Genn, the only father I ever knew. But other times it's like a hard rain pounding down on me, and all I can do is let it fall.

Memory, I've learned, is responsibility, and responsibility never lets you forget.

But today, I've promised Mercy not to dredge up the past. Today is for her, the last day in a while, it may be, for us to get out and hike the canyon trail. To my last-minute question about her fitness for the climb, she only rolls her eyes. I throw my legs from bed, testing my right foot as always before trusting my body to it. Then I rise and dress quickly, hoping we can reach the top before the sun gets too high.

I offer Mercy my arm. She takes it, though not without an ironic smile. Bracing myself with the crutch I've carried these past ten years, I exit the apartment with her.

We walk through the city. Few are up this early. Keely, fifteen years old and already taller than me, hammers away at a bent windmill blade, his bronzed back and shoulders shining with sweat, his blows ringing above the quiet chorus of bird song. Later, he'll join Adem and his crew on one of the many urban improvement projects our chief engineer always seems to have dreamed up the night before. We nod at a few other early-morning walkers, and they smile at Mercy's enormous belly. I'm glad to be anonymous beside her. I'm glad we're the only ones heading out of the city this early. My history's not exactly a secret among the newcomers, but sometimes I still feel uncomfortable in their presence.

We reach the foot of the trail and begin our climb. If I thought Mercy's burden might slow her down, I was dead wrong. It seems to propel her even faster than usual, and the arm I've lent her becomes less a means of support and more a way for her to drag me along. For easily the thousandth time, I marvel at her energy, her life. I give thanks that this is the woman who chose me to father her child.

But I have to admit, I do worry who that child will be. *What* that child will be. I carry both human and Skaldi genes. What combination of traits will our child possess? The first time I watched a lumpy appendage roll across my wife's stomach, it really did look like an alien creature. Tyris assures us the pregnancy is progressing normally, but she has no way of seeing inside. No way of seeing ahead. And neither do I.

What will my child be? What choices will he or she make? Will our city stand or fall? Will we leave in search of elsewhere, or stay right here? Will we live to see the world renewed, or spend our lives in the shadow of its final days?

We dwell in the past, it may be, because it holds so many fewer secrets than the future.

The sun breaks upon us as we exit the trail and stand on the canyon's upper rim. To the south and east, the impact zone—too far to see—rolls in black and undisturbed silence. The altar, if we could glimpse it, would glitter in the late-morning sun like a crown of darkness. But we face away from those icons, away from the sorrows they hold. This is not a memorial. Not a vigil. I could ask Mercy why we're here, but what answer would she give me?

We're here, she would say, as she's said to me so many times before. *We have this moment. It's the only thing we do have, the only thing we're given. We'll never be more alive than we are right now. Hold on to it, Querry. As long as you can, until you have to let it go.*

I stand behind Mercy, my arms wrapped around the life within her, while she lifts her head to the sunlight and laughs, fearless and free.